The Life of Ely

"This is my first non-fantasy book that was originally written as a screenplay. This story is sort of my 'baby'. There are a lot of personal connections in the story that make it very important to me. I sincerely hope that you get as much enjoyment from reading it as I did in creating it."

Jason McWhirter

A Twiin Entertainment Book

Other books by Jason McWhirter

The Cavalier Trilogy (Fantasy Genre)

Book One, *The Cavalier*
Book Two, *The Rise of Malbeck*
Book Three, *Glimmer in the Shadow*

Published by Twiin Entertainment
www.TwiinEntertainment.com

Cover photograph copyright:
Isoga/Shutterstock.com
Author Photo: Jason Halvorson
Edited by Linda McWhirter and Sarah Finley
Cover designed by Twiin Entertainment

The Life of Ely

Dedication

This book is dedicated primarily to Rick Selfors, my middle school shop teacher and wrestling coach, my mentor, my colleague, and my friend. His dedication to his profession and his positive impact on thousands of students cannot be measured.

Author's note

Some people might think that Mr. Seljin, one of the main characters in this book, might represent me, or maybe Mr. Selfors to whom I've dedicated this book. But the reality is, that although his character may be somewhat autobiographical, he represents aspects of many of my former mentors, such as coaches, teachers, and colleagues I have known over the last thirty years. And although Mr. Selfors, known as 'Sel' to his students and friends, was the main inspiration for the character of Mr. Seljin, his personality also includes the traits of those I have had the pleasure to know and work with throughout my years as a student, athlete, and educator.

The other characters in the book are also fictitious, though they too were often created from bits and pieces of various people I have known throughout my career. Ely was not one of my students; his character merely reflects many of the traits and conditions of some of the students that I have encountered over the last eighteen years of teaching.

The Life of Ely is fiction, but like historical fiction it contains pieces of truth and reality, rearranged in a way to create a coming of age story that sheds light on the struggles of some students, as well as the amazing ability of some of our dedicated educators and coaches who manage to make a positive difference in their lives.

And so, I not only dedicate this book to Rick Selfors, but also to the educators, coaches, and others who work so hard to improve the lives of our struggling students, not just by trying to teach them something useful, but also providing support and the tools necessary to build a life for themselves. These people deserve our thanks, and this book is for them.

The Life of Ely

One

There are only a few things in my life that I've figured out to be certainties. You're born into a life of which you had no choice, you grow older every day, and then you die. Everything in between, is up to you. As the old saying goes, modified by me of course; life is a blank slate, and you're the writer.

I'm a big movie fan, and I read a lot of books. You tend to find things to occupy your mind when you have a shitty life…an escape from the realities of your own world. One of my favorite movies, Shawshank Redemption, had a line that I think of almost daily. It helps me sometimes when I think things couldn't get any worse. Andy Dufresne, played by Tim Robbins, says in the movie, "Get busy living, or get busy dying." It's so simple, but most truths are, and it makes so much sense. It helps me focus on the possibilities that life can offer, not the negative stuff that seems to be shoveled in my direction every day. It helps me put my life in perspective and makes me realize that no matter how bad my existence is, someone has it worse. All you need to do is turn on the five o'clock news, open a newspaper, or scan the Yahoo main page and you will see daily proof that your life, no matter how bad it seems, is better than some. Unfortunately, it's sometimes difficult to have this perspective when you're walking through knee deep shit. Some people need a guide to help them, while some can do it on their own. It reminds me of the difference between a Theravada Buddhist and a Mahayana Buddhist. The Theravada, thought to be the original branch taught by Siddhartha Gautama, the Buddha, believe that everyone can reach enlightenment on their own if they follow the Four

Noble Truths and Eightfold Path as taught by Buddha. The Mahayana Buddhists believe that you need help to reach enlightenment. So they worship the Buddha, and other Buddha's, in order to find the path towards enlightenment. But unfortunately I didn't know much about Buddhism in eighth grade, so this so called Eightfold Path did me no good. But I think both sects of Buddhists would agree with Andy and say, "get busy living, or get busy dying."

There is something else that I try to remember when things get bad. I think about how insignificant we really are. I know we don't want to think about it, but the reality is that what we do now will generally not matter in a hundred years, unless of course we invent something world altering or we do something horrible enough that our actions are taught in history classes hundreds of years later. What are we really in the scheme of things? We're nothing, just a collection of atoms rolling around for a set number of years until our cells' DNA code tells us it's time to die. It's our emotions that make us more than that, but at the same time make us susceptible to believing that we deserve better. I believed that, that I deserved better, and yet I could not pull myself from the muck on my own. I needed help, and unlike many others in the world, I was lucky enough to find that help. I found my Buddha, or Buddha's actually, and because of them I survived.

Here is my story.

Ely Carter

The Life of Ely

The setting sun reflected off the mirror-like water of Vaughn Bay, casting a crimson and orange glow behind the Olympic Mountain range as the sun descended behind the evergreens on the opposite shoreline. Several dozen boats filled the quiet marina, creaking and whining as they rubbed against the oiled pylons and weathered planks of the dock. The rickety dock led to an old single lane road separating the marina from a rustic country store.

Ely Carter, a young, round faced fourteen year old, sat on the curb outside the country store. His frayed, gray sweatshirt barely concealed his two hundred and fifty pound body. Khaki shorts and dirty worn out sneakers mirrored the overall appearance of the store behind him.

A light scattering of freckles highlighted the boy's pale and pudgy face. He would be considered a five or a six on the rating scale for appearance, average and relatively non-descript. His overweight body and double chin, however, dropped him significantly lower on the middle school scale, probably to a three. But in that world the difference between a three and a six is really insignificant; either rating making you a pariah, or at best a ghost, a fluttering apparition in the school's hallways that no one seemed to notice, making Ely painfully aware of his virtual invisibility.

The old store had definitely seen better days. There were only two cars parked outside; one a rusty pickup truck, and the other a paneled station wagon, both old and dilapidated, covered in dirt and grime.

Ely was sitting, crouched over and sobbing quietly in his hands. He lifted his head up and wiped his bloody nose with his sweatshirt, completely oblivious of the stunning sunset before him. Flakes of dried blood covered his upper lip and one eye was swollen partially shut and beginning to turn purple. Blood from his nose made a red streak across his old, threadbare sweatshirt. The boy's brown disheveled hair hung in loose curls over his face. With bloodshot eyes he scanned his surroundings with a look of utter despair.

A scrawny man with long, greasy hair, dressed in dirty pants and a flannel shirt, walked out of the store carrying a half-rack of beer. His white undershirt was stained with a mixture of dirt and yellow sweat, yet it looked to be the cleanest part of his clothing. A cigarette dangled from the corner of his mouth. As he walked by Ely, he stopped casually, flicking his cigarette on the ground at Ely's feet. He glanced down at the boy with a look of mild disdain, "What the hell's your problem kid? Christ, what do you have to cry about?"

Ely glanced up at the man, barely registering his words through the sorrow that draped him like a heavy coat.

"Pussy," the man muttered under his breath. Shaking his head, the lowlife turned and got inside his pickup truck. As Ely watched the truck drive away a little girl suddenly plopped down next to him on the curb. She looked like she could be about seven.

"Hi, I'm Laura," she announced.

Ely wiped his nose again and stared at her. The last thing he wanted to do was have a conversation with a little kid. He was not in the mood to interact with anyone let alone a young child who couldn't possibly understand what he was going through.

"What's wrong, why you cry?" she continued. Her long dark hair was pulled back into a pony tail, and though one of her cheeks was smudged with dirt, it did nothing to diminish her angelic expression. It was as if she really cared about why Ely was crying.

Ely didn't know what to say, so he didn't say anything. But she wasn't going to let him off the hook so easily.

"You can tell me. I cry all the time, especially when I watch sad movies."

"I…hurt myself," Ely stammered, again wiping his runny nose on his sleeve.

"I fall and hurt myself sometimes. See this," she said, pointing at a scab on her elbow. "I was running fast and tripped. It hurt really bad."

"I'm sorry," was all Ely could think to say.

"Are you okay? My momma has band aids. They have little bears on them."

"No, I'm fine," Ely responded.

From behind them a voice interrupted their conversation. "Hey, there you are!"

Ely and Laura turned to see a young boy, about Ely's age, walk up behind them. The boy was thin and handsome, sort of a Justin Bieber look alike, and his smile seemed genuine to Ely, although he had seen so few smiles in his life that he could not be sure. "Laura, don't run off while we're in the store, okay."

"Okay, Jeff," Laura said with mock contriteness. "I was just bored."

Jeff glanced over at Ely. "Hey, is my sister bugging you?"

"No," Ely replied softly, not looking up from the ground.

"He needs a band aid," Laura said.

"It sure looks like it. What happened to your face?" Jeff asked.

"Nothing, I just fell."

Jeff looked intently at Ely for a second before lifting his sister up from the curb. "My name is Jeff. I don't recognize you. Are from around here?"

"I just moved here a couple of weeks ago," Ely murmured.

"You going to Key Peninsula Middle School then?"

"Yup."

"In that case, it looks like I'll see you tomorrow," Jeff said, holding his sister's hand.

"Yeah," Ely sniffled again, "maybe."

"What's your name?" Jeff asked.

"Ely."

Just then two women in their late thirties emerged from the store carrying a few bags of groceries. One woman was tall, with long straight sandy blonde hair and a clean face devoid of makeup. She was naturally pretty, but with the type of beauty that would not make her stand out, appearing almost average, until you took more than a passing glance at her and noticed that her strong features were anything but average.

The other woman was short, almost stocky, with short cropped hair and an angular face. She looked the complete opposite of her companion, except for when she smiled. Both women had glowing smiles that lit up their faces.

"Come on you two, let's go," the taller woman said.

"I have to run, Ely. I'll see you around," Jeff said, walking towards the station wagon with his sister in tow.

Ely glanced up, nodding briefly before returning his gaze to the ground. His mind was cluttered with many images, mostly unpleasant, but Laura's face managed to peek through his thoughts, staring at him with what seemed to be genuine concern. *Kids*, Ely thought, they are so innocent, so full of goodness. *How do they lose it?* he asked himself. *It gets beaten out of them*, he answered back almost immediately.

A voice derailed Ely's train of thought. "Here you go, it's clean." Ely looked up to see Jeff standing near him holding out a white handkerchief.

"Thanks, but I don't want to dirty it."

"Go ahead; it's for my allergies in case they act up. I have several more in my backpack. Besides, you need it more than me." Ely looked up at the towel skeptically. "Don't worry; I haven't blown my nose on it or anything," Jeff smiled and tossed the handkerchief on Ely's lap. "You can have it. See you tomorrow," he said, racing back to the car as the engine started.

"Okay," Ely responded, this time with a little more assurance.

Two

Picture a jar with marbles in it. Every marble represents a reason for living. Each little glass ball is a dream, a goal, an idea, a compliment received, a word of praise from a parent, a kind gesture from a stranger, the feeling of accomplishment from a task well done. A jar, a life, filled with everything good and kind that has come from others and one's own consciousness.

Every time something positive happens, a marble is added. Every time something bad happens, a marble is taken out. The idea being that as you live your life more marbles should be added than taken out. At least that is the type of life that people 'should' live.

My jar was nearly empty. I had a few marbles in the jar of life. Some came from my mother who struggled to make my life better. But she too had a jar that was nearly empty. I didn't know it at the time, but it's hard for someone with few marbles to fill another's jar. She tried as hard as she could. I know that. But as she added marbles to my jar, marbles were taken from hers, and before long that drain on her jar affected the input of mine.

I received a few marbles from various teachers who did their best to be kind and help me, but their presence in my life was just a temporary blip in time as I moved from school to school and grade to grade. They did their best, but they just couldn't add marbles to my jar at the same rate they were taken out.

It should be known that for someone like me, each marble added to my jar felt as if it weighed ten pounds, its impact so much greater for me than for someone who already

13

had lots of marbles in their jar. One more marble in their jar would not be noticed so much. But one marble rolling around and clinking against the glass walls of an empty jar resounded like cathedral bells on a Sunday morning.

My jar was empty that morning as I sat on the curb of that store. But a marble was added that day, and its presence had a huge impact on my life, an impact that no one, not even myself, would fully understand until later.

Ely Carter

————————————

The dilapidated trailer sat on cinder blocks tucked into the corner of a small parcel of land, surrounded by overgrown grass and shaded by several large oak trees. A long dirt road, filled with pot holes, snaked its way through the heavily wooded lot until it made a loop in front of the old worn down single wide. The un-mowed grass around the trailer was choked with weeds, and it was obvious that no one had cared for the home or the land for many years.

The trailer was streaked with grime and mildew and a few of the windows were cracked and had been repaired with frayed pieces of duct tape. Several rusted derelict cars littered the front yard, and intermingled amongst the cars and weeds were various rusty automobile parts. A fender, some hub caps, and even an old axle lay peeking from the overgrowth of foliage.

The inside of the trailer was old and run down as well, though it looked as if someone had done their best to make it clean and organized, an effort equivalent of trying to polish a dog turd, impossible, and to most, not worth the effort.

The small living room was furnished with worn mismatched furniture arranged around a little television in the corner with rabbit ear antennas. A worn recliner sat before it, flanked by garage sale end tables covered with empty beer cans and several ash trays overflowing with cigarette butts.

The tiny kitchen could barely accommodate the small round breakfast table and four rickety chairs. It was relatively clean but everything was so stained and nicked up that it was difficult to tell.

Two bedrooms and a bathroom made up the rest of the home. In contrast to the rest of the aged trailer, one of the rooms reflected a desire to make the best of what it had to offer, which wasn't much. Like the rest of the trailer, the room was old and the carpet stained, but it was as immaculate as it could be under the circumstances. Nothing littered the floor and everything had been meticulously arranged to provide an orderly functional space in an otherwise chaotic life.

An aged rickety book shelf lined one wall and several dozen books filled those shelves in perfect order, organized alphabetically by the author's name. On closer inspection one would see that every single book was either a fantasy or science fiction novel. Several of the classics were there, like *The Hobbit* and the other Tolkien books, along with those of C.S. Lewis and Isaac Asimov. There were handfuls of others that would seem obscure to a casual observer, but to a fellow fantasy aficionado they would bring a smile of recognition, books by David Gemmell, Robert Jordan, E.E. Knight, Terry Brooks, and Jim Butcher, just to name a few. All of the books were old and worn, as if they had been purchased from a used book store. But their careful and organized display suggested that they were much more than junk to their owner.

Any observer would have also noticed that the thrift store clothes of the occupant were neatly folded and stacked by color and type. The short sleeve shirts were stacked together. Sweatshirts were organized on the top shelf in the closet and jeans were folded and stacked perfectly inside one of the drawers.

A tiny desk was tucked into a corner of the room. The space occupied by the desk, the bed, and the chest of drawers left only a patch of carpet showing. It would have been just enough room for a small child to lie down and make a snow angel. It was a small room.

On the desk was a neat pile of books. One was a monster manual from the Dungeons and Dragons game. Another was a book titled *The History of Ancient Weapons*. On top if the pile was a black book three times as thick as the rest. In gold filigree writing the cover read, *Shakespeare's Sonnets, a Complete Collection*.

Nestled against the wall at the back of the desk was a stack of compact discs from various classical composers. Bach was there, along with Beethoven, Mozart, and Tchaikovsky. There was a set of battered headphones plugged into a scratched up compact disc player that had been wrapped in duct tape to keep the battery plate in position.

An alarm clock buzzed and the blinking 'six o'clock' pulsed with the annoying sound. A form stirred in the patchwork quilt on the bed and a big hand reached out and slammed on the end table, frantically searching for the blaring clock. It missed once before finding the snooze button, silencing the piercing sound.

Ely awoke with difficulty, unable to completely shake the grogginess that threatened to pull him back into bed. But he slowly managed to slide out of his blankets and sit up on the edge of his bed. He rubbed his eyes, scratching the top of his head. One eye was still puffy and blue, but his lip was almost healed with only the remnant of a small cut remaining. A few other minor scrapes and bruises were apparent on his freckly face. He took a couple of deep breaths, looked around the room through sad, tired eyes, and then slowly sat up, moving more like an old man than the adolescent he was. His mind and his body wanted nothing more than to retreat back into the blissful sanctuary of sleep.

Ely put on a pair of jeans, a t-shirt, and some ragged sneakers and moved out into the living room. Before he exited his room he grabbed the backpack lying on the floor by his bed, slung it over his shoulder, and walked into the kitchen.

The kitchen was empty, as it always was at this time in the morning. Usually his mother, Mary Carson, was working at the local grocery market.

She typically worked the late night shift and didn't get home until seven in the morning, and would go straight to bed. Sometimes she would even stay longer if she had a chance to pick up a few more hours at work. Ely sighed as he scanned the mess in the kitchen, knowing the source of it as he glanced into the living room. There he saw his father, Bill Carson, sleeping in the recliner, his mouth slightly open, snoring loudly.

Bill was a big man, around six foot five inches and he weighed close to three hundred pounds, most of the bulk stored in his belly, sustained by large quantities of beer each night. A tank top that had once been white managed to cover only about three quarters of his bulging abdomen. The table next to his chair, and the carpet around the recliner, were littered with empty beer bottles.

Drunk again, Ely thought to himself. He felt bad for his mother. She had to come home to such a messy kitchen…again. He knew the situation all too well. She would clean up, and he would yell at her for whatever reason. Then she would make him some breakfast while he sat on his ass and watched television, getting drunk again. He had been out of work for nearly two months now. Bill was a mechanic who couldn't seem to hold down a job anywhere. In fact they had moved to Key Peninsula because he had managed to find a job working at a local gas station. But after just two weeks of work he was fired for drinking on the job.

Ely glared at his passed out father with unmasked disgust before turning for the door. He knew there would be no food to eat for breakfast as his father would've eaten whatever dinner had been prepared last night, and he didn't have time to make anything, even if there was something to cook. Maybe he could get breakfast at school. He wouldn't have enough money but he could fill out the paper work for free and reduced lunch. He had a lot of experience at that. He had done it many times, in all the schools he had attended. His family primarily lived off his mom's salary alone, and what she earned as a grocery store clerk was pretty minimal. But it would take time to fill out the paper works, so he knew he would go hungry this morning, but that too was nothing unusual. It was just another day in the life of Ely.

He was just about to leave when he noticed a note on the kitchen table. Under it was two dollars. The note was from his mother, "Ely, I'm working a double shift so I won't be home when you get up. Sorry I could not be here to make you breakfast. I hope you have a good first day at school. Here are a couple bucks for lunch. I love you, honey, Mom." Ely smiled and tucked the money in his pocket before exiting the trailer, the thin metal door slamming shut behind him.

A long line of bright yellow busses were lined up in front of the school as kids flowed out of them by the hundreds. Ely stepped out of his bus to join the ranks of his new classmates. Standing taller than most, he stopped and looked around. More than a few of the students took notice of this big newcomer, but none made any effort to acknowledge him. Bright eyed teenagers milled about in their new school clothes and stylish shoes with their cool backpacks slung casually over one shoulder. Ely sighed in frustration as he looked down at his worn pants, dirty sneakers, and old, outdated backpack. He tried to keep his clothes clean, but even laundry detergent can't make thread-bare clothes and holes disappear.

The school was definitely in the boonies, surrounded by acres of evergreens, sparsely populated by small homes and modest residential developments. There were a few more affluent homes on the waterfront acreage of the Puget Sound. The school building itself didn't look like a rural school, however. It had been almost entirely constructed of concrete, perhaps in an attempt to give it a contemporary look, but more likely it was done to save money, and Ely couldn't help but think that it looked somewhat like a prison, this time a prison in the woods. He smiled to himself as he thought about how fitting that was; after all, every school he had ever attended had been sort of a prison for him. His previous schools weren't necessarily all bad, but most of his experiences and memories were not so great. The collection of these unpleasant memories had accumulated over the years, forming the thick walls of his own personal prison.

Ely put his head down and followed the stream of students through the main doors. Inside they clustered together in their various groups, formed by grade level, and social standing, chatting excitedly in the commons area as they looked over their schedules and talked about their upcoming classes.

Ely glanced around and saw various tables occupied by teachers who were giving out schedules. The tables were labeled in alphabetical order. Ely quickly found the table labeled A through D. He picked up his schedule from a smiling younger woman with short dark hair and glasses and moved off into a quiet corner to be by himself.

His first class was history. Well that was good, he thought. History was his favorite subject. He loved to read about the past as it helped him forget about the present. He had no problem remembering obscure events, dates, and details, things that most students his age found rather useless or boring. But for Ely it opened a door where he could view humankind over time, and attempt to understand the vagaries of human nature. Why people behave as they do, why some people have such a capacity for good while others can do the most horrible and despicable things, why people act differently in groups than they do as individuals. History provided an endless list of questions. Studying historical events and people had always helped Ely focus on finding the answers to those questions, and for some reason that search minimized his own insignificance and helped him realize that he was not the only nameless pawn on the chess board.

He glanced up from his schedule and noticed that some kids were moving off down the halls, probably looking for their lockers. His history class was in room 116 and on the back of the schedule was a map of the school. Well at least this school thought ahead. He had been a new student in a new school before and there was nothing more embarrassing than walking into a room late because you couldn't find it. He could vividly remember several times where he had done just that. The teacher would stop his or her discussion as the rest of the class stared at the new fat kid. He couldn't actually hear what some students mumbled to each other, but he could read the looks on many of their faces as he made his way to an empty seat while the teacher resumed his or her class introduction. At least this time that wouldn't happen to him.

Ely walked down the noisy crowded hallway, turning this way and that, trying to figure out where to go. He studied his class schedule and map, then looked up as he tried to get his bearing among the throngs of students moving through the halls. One of them bumped into him, knocking his pack off his shoulder, but Ely just ignored it, picked his backpack back up, and hesitantly moved on, now realizing that he was on the wrong side of the school. He needed to walk around the circular hall to the C wing located on the opposite side of the clearly labeled library.

The sound of the bell quickly sent kids scattering in different directions. Ely looked anxiously down the hall, then to his left through the library, trying to figure out which direction to go. It looked like he could walk through the library to get to the C wing, but he wasn't sure if the doors would be locked.

"Can I help you find your class?" he heard a man's voice next to him.

Ely turned to face a smiling man wearing grey slacks and a blue button up shirt. The man was handsome in an outdoorsy way, maybe thirty years old, with several days of unchecked stubble. His unshaven face was angular and strong and on most people it would have looked unkempt, but on him it somehow looked dignified and tough all at the same time. His dark brown hair was shaved short and that made him look younger than his years.

"Um, yes sir, my schedule says I have Mr. Seljin," Ely muttered.

"Well, that's easy," the man said. "That's me. I'm heading to class now so why don't you follow me."

"Okay," Ely replied shyly.

Mr. Seljin headed through the library doors and led Ely across the floor. Mr. Seljin noticed Ely looking intently at all the books. "You like books?" he asked.

"Um, yes, a lot, sir."

"Call me Mr. Seljin, or just Sel, I'm definitely no *sir.*"

"Um…okay, sir, I'm mean, Mr. Seljin," Ely stammered quickly.

"We have something in common. I love to read as well. What's your name?" Mr. Seljin asked as they neared the double doors on the other side of the room.

"Ely."

"Well it's nice to meet you, Ely. Are you new around here? I don't recognize you."

"Yeah, we moved here from Seattle," Ely replied as they moved through the doors into another hallway filled with students hurrying to their classes.

Mr. Seljin led Ely across the hall and into another hallway that branched off from the main one. They danced and dodged as they maneuvered their way through the stream of students hustling to class. Most moved aside when they saw Mr. Seljin, smiling at him or calling out a casual "Hey Sel," before moving down the hall to be swallowed up by the swarm of kids.

As they neared Mr. Seljin's room, Jeff, the same kid that Ely had met at the convenience store the previous day, emerged from the throng of students and greeted the young teacher.

"Hey Sel, I'm so glad I have you this year," Jeff said enthusiastically.

"Cool," Sel replied. "I have you first period?"

"Yeah. So how was your summer?" Jeff asked.

Ely hung back, unsure if he should enter the classroom or say hi to Jeff. The dialogue between the two was interesting. Ely hadn't heard many student- teacher interactions like that before and it intrigued him. Obviously this Mr. Seljin was respected and his behavior with the students around him seemed very casual, almost effortless. Ely was actually looking forward to class, something that he had not experienced in a long time. At least he wasn't invisible to this teacher. Ely knew that it probably wasn't fair to assume or imply that all his other teachers didn't *see* him. They probably did, and they probably cared, but most of their time was spent trying to teach their subject matter while dealing with the more vocal or unruly students. The quiet ones like Ely easily slipped through the cracks. It isn't their entire fault; they are given a pretty difficult task. There was no other job that Ely could think of that required someone to teach information to a group of young people, most of whom could care less about it. Combine that task with dealing with the issues of behavior, puberty, a few crazy parents, family problems, and the handful of kids in each class who were so messed up that teachers often spent a disproportionate amount of their time disciplining and counseling rather than actually teaching.

"It was good," Sel answered. "Went by too fast though. Hey, I want you to meet one of our new students this year. This is Ely."

"Yeah, we've met. What's up Ely? Your face looks better," he said, glancing sidelong at Ely.

"Hey, yeah, it was nothing. It's better now," Ely said, glancing quickly at Jeff before looking away.

"I noticed you have some bruising, what happened?" Sel asked.

"I tripped and fell," Ely said, a little too quickly.

"Really?"

"Mmm, huh," Ely stammered, looking down at the ground.

Mr. Seljin glanced at Ely momentarily as Ely avoided his gaze. "Okay Ely, why don't you go in and take a seat before the bell rings."

Ely didn't say a word as he left the two by the doorway.

"Jeff, do me a favor, would ya? Help him out if you see he needs anything."

"Oh, come on, Sel, I'm not a baby sitter," Jeff protested.

"Imagine being in a new school for the first time. People know you. You're an eighth grader and the captain of the wrestling team. He doesn't know anyone. Put yourself in his shoes," Sel said.

"Empathy, right?" Jeff asked.

"That's right, you remember, good work," Sel replied.

"I remember you talking about that last year in practice. You said to treat your opponent with respect, whether you win or lose. Treat them how you would want to be treated if you had lost. Put yourself in their shoes. Empathy," Jeff finished with a flourish.

"That's right."

"Okay, I'll keep an eye on him," Jeff relented. "Besides, we're going to need some unlimited wrestlers this year and he definitely looks like he fits that category."

"That's what I was thinking. Speaking of, what are you weighing now?"

"A little over one thirty five."

"That's good. Only three months away. Plan on making it on the Hall of Fame again?" Sel asked.

"I better. Oh man, I can't wait for wrestling season," Jeff said as he clenched his fists excitedly.

"Me too; remember, you have to keep your grades up. How's your math coming along?"

"Sel, you know I struggle in math," Jeff replied, his enthusiastic smile all but disappearing.

"I know. That's why you have to work on it. It's no different than any skill, perfect practice makes perfect," Sel said as the final bell rang. "Go have a seat. We'll talk about this later."

"All right, Sel," Jeff said as he walked into the room.

Mr. Seljin waited for a second as he looked in the hall for any stragglers. The hall was empty so he strode toward his door, stopping momentarily to glance at his bulletin board outside his room. On the board was a cut out caricature of a huge muscle-bound wrestler holding up a stack of books. Above the drawing was written, 'You have to be strong to keep your grades up'. Sel smiled at the picture and then entered his room.

The first half of the day went by quickly for Ely. No one talked to him and the monotonous teacher introductions became just a series of incoherent words linked together as he let his mind drift away to the heroes of distant fantasy realms within his books, where the courage in one's heart and the strength of one's sword saved the day. He loved fantasy and he read it constantly. It was easy to project himself into one of these worlds, where he was the hero feared by villains, and swooned over by buxom maidens.

Several times throughout the morning, when he didn't think the teachers were watching, he would read from his book under the desk. Most of the day was just filled with introductions, going over the curriculum, and reading through the syllabus, all of which Ely didn't think was that important anyway.

The only class where Ely actually listened was Mr. Seljin's class. He showed a PowerPoint presentation introducing himself so the new students could know him better. Ely thought that was interesting, not just because of the PowerPoint, but because of the concept. Teachers often wanted to develop this 'relationship' with their students but they rarely shared anything about themselves. It made sense to Ely. After all, it should be a two way street. How could someone really know or respect a teacher if they knew nothing about him or her?

One thing that really piqued Ely's interest was the fact that Mr. Seljin had shared with everyone that he was an avid fantasy reader and that he collected fantasy books. That really surprised Ely, as he had never met any adult who read the type of books he liked; nor had he met anyone with the same passion for fantasy. And yet it looked as if this new teacher might have something in common with him. This too was a strange concept, as most of his previous teachers, no matter how hard they had tried, seemed liked aliens from another world. Ely was smart enough to know that he probably wasn't giving them the benefit of the doubt, as they very well could have had similar backgrounds or even interests, but they seemed so separated from his reality that they were never able to make a connection with him.

It was during his lunch break when Ely ran into his first problem. Ely had bought a piece of pizza with his two bucks and had gone outside to find a spot to read his book and eat his lunch. He found a big rock next to a basketball court and sat down next to it, leaning up against it to read. It was a good spot as it sheltered him from the sun, and the only activity going on was a basketball game between a few boys on the nearby court. The noise they made was nothing compared to the commotion inside the common room and Ely figured this would be a great spot to relax with his ear phones on, and drift away into the fantasy world his book had created. Ely took a bite of his pizza, settled his taped up ear phones over his ears, and turned on his classical music. Today he was listening to one of his favorites, Beethoven's 9th symphony.

He had only gotten a few pages into the book when a basketball bounced towards him from the court and bumped into his leg.

"Hey, throw us the ball back!"

Ely shifted his weight, took off his headphones, and looked over at the boy moving towards him. He was nearly six feet tall and stocky like a football player. The big kid wore baggy pants and a long white basketball jersey. He was sure the number and colors of the jersey meant something that he should know, some famous basketball player, but it might as well been written in Orcish as it meant nothing to Ely. He had on a fashionable straight brim hat that was turned sideways, just enough to be cool. There were five boys standing behind him waiting for Ely to return the ball to them.

Ely reached out with his right foot in a feeble attempt to kick the ball back to the big boy, but he grazed the ball with his foot and it shanked to the right, down a long gradual hill, slowly rolling all the way to the rear entrance of the school.

Time slowed momentarily as Ely watched each rotation of the ball as it rolled farther away from the basketball court, away from the boys who were now glaring at Ely.

"Hey fatty, why did you do that?" the boy yelled angrily as he strode towards Ely, the other boys close on his heels.

"I didn't mean to, I...I'm sorry," Ely stammered.

"You're sorry?!" the boy said, leaning menacingly over Ely. "Why don't you pick your fat ass up and go get it."

Ely slowly got up to do just that, and as he stood the boy whipped his hand out and grabbed Ely's book out of his hand.

"Hey, give that back!" Ely protested.

"Who the hell reads during honor time? And nice CD player," he sneered.

"Give me my book back."

"Go get the ball first. Maybe you'll lose some weight on the way over there," the boy said laughing. His friends joined in with their own versions of put-downs related to his weight, nothing Ely hadn't heard before.

Ely sighed and turned around to get the ball. Just as he did, the bully kicked Ely in the back of his right leg behind the knee, causing his leg to buckle. He lost his balance and fell forward, landing face first in the dirt and hitting his chin on a rock. Ely lay there for a moment, tears welling in his eyes, and dirt covering his face. His chin hurt but he choked back the tears, not wanting this bully to humiliate him further by seeing him cry.

"Hey!" a voice yelled from the side.

Ely glanced up from the ground and saw Jeff and another big kid stride purposefully towards them. The boy next to Jeff was black, one of few black students that Ely had seen in this rural school. He must have weighed close to two hundred pounds, and very little of it was fat. He was about the same size as the bully that had just kicked him to the ground.

"Leave him alone, Adam," Jeff said as he walked over and stood next to Ely's prone body.

"We're just having fun, Jeff, don't worry about it," Adam said, his bravado quickly vanishing.

Ely thought that was interesting since Jeff weighed considerably less, and was at least a head shorter. But his words carried a certain weight that did not reflect his smaller stature and Adam clearly felt the power of his character just as Ely did. There was something about this Jeff kid that said, 'don't mess with me.'

Jeff and his friend stepped in between Adam and Ely, making their intent clear. Jeff possessed an air of confidence that the rest of the kids respected. Their body language lost its aggressiveness, and suddenly messing with this new fat kid didn't seem like a good idea. "Go have fun somewhere else, Adam," Jeff said again.

"Why do you care?" Adam sneered.

"Sel asked me to help him out," Jeff replied smoothly, stepping meaningfully closer to Adam.

Adam looked down at Ely with disdain. "Whatever," he said, glancing back at his friends. "Let's go."

Adam threw the book on Ely's back and walked away with his friends, laughing all the way.

Ely slowly got up and quickly wiped away the tears from his eyes before he turned towards Jeff.

"You alright?" Jeff asked.

"Yeah, thanks," Ely replied softly.

"No problem. Adam's a punk. Don't let him get to you," Jeff said.

"Okay," was all Ely could think to say.

Jeff and his friend walked off and left Ely to his thoughts. He first wiped the dirt off his book and then tended to his pants and shirt, doing his best to brush off the dust from his clothes. With dirt still smudged on his face, he looked over at Adam and his friends as they walked away.

"Here we go again," Ely muttered with sad resignation.

Three

What is it with so many kids and their ability to be total, uncaring, selfish jerks? I mean, don't get me wrong, there are always nice kids in schools, but they tend to be quiet, phantoms hiding in the shadows of the pricks. No one really sees that they don't think like the jerks do. So, to the kid who is the brunt of a bully's harassment, it seems like they're all in it together, that no one really cares, even though that is not really true. But while you're dodging all the shit some people are throwing at you, you never really notice the other kids, the passive bystanders, who are looking at the scene with disdain, too afraid to intervene. You don't have the time because if you relax one second, crap will hit you in the face.

And then there are anomalies like Jeff. A popular kid and star athlete who didn't really care what people thought, and acted according to his own conscience, his own set of rules. That behavior in middle school politics is not very common, and potentially a major risk in the social world of the adolescent. But Jeff didn't seem to care and the social science side of my brain always asked why. What makes someone like that? Is it something inherent, or is it how they were raised? What makes someone the antithesis of a kind and caring person? Why do some kids, and adults too, I guess, treat others so rudely and cruelly. Then throw another variable into the equation. Why do some of those horrible teenagers turn into great and wonderful people later in life? Can that dichotomy be chalked up to adolescent hormones? Those poor hormones, they seem to be blamed for all the negative behaviors of young adults. I don't know the answer, but whenever I view the world through a dark lens, and I feel

*that the human race is doomed, I think of people like Jeff,
and a scarce few others, and my outlook about the world and
its human interactions suddenly becomes a little brighter.*

Ely Carter

———————————————

      Ely was in a pretty bad mood as he walked
along his long dirt driveway. He wore his
headphones and the classical music helped drown
out the problems of the day. The melodic notes
calmed his senses as one foot in front of the other
carried him up the mile long driveway closer to his
mobile home.

      But the music couldn't totally erase the day.
His chin was hurting and beginning to bruise, and he
was already dreading the next day that might bring
about another possible run in with the bully from
the basketball court. But to be honest, he had had
much worse days. All in all he had several classes
that he really liked, and Jeff's presence, although a
bit uncertain at this point, was definitely helpful. Ely
chuckled to himself, finding it ironically amusing
that he considered a day where he was nearly beat up
by a bully to be a 'good' day. It wasn't really funny
of course, but it helped Ely deal with the biting
reality a little better.

      Before Ely knew it, he was walking up the
rickety wooden steps to his porch and front door.
His mind had drifted off somewhere and he almost

didn't notice his father sitting in the recliner in front of the television.

Bill was wearing baggy worn overalls covered in grease and a sleeveless flannel shirt that nearly covered his classic stained white tank top that was his usual attire. Ely wondered if he took it off whether there would be an outline of clean skin underneath it shaped like the shirt. His father held a beer in one hand and a lit cigarette dangled from his lip as he glanced at Ely.

"While you're up, get me a beer," his father said.

Ely set his backpack down and went to the refrigerator without saying a word.

"And don't go hiding in your room like a little girl. All you do is read. Do those damn dishes and make yourself useful."

"Where is mom?"

"I guess she's still working, probably picked up more hours. She better be home in time for dinner, I'm starving." He reached out to grab the beer that Ely had brought him. Ely turned to go without looking at his father but Bill grabbed his hand roughly and turned him about.

"What the hell happened to your face?" he said, his voice rising in anger.

"You hit me, don't you remember?"

"Hell yeah, I remember. Don't get smart with me. I'm talking about the cut on your chin." Ely noticed his father's words were slightly slurred.

"Nothing happened. I fell and scraped it," Ely muttered.

"Jesus Christ, you got your ass kicked again! God dammit, what kind of pussy are you!?"

"Dad, I didn't do anything," Ely protested.

"That's the problem, you didn't do anything! You have to stand up for yourself. I ought to beat that pussy attitude right out of ya. I thought the beating I gave you the other day might have done ya some good. Looks like you need another lesson."

Bill stood up with his beer in hand and Ely backed away in fright as his father slowly found his balance.

"Dad, please, it won't happen again," Ely stammered as he stepped further away from his drunken father.

"Don't back away from me, boy! Come here and take it like a man! It'll be worse if you don't get over here right now!" Bill yelled.

Ely, with his lower lip quivering, slowly stepped toward his father, whose hand flew out and slapped him roughly across the face. The blow was just hard enough to sting, but not do any real damage. Ely's head snapped to the side. Tears began flowing freely down his face leaving wet rivulets down his cheeks. Then his dad slapped him again with the back of the same hand.

"Don't cry like a girl! You'll thank me for this someday. It'll make you tough!" Bill yelled, swaying in his drunkenness.

Bill slapped him a third time, this time a little harder. Once more, he hit him with the same hand. This time the force of the blow was enough to knock Ely off balance, causing him to stumble to his right. He nearly fell before he caught himself on the corner of the end table.

Ely looked up at his father, blood now dripping from his damaged nose. Breathing hard, he tried to keep control, knowing that to do anything other than that would just bring more pain.

"Now get your fat ass in the kitchen and do those dishes before your mom gets home. And wipe off your nose; I don't want blood on anything!" His dad then fell back into his chair as if nothing had happened.

Ely walked into the kitchen and stood in front of the sink. He put his hands on the kitchen counter, gripping the edge so tightly his fingers turned white, focusing all his pain and anger on that one inch lip of wood and laminate.

Ely looked back at his father with growing revulsion. Bill was again seemingly mesmerized by some stupid television show, draining another beer can as if Ely did not exist. Ely turned back and stared into the cracked mirror that hung to the left of the sink. The face staring back at him was bloodied and sad, but the eyes blazed with a smoldering rage.

Ely did the dishes quickly so he could remove himself from his father's presence. He was feeling a mixture of emotions heavily dominated by anger and fear. He needed to get away, to escape into a book or music, or to fall asleep and dream of something better than his life. Getting the dishes done quickly would accomplish that goal, as he knew his father would leave him alone, at least for a while.

Later he lay on his back in bed, staring at the ceiling, listening to Beethoven's Moonlight Sonata.

Suddenly there was a pounding at his door. "Turn that shit off!" his father yelled through the door before stomping off to resume his place in front of the television.

Ely sighed, leaned over, and plugged in his head phones, putting them on and cranking up the volume. The lilting notes of the piano began to sooth his mind, and he closed his eyes, losing himself in the music which, at least for a while, helped him shut out the pain.

***

The scanner at the checkout stand beeped, echoing softly in the silence of the nearly empty Safeway grocery store. Mary Carson scanned the youth's purchases with practiced monotony. It was late, or early, depending on your perspective, nearly 3 A.M., and the only ones in at the local country store were Mary, John, the manager, and the young customer staring back at her with a stoned smile. The boy looked to be about sixteen. His long black hair hung loosely around his shoulders, and his bloodshot eyes made him look as if he was suffering from some severe allergy.

Mary Carson was overweight, at least eighty pounds heavier than her five foot six frame should handle. But despite her large body, her face was kind, gentle, and above average, definitely not uncomely as you might expect on someone so big. Her eyes were a brilliant green and her long eye lashes accentuated their beauty. Her pudgy face did nothing to dampen her bright smile.

"Get some late night cravings?" Mary asked.

The kid giggled in response. Not a young girl giggle, but the kind so often portrayed in Cheech and Chong movies, the 'I'm stoned out of my mind' giggle. "Yeah, I kinda got the munchies. My friend, Mary Jane and me, get hungry late at night."

Mary smiled wanly, as she took his money and finished bagging the food. "You take care. You and Mary Jane have fun now."

He was still giggling as he left the store. "We will, and thanks."

Mary shook her head and yawned, stretching her back at the same time. The late nights and long hours standing on her feet really bothered her back. She knew her weight didn't help either. She kept telling herself she was going to lose some weight, but she never got around to it. Plus, Bill didn't like healthy food. He always wanted pizza and other processed food. Anytime she made something healthy, he got angry and took it out on her. After a while she just gave up. Bill always called her fat and she knew he was right, but she didn't have any extra time, and the few moments she did have were spent taking care of her unemployed husband. She sighed and reached up for the phone near her register.

"John, it's nearly three o'clock. Thanks for the extra hours but do you mind if I go home now?" Mary asked over the phone. "Okay, thanks, can you come and relieve me?" Mary yawned again. "Great, I'll see you in a sec."

The Life of Ely

Mary hung up the phone and walked over to the magazine and book section of the store. They had a small section of fantasy and science fiction books and Mary scanned them slowly, looking for a book for her son, Ely. They all looked the same to her, so she grabbed one that had a new copyright.

She walked back to the checkout stand where John was now logging in at the register. He looked up and smiled.

"You buying a book before you go?"

"Yeah. My son loves fantasy books."

"Oh yeah? What book did you get?"

"Oh, I don't know. I just grabbed one. They all look the same to me," she said as she held it up for him to see. John checked the book through the scanner and he took her ten dollar bill. "All the covers have some big strong guy with a sword and some beautiful girl hardly wearing any clothes standing near him."

John gave her the change and put the book into a bag. "Yeah, I guess they do. Perhaps that's why they're called *fantasy* books."

Mary laughed. "I hadn't thought of that," she said, smiling back at him. "Good night, John."

"Good night. Drive carefully. That highway is really dangerous. It's like the autobahn for drunks…especially this time of the night. And get some rest."

"I will. Thanks, John."

Mary made it home safely and it was all she could do to keep her eyes open. The lights were all out, which was nothing unusual for this time of

40

night. She was hoping they would be out; that meant that Bill was asleep. If he were still up this late it would mean he was in a foul mood, probably drunker than usual, which meant he would most likely take it out on her.

She entered the front door quietly and set her keys on the kitchen table. Looking over by the television she noticed that Bill was still there, snoring loudly in his recliner, beer cans and cigarette butts littering the space around him. She frowned briefly before moving down the hall toward the bedrooms. She clicked on the hall light before turning toward Ely's door.

Mary cracked open his door and a thin ray of the hall light shined into the room. She quietly stepped inside and set the book down on top of his desk, the light from the hall hitting it perfectly as if it were a magical artifact.

"Good night, son," she whispered. "I love you."

She walked out quietly and slowly shut the door, extinguishing the thin ray of light and returning the room to darkness.

***

The door to enter Mr. Seljin's room was a collage of various pictures and quotes. The dominant piece was a drawing of a muscular upper body with a hog's head, complete with massive tusks and course hair. The quote above it read, 'Key Peninsula Wrestling', and below the head it said, 'Fear the Hog!'

It took a long while for Ely to know what the hog reference was even about, and he always wondered about it considering that the school's mascot was a cougar, not a hog. Eventually he learned that it was a reference to a television series in the seventies called *Welcome Back Kotter*, and that Mr. Kotter was a teacher who taught a class of students with behavior and academic issues. Mr. Kotter referred to them as the *sweat hogs*, the tough kids in the school, the ones that were a challenge to teach. So Mr. Seljin started calling the wrestlers Sweat Hogs, in reference to the show, because in reality many of the kids that were wrestlers were just the sort of students that would have been in Mr. Kotter's class anyway. And the wrestlers accepted the name with honor, never really knowing exactly what the connection was, but trusting in Mr. Seljin that the name was given to them because they were tough. They were Key Peninsula wrestlers, and that meant something at this school.

It was first period, and Mr. Seljin was giving a lecture, his eighth grade students busy taking notes. He moved slowly through the aisles, lecturing and advancing the PowerPoint slides with a remote as he spoke.

"Alright everyone, let's do a quick review of what we covered today," Sel said as he completed the last slide.

Cisco, Jeff's friend, raised his hand.

"Yeah, Cisco, go ahead," Sel prompted.

"Sel, why do we have to copy the notes during these lectures? Why don't you just copy off the slides for us?"

"I've already talked about this, Cisco. Who can help Cisco understand my reasoning for writing notes?" Sel asked the class.

Shannon, a cute red headed girl with blue eyes and dimples, raised her hand. Sel just nodded at her, giving her the go ahead.

"When we write it down it helps us remember the information. It forces our brains to remember the stuff. I think you said it helps imprint it on our minds," she explained.

"Very good, Shannon, I'm glad *someone* was listening," Sel said, looking pointedly at Cisco, but smiling nonetheless.

"Ah, come on, Sel. I'm listening. Well maybe not yesterday, but I am today," Cisco replied with mock innocence.

"I'm glad you're listening today, Cisco, I guess I can't have everything," Mr. Seljin laughed. "Besides, note taking skills are important. You are all going to be in high school next year and I need to prepare you for that. Anyway, let's get back to our review. When was Jamestown established?"

Several people raised their hands, including Jeff Hanson.

"Go ahead, Jeff," Sel said.

"1608," Jeff answered.

"Close, very close. Anyone else?" Sel asked a second time.

Again, several hands went into the air. Mr. Seljin paused for a moment as he scanned the faces. He stopped on Ely who was looking down at his desk, seemingly not paying attention.

"How about you, Ely," Sel said.

"1607," Ely said quickly, not looking up.

"Good," Sel responded. "Now, can you explain some of the problems they faced when they arrived in Jamestown?" Sel continued.

Ely was still staring at his desk. "They built their town on a swamp," he said softly.

Adam, the same kid that had bullied Ely by the basketball court, interrupted him. "What's wrong with that?" he asked, as if it was the stupidest thing that Ely could have said.

"Adam, please don't interrupt," Sel said sharply.

Mr. Seljin was impressed. They had talked about the various problems the first settlers had encountered, but they had yet to discuss that issue. He had planned on bringing it up tomorrow when they studied the English colony in more detail. Ely must have read ahead, or maybe he had learned it before in his previous school. Nonetheless, he was impressed that he would bring up something that they had not actually discussed. "Ely, go ahead, finish what you were saying."

Ely looked up shyly at Mr. Seljin and then glanced quickly at Adam, his look clearly telling Mr. Seljin that the two had already had a run in. "Go ahead. You're right, so please tell the rest of the class why building on a swamp was a mistake."

"Well," Ely stammered. "The swamp was infested with mosquitos."

"That's stupid! What the heck is the problem with a few bugs?" Adam blurted out again.

Mr. Seljin turned his angry eyes on Adam, and gave him a stare that immediately shut the bully's mouth. "Adam, I asked you not to interrupt, and I mean it. One more outburst and we are going to have a problem. Do you understand?"

The entire class was silently staring at Adam. Mr. Seljin's glare was famous, and everyone in the room felt the heat from it. And the wrestlers in the room, including Adam, had seen that glare on more than one occasion, and it usually meant that something bad was going to happen. It had the desired effect on Adam and he nodded his head in acknowledgement, his mouth clamped shut.

"Go ahead, Ely, finish your comment," Sel continued, his glare disappearing as he turned back to Ely.

"Mosquitos carry malaria, which is a deadly disease. Many people died of malaria. Only thirty four of the original one hundred and four were alive after the first year," Ely said, suddenly finished.

"Excellent, Ely, I'm very impressed. Now," Sel said to the rest of the group, "were there any other problems?"

John, an athletic looking boy with a messy mop of light brown hair, raised his hand enthusiastically.

"Go ahead, John," Sel said.

"They didn't have enough women," John blurted, in his mock 'gangster wanna be', voice. Everyone knew John and liked him. He had a definite style about him, talking in a mixture of surfer lingo and rapper style. He was funny and kind, and not afraid to get involved. "If I was there, I'd…bam!, take control. I'd have all the ladies. You know what I'm sayin' Sel?"

Most of the kids began to laugh, including Mr. Seljin, who, no matter how hard he tried, could rarely hide his smile when John spoke, which was quite often. During the laughter, he noticed that Ely was not participating and still looking down. That is when he noticed that he was reading a book under his desk.

"Well, that is true, they didn't have many women at first; however, that wasn't one of the main problems during the first year. What were some of the serious problems they faced?" Sel asked as the laughter subsided.

"Come on, Sel. You can't get more serious than that. You're crazy, man," John added with a flourish of his hands. He liked to talk with his hands and the kids just loved it.

They began to laugh again when the bell rang, ending first period.

"All right everyone, no homework tonight. We will get into Jamestown, Virginia in more detail tomorrow. Have a good day," Sel said, excusing everyone from class.

Everyone got up, gathered their things, and moved for the door like a herd of sheep. There was an occasional "Bye Sel," mixed in with the usual middle school banter as the kids left the room.

Mr. Seljin walked over to Ely as he was walking toward the door. "Hey Ely, can I talk to you for a second?"

Ely turned shyly, looking up briefly as if he might be in trouble. "Yeah...sure."

"I have a favor to ask you."

"A favor?" Ely responded, looking up, his eyes making eye contact for more than a fleeting moment.

"Yes. I noticed that you were reading during class." Ely looked away again. "It's alright," he continued. "I don't want to discourage you from reading. I think it's great that you're a reader. I just can't have you doing it during class, okay?"

"Okay, I'm sorry," Ely whispered. It was weird. Ely felt like he had let Mr. Seljin down. He felt guilty. It was a strange feeling to Ely as he realized that he felt guilty because he actually respected this man. Respecting adults in general was new to Ely, and it would take some getting used to.

"It's no problem. Do you mind me asking what book you're reading?"

"Oh, it's just some fantasy book."

"That's great. Don't you remember from my presentation? Fantasy is my favorite genre. I have so many fantasy books that you'd think that is all I ever read. I'm a certifiable fantasy nerd. What's the title of this one?"

"It's called *The Path of Daggers*, by Robert Jordan. You really do read fantasy books?" Ely was clearly surprised, and maybe even a little impressed. He remembered Mr. Seljin saying that in his first day presentation, but he didn't really believe it. It seemed too far-fetched. But maybe he did read fantasy. That realization seemed to create a change in Ely's demeanor. Where he was typically quiet and shy, he was now smiling and asking questions.

"I told you I'm a fantasy freak. In fact, I've read Robert Jordan's entire series. You want me to tell you what happens to Rand Al'Thor?" Sel teased.

"No," Ely blurted out with a laugh. *He really did read these books.*

Sel sat on the edge of the desk next to Ely. "So, what are some of your other favorite books? Don't worry about class. I'll write you a pass. It's my planning period."

"Oh, okay. Well, *The Hobbit* goes without saying for any fantasy reader. I like *Druss the Legend*, by David Gemmell, Terry Brook's first *Shannara* books, and I also like Jim Butcher's *Codex Alera* books."

"You have good taste," Mr. Seljin offered. "I've read them as well, and of course I've read *The Hobbit*. Like you said, that goes without saying."

Ely looked at Mr. Seljin with something akin to awe. Three minutes ago he was bored and alone and now he was talking about his passion with one of his teachers. "Wow, I can't believe you actually read those kinds of books."

"You better believe it. I even played Dungeons and Dragons all the way up until I went to college," Sel added with a smile.

"Really? I have some of those books, but I don't play."

"Why not?" Sel asked.

"Well, I don't have anyone to play with," Ely murmured.

Sel looked at Ely again as the young boy once again reverted his gaze to the floor. He had had him, even if it was just for a moment. He found the spark inside him and now it was just a matter of nurturing it to a flame. "How many books do you have?" Sel asked, changing the subject.

"Not too many. I can't afford to buy them, so I have to get them from the library. They don't really have much of a selection."

"You got that right. Their selection of fantasy books sucks," Sel said bluntly. Ely laughed, not used to hearing a teacher talk like that. "I'll tell you what. I have tons of books. Why don't I bring in some of my favorites and you can borrow them. You have to read R.A. Salvatore's *Dark Elf* books and Elizabeth Moon's *Paksenarrion* series. You'll love them."

"Really? You'll let me borrow them?"

"No problem. As long as you tell me one thing."

"What's that?"

"Why do you like to read fantasy books so much?"

"Oh…I don't know," Ely responded.

"Yes you do," Sel said smoothly, smiling at Ely. "Come on now, my books are important to me. I don't want to loan them to just anyone. I want to know if you're worthy of them."

"Okay, I think I see what you mean. Well," Ely said, thinking. "I guess I read them to escape, to go somewhere else. You know, to disappear."

"Yes, I do know. When I get stressed out, the first thing I want to do is escape into one of my books. I want to bury myself in a story and go to a different world where the stresses of my life don't follow me."

"All the books have heroes," Ely continued, "someone who is pure of heart, who is strong and unbeatable in combat. I like to pretend that is me."

"Well that is the answer I was hoping for. The books are yours."

"Cool."

"I've kept you long enough. Let me write you a pass to your next class." Mr. Seljin walked over to his desk to grab a sticky note. "What class do you have now?"

"I have Mr. Helgrin."

He wrote a note and handed it to Ely. "There you go."

"Thanks," Ely said, taking the note and moving toward the door.

"Hey, Ely."

"Yeah," he responded, turning back to Mr. Seljin.

"You ever thought about wrestling?"

"No," he said simply.

"Well, we sure could use you. We need an unlimited wrestler. Why don't you think about it," Sel offered.

"I don't think I would be a good wrestler. I don't know anything about it." Of course Ely had no idea what an unlimited wrestler was, but he figured it had something to do with his size. Either way, wrestling didn't even remotely sound like something he would like to do, let alone be good at. Who in their right mind would put on a pair of tights and wrestle other guys in front of lots of people? Just the visual image of his own body stuffed into a spandex suit made him cringe; he could only imagine what it would do to others.

"Hey, even heroes have to start somewhere. Just think about it, okay?" Sel asked.

"Okay, thanks."

"No worries. I'll have your first book tomorrow," Sel said as Ely turned to leave again. "One more thing, Ely."

"Yeah," he said, turning toward Sel with a smile.

"What happened to your face? Did you fall again?" Mr. Seljin asked with concern.

Ely's smile disappeared quickly. "Yes, I'm pretty clumsy."

"Looks like it hurt. If anyone gives you any problems, you let me know, okay?"

"Okay," Ely said softly, turning and walking out the door, leaving Mr. Seljin to his own thoughts.

Four

Why the hell would anyone want me to wrestle? I remember rolling that idea around in my head for a while. I'm fat, socially inept, and more than likely not a very good athlete, although I've never really tried, so who knows. But I have to admit that it felt good that he asked.

Why was that? Why did it feel good that he asked me to wrestle? I thought about that for a while too. Why did it feel good to be asked to do something that I probably was not going to do, and that if I did try, I would more than likely fail miserably at? Here is what I concluded:

I have never been asked to do anything before. No one has ever picked me to be on their team in physical education class. No one has invited me over for a birthday party, or to go see a movie. Well, that's not totally true. I remember in second grade I was invited to Billy Marsden's house, but that doesn't really count. Pretty much everyone in our class was invited. Anyway, after I really thought about it, I realized that no one had ever asked me to be a part of something, to join them, to be included in something. It felt so good to me because finally I felt like someone actually wanted me to join them in a common cause. It didn't really matter what it was. He could have asked me to join a satanic cult, and it still would have felt good.

I mean, think about it. Most people go through their lives taking for granted that people actually want to hang out with them. They get invited to parties, people actually talk with them at lunch, or they take it upon themselves to join clubs, teams, and other organizations. I was so used to being alone, that the idea of anything else seemed like it was out of the question.

Now, I'm not looking for a pity party. I realize that most of my fate was brought on by me. But I also realize that my actions in life were a reflection of what I thought was possible. Since my self-esteem was at an all-time low, and I really had no positive experiences that would support the fact that I could be a part of something, I simply believed that it was impossible, and that no one would want me even if I tried.

Let me just say that that the words, "we need a wrestler," could have been chanted by Gregorian Monks and stamped in gold and hung above my bed. This simple phrase was the catalyst for positive change in my life. It got me thinking that maybe I could do something out of my comfort zone, and that maybe there could also be some friends beside me while I made that leap of faith. I didn't really believe that right away, but unbeknownst to me, the fuse was lit.

Ely Carter

———————————————

Several weeks had passed and Ely was going through the motions as he always had. His daily goal was to be invisible, to keep his head down, and move through the halls without any incidents. For the most part he was successful. Several teachers made efforts to talk with him, as they always did. He liked most of his teachers, and in fact, two, in his opinion, were very good. They laughed, enjoyed their jobs, and truly seemed to care about the success of their students. One was Mr. Seljin, and the other was his language arts teacher, Mrs. Overmeyer. She was the soft spoken, motherly type, who treated every student like they were her son or daughter.

Things at home were okay as well. At least he hadn't been hit lately. He managed to stay away from his father and most of his time was spent in his room reading and listening to music. That was the one thing that he looked forward to, the opening of a book, the smell of printed paper, and the feel of a glossy cover in his hands. Every night he would escape into a different realm and dream of alternate worlds, attempting to bury the realities of his life beneath the courage and honor of a fictional character.

Ely would read during any spare moment he could find at school. One day Ely was sitting at a table by himself, reading a book that Mr. Seljin had given him and listening to his head phones. His face had completely healed and no one was paying him any attention. Most of the kids had eaten and were now either in the gym, or on the field taking advantage of the last ten minutes of honor time. For some reason the half hour of free time they had after lunch was called 'honor time'. It was still pretty loud, but Ely's headphones muffled the chatter and Mozart's delicate notes did the rest.

Suddenly three boys sat down next to Ely, forcing him to look up from his book. Jeff was smiling at him, and Cisco, Jeff's buddy that had helped Ely with Adam a few weeks ago, was there, along with John, the funny kid from several of his classes. Ely looked at them a bit apprehensively, but didn't say a word.

"Hey Ely, how's it going?" Jeff asked.

Ely took off his headphones. "Fine."

"We have a question for you," Cisco added.

Cisco was a handsome black kid that must have weighed close to two hundred pounds. But he wasn't really fat, just big, close to six feet tall with broad shoulders and meaty looking arms. His smile was genuine, and he seemed nice enough, but Ely had his reservations, as he always did when it came to other kids.

"Okay," Ely said apprehensively.

"Have you ever thought about wrestling?" Cisco continued.

Here was that question again. Why does everyone want me to wrestle, Ely thought? Can't they see that I'm fat and not really the athletic type?

"No, not really."

"Well," Jeff said, cutting in. "All three of us are the captains this year, and we want you on our team. Right now we have no unlimited wrestlers."

"What's an unlimited wrestler?"

"It's a weight class," John explained. "Cisco weighs one hundred and seventy pounds, but we need someone who weighs more than that for our last weight class."

"You want me to wrestle because I'm fat?"

"Ely, it's not like that," Jeff reasoned. "There are seventeen weight classes. It starts at seventy eight pounds and goes all the way to unlimited. If we don't have an unlimited wrestler, then we have to forfeit the match for that weight class, and the other team gets six points. We can't let that happen against Kopachuck."

Ely knew that Kopachuck Middle School was another school in the district and the main rival of Key Peninsula Middle School, especially for the wrestling team.

"We have a kick ass team but we need an unlimited wrestler," Cisco said.

"It's hard to find kids that are—"

"Fat," Ely said, interrupting Jeff.

"Big boned, like me," Cisco said, flashing Ely a dazzling smile.

"I don't know. I'm not a good athlete. Besides, I don't think my mom would let me. We can't afford it." Ely was being pretty honest with these guys. He wasn't sure why. He never talked about family stuff. But then again, no one had ever really talked with him before so he never really had to. There was something about these guys, an aura or something, that made Ely believe that he could trust them. For some reason he didn't think they would judge him, so he just spoke up without much thought.

"Mr. Seljin would take care of all that for you," Jeff said. "We need you, man."

All three got up to leave.

"We're going to keep bugging you," Cisco promised. "If we are going to beat Kopachuck this year, we will need an unlimited wrestler."

"I…I don't know," Ely stammered.

"Just think about it," Jeff said. "See ya, Ely."

"Later dawg," John said.

"Later," Cisco added.

And then they were gone. Ely looked down at his book and flipped it over to the cover. The title of the book was Homeland, and on the cover was an amazing painting of a dark elf, or Drow. In the fantasy world Drows were distant cousins of the fairy tale elf, but inherently evil. Their skin had turned dark from adapting to thousands of years of living underground. Lack of sunlight normally meant white skin, but the Drow had evolved to become hunters in the night, their dark skin allowing them to become literally invisible in the dark caves in which they lived. Drizzt, the dark elf, was standing at the gates of some underground city, grasping two silver scimitars in his hands. Ely had just started reading the book and was thoroughly enjoying the story.

Drizzt was an anomaly amongst his people. He was not evil, and so far the beginning of the book was about how he was going to survive in the violent merciless world of the Drow, while still holding onto his principles. Ely was particularly excited because this book was just the first in a very long series and Mr. Seljin had the whole set, and that they would be at his disposal as he burned through the pages.

Ely slowly traced his finger along the outline of Drizzt. "Did you hear that, Drizzt?" Ely whispered. "They said they need me."

Later that day, Ely was sitting in Mrs. Overmeyer's class. Mrs. Overmeyer was in her late fifties, with short cropped blond hair, glasses, and the cheerful demeanor of a solicitous mom. If you were an orphan and you could pick your mom from a lineup, you would pick Mrs. Overmeyer. She was standing at her podium explaining the day's schedule.

"Okay," she began, "It's time for our book reports. Remember, your assignment was to write a one page report on a character in the book you chose to read. I wanted you to reflect on what you liked, or didn't like about the character. Critique the character's flaws as well as their good qualities. I'm looking for some personal insight here, some emotional connection to the character you've chosen." Her students were just staring at her with blank expressions as she paused. "Would anyone like to volunteer first?"

John, Jeff's friend, grabbed his report off his desk and headed up to the front of the class. "I got your back, Mrs. O."

"I assume that means that you'll go first," she said laughing.

"You got it."

"The stage is yours," Mrs. Overmeyer replied as she stepped away from the podium and moved to her desk.

"Okay," John began. "The book I read is called, *A Stolen Kiss*, by Wanda Jerasich."

John held up the book for all to see, exposing the cover which clearly identified it as a cheesy, young adult, romance novel. Everyone in the class laughed, and even Mrs. Overmeyer, although she tried to stifle it, chuckled behind her desk.

"Alright y'all, quiet down now," John continued. "Okay, the character I chose was Brooke. She is this eighteen year old hotty. I picked her because…well, she is smokin', plain and simple."

Again, everyone laughed.

"Mrs. O, do I have to read my report or can I just talk about it?" John asked.

"Whatever is easier for you, John," Mrs. Overmeyer said. "I do hope that you have some more personal reasons for choosing Brooke other than the fact that she's hot."

The class giggled some more. Clearly she was having fun as well. Even Ely, who had his head down, looked up briefly, and cracked a smile.

"Oh, don't worry, teach, I got some shi...stuff," John added quickly. Mrs. Overmeyer gave him a quick, *watch it*, look, before he continued. "So, I picked Brooke because she reminds me of my sister—"

"You think your sister's hot?" Jeff interrupted. "Gross, dude."

"She is hot, man," Cisco added. "I'd love to—"

"Hey!" Mrs. Overmeyer reprimanded.

"Sorry, Mrs. O," Cisco said. "But she is definitely a ten."

Again the class laughed, and now Ely was also smiling and looking on with genuine interest.

"I'm not saying I think my sister is hot, you perv. And don't talk about my sister like that," John said with a grin. "I mean, this Brooke chick had a lot of problems with guys, just like my sister. My sister is always complaining about guys. Brooke would lock herself in her room and write in her diary about all of her boyfriends and such."

"Does your sister do that?" Jeff asked.

"Heck yeah. I've even read her diary. Good stuff. But most importantly, I liked this Brooke character because she reminds me of my sis, and since my sister left for college, I sort of miss her."

"Oh, how sweet," Jeff teased.

The guys in the class laughed. But most of the girls smiled and thought it was cute, expressing themselves with a series of *ahhhs, that's so cute…*and *ooohhhhh*.

"Shut up, Jeff. Mrs. O said she wanted it personal. Anyway, that's all I have," John said.

"Thanks for sharing that, John," Mrs. Overmeyer said. "Let's give him a hand." The report was clearly too short, but the class knew that Mrs. Overmeyer was probably just happy that she got a report from John at all. School wasn't really his strong point.

The class clapped loudly as John made his way back to his desk.

"Okay, who's next?" Mrs. Overmeyer asked.

Everyone looked down at their desk hoping she wouldn't call on them.

"Since I have no volunteers, why don't we hear from….Ely."

Startled, Ely looked up. Suddenly his heart was pounding and he could feel his face turn red. He hated doing anything in front of the class. It was hard not to feel self-conscious, embarrassed, scared, and a plethora of other emotions when you were standing in front of a group of people, especially your peers.

But he had no choice. He knew everyone had to do it eventually, so he took a deep breath, grabbed his paper, and walked to the front of the class and stood behind the podium. He set his paper down on the podium so his shaking hands wouldn't divulge his nervousness. Taking a deep breath, he began his report.

"The book I read is called, *Homeland*, by R.A. Salvatore," Ely began, his voice shaking as he held up the book. "The character that I chose to do my report on is Drizzt Do Urden."

Scott, a young blond haired kid sitting in the back raised his hand.

"Yes, Scott?" Mrs. Overmeyer asked.

"Drizzt do who?"

"Drizzt Do Urden," Ely said again. "He is a dark elf." Ely turned to Mrs. Overmeyer. "Do you mind if I just read my report? It might make more sense."

"Sure, Ely, go right ahead."

Ely looked down at his paper and began to read. "The character that I chose from my book is a dark elf named Drizzt. This story takes place in a fantasy world called the Forgotten Realms. Drizzt is a good and honest warrior, who's alone in the world and a member of a race that's inherently evil, whereas his heart resonates all that is good in the world. Drizzt is a Drow Elf, which is a distant cousin to the elves that we often read about in fairy tales, or see in movies like The Lord of the Rings. He is an anomaly amongst his people, surrounded by greed and the desire to appease their Goddess, Loth, known as the Spider Queen. Drow Elves are the epitome of evil, and the only thing they care about is personal gain, power, and making their dark deity happy. They will do anything to achieve this, even kill their own family members." Ely paused and looked up into the silence, expecting to see boredom on the student's faces. To his surprise, most of them were actually listening, so he quickly glanced back down and continued. "Because the Drow live miles underground, their skin has adapted to the lightless world by turning black, enabling them to better blend in with the darkness, and their eyes have adapted as well, for they can see in the dark. To survive in this harsh and dangerous world you have to learn how to adapt, but most importantly to fight. In this story Drizzt faces the evilness of his people and struggles to hold onto his principles and morals and survive at the same time. Drizzt is an exception among his people, for he's not evil. He cares about life and feels empathy and compassion. But do not mistake his kind heart and gentle spirit for weakness. His skill in battle is unmatched, and he fights with two scimitars, which are curved swords. No one can best him with the blade. I chose Drizzt because he has to fight to hold onto his values, to his goodness. He has strength, speed, and power, and he uses these skills to uphold good and protect the weak. I chose Drizzt, because, like me, he was born into a situation that he doesn't like, and unlike me, he embodies power and courage. He uses these traits to change his life. He embodies characteristics that I would like to emulate in life." Ely stopped and slowly looked toward Mrs. Overmeyer. "Ummm…that's it, the end."

The class, along with Mrs. Overmeyer, sat staring at Ely. Even the kids, who started off not listening, now sat, attentive and speechless.

"Wow, Ely," Mrs. Overmeyer said. "That was very well written. Nice job expressing yourself. Give Ely a hand, class."

The class clapped as Ely made his way back to his seat. As soon as he sat down, Jeff leaned over and whispered to him. "Dude, that rocked. Anomaly, deities, resonates, I didn't know what you were talking about half the time and I still thought it kicked ass."

"Thanks," Ely said, clearly uncomfortable with the attention.

"Okay, who's next?" Mrs. Overmeyer asked. The clapping stopped abruptly and everyone went back to their, *don't pick me*, look. No one wanted to follow that report.

The walk home from school was typical. Ely put one foot in front of another, wearing his headphones as he listened to more of his favorite classical composers. Today it was one of Francesco Cavalli's baroque compositions from the 1600's. As usual the music put him into a meditative state as he closed the half-mile distance to his mobile home, simultaneously navigating the clusters of mud puddles and potholes as he read his book.

As he neared his run-down home he saw his father working on a car in the driveway. He was sweaty and covered in grease and grime. Ely, hoping to avoid the typical barrage of insults from his father, took off his headphones and tucked his book under his arm. Keeping his head low, he walked briskly past his father, hoping to enter the home unnoticed. It was a fairly typical event for Bill to tease Ely about his music or his 'stupid, children's books', as he so eloquently put it.

"Hey, boy! Put your shit in the house and come out here and chop that wood over there," he grunted as he peered over the hood of the car at Ely.

"Okay," Ely responded without pausing.

He walked into the house to see his mom at the kitchen counter doing dishes.

"Hi, hon, how was school?" she asked, keeping her back to him.

"Okay. Mom, can I ask you a question?"

Mary turned around and faced her son. She looked exhausted and it was obvious she had been crying. Her left eye was beginning to swell and turn red. She forced a smile, as if she could camouflage the pain from her husband's abuse. Ely knew that he wasn't the only one being hit in this family. The funny thing was, it hurt him more to see his mother in pain. He got angrier looking at her swollen eye than he did his own.

"Of course," she responded.

"I was," Ely paused as the anger began to rise within him. Her eye was slowly closing and it was obvious that she had just been hit. "Did he hit you again?"

"It's nothing. It looks worse than it is, really."

"Did Dad hit you again?" Ely persisted.

"Well, we got into a fight. I shouldn't have spoken to him as I did. He's really stressed out about not working and I instigated him. I'll be fine."

"He shouldn't be hitting you, Mom. Why do you let him? He paused for a moment, his anger almost palpable, "Someday I won't let him hit either one of us," Ely said softly, his voice shaking with emotion.

"Ely, I said don't worry about it. It's really nothing. Now, what was your question?" Mary asked again, obviously wanting to avoid dealing with the elephant that was in the room.

"I want to join the wrestling team."

"Really? You've never shown any interest in sports before."

"I know. But the coach and some of the wrestlers said they need me," Ely said, almost pleading.

Mary sat down at the kitchen table. "Oh, I don't know, son. What would your dad say?"

"I don't care what he says. What do you say?"

"Will it cost anything? We just don't have any extra money right now."

That got Ely frustrated. He wanted to say that his dad spent money every night, his mother's money, on beer and cheap whiskey. But he knew that it would just upset his mother by causing her more stress. She was obviously not up to a confrontation that she was not able to win, especially right now. "I don't think so," Ely reassured her. "The guys said that Mr. Seljin would take care of everything if money was an issue."

"We'll see. Okay?"

"We'll see what?" Bill asked loudly as he pushed open the door. "Get me a beer, Mary." He was covered in grease from the car but it didn't stop him from plopping down at his usual place in front of the television. "So what are you guys talking about?"

"Ely wants to join the wrestling team," Mary said.

"Are you serious?" Bill asked incredulously.

"Yes," Mary began.

"I wasn't talking to you," Bill interrupted her. "I was talking to Ely. Come over here, boy." Ely got up from the table and walked over to his father, his earlier bravado rapidly melting. "You want to join the wrestling team?"

"Yes," Ely said.

Bill looked him up and down. The atmosphere of the room was tense and coiled like a snake. Both Mary and Ely didn't know if he would be relieved that his son was finally doing something he would approve of and say yes, or hit him for daring to ask.

"Okay," Bill said. "It might be good for you. Toughen you up a little. Maybe you'll lose some fat and turn into a man after all. Now go chop that wood."

"Okay," Ely said as he turned away. Mary had resumed washing the dishes as Ely walked up behind her. He hugged her briefly and kissed her on the cheek before he left through the screen door.

Mary stopped scrubbing the pan and stared ahead through the dirty kitchen window as a lone tear slowly trickled down her cheek.

Five

Well, as I suspected, I got my ass kicked. Luckily, I was so used to ridicule that the taunts I got from kids, even from a few of my own teammates, did little to shock me. Not that it was okay. I mean, I'm fat, it's pretty obvious. But when you put on a spandex singlet for the first time, you really learn a lot about yourself. Even the guys that were in great shape always looked skeptical when they held up the scanty uniform for perusal. Those tight suits didn't hide anything, and I mean that. So, for someone like me, who had a lot of extra physical topography, the singlet became my other antagonist at every match. I glared at it with a sense of futility. As I stretched it over my ample body I mentally swore at it, calling it all kinds of names that should never be used to describe an article of clothing. I really hated that thing. The other wrestlers couldn't always disguise the fact that they found it morbidly fascinating to watch as I attempted to tuck my fat folds into the spandex. It was like squeezing a sumo wrestler into a Ken Doll tuxedo. Their stares hurt and embarrassed me, but when I looked at myself in the mirror I could hardly fault them. I looked silly, stupid, and, well…fat. I looked the complete opposite of tough. I certainly didn't look like the drawing of the wrestler on Mr. Seljin's door.

But, strangely enough, the embarrassment I felt would always disappear as I stood toe to toe with an opponent.

Suddenly, nothing would matter except what I was going to do in the next six minutes. I no longer worried about the way I looked. It was as if I had entered a meditative state. All the sounds disappeared except for the pounding of my heart and the muffled yells of Mr. Seljin and my teammates.

I always lost, but there were several occasions where I won points for my team, sort of, anyway. Wrestling was one of those weird sports that kept two scores. You wrestled your match as an individual, but the points you earned for your team were added to your team total to determine if your squad won the match. So it was possible that you could win your individual match but your team could lose the meet. Or you could lose your match but your team could win. If you won your match by less than eight points, you gained three points for your team. It was a win by decision. If you won by more than eight points, then you earned four points for your team. That was a win by major decision. If you won by fifteen points or more, it was known as a technical fall, which earned five points for your team. And lastly, if you pinned your opponent, six points would be added to the team score. With that in mind, you could lose to your opponent and still gain points for your team. My goal was to go out there and not get pinned. If I did that, then I technically earned anywhere from one to three points for my team, which could be the deciding points in a match. If I wasn't there we would have to forfeit the unlimited weight class, which would mean that the other team would always get six points. But if I could keep myself from getting pinned, and lose by less than eight points, then I actually earned three points for my team.

Isn't it strange that that was my goal, to lose, but by as few points and possible? Don't get me wrong, I did get pinned. But those times where I was able to fight off my back and struggle through the third round without getting pinned felt amazing. Mr. Seljin always congratulated me, and made it a point at practice to talk about how I had supported the team by not giving up, by having enough courage to come out and wrestle, participating in a sport that many would not even try. I was actually earning points for the team by doing my part. I'm not sure if all the kids bought it or not, but I did, and it felt really good.

Most of the wrestlers did listen to him though, and seemed to hang on his every word. After his speech there were a few kids that actually congratulated me and patted me on the back. It felt good. Jeff was always the first one to encourage me. For some reason he was one of the few people I could hear cheering me on. His voice echoed in my head and there was more than one occasion that he gave me the courage to lift my shoulder blade off the mat, or to get away and earn the point I needed to shave my opponent's lead from a technical fall, to a major decision, earning the team one more point. Cisco was close to my weight so he worked with me on occasion. He was tough on me, but he too encouraged me to work harder.

I was still occasionally teased about my weight, my talent, or lack of it, and sometimes for the way I smelled. I wanted to shower at school, but I was too embarrassed. My dad only let me shower every other day because the water bill was too high. I had deodorant but it wasn't always enough to mask my body odor.

Adam, the jerk that had made it his job to harass me, capitalized on any opportunity he had to bully me. I can hear the taunts in my head. 'Hey shit stain', 'How's your stupid book, dork?', 'Nice pants, dipshit', 'You smell like my ass,".

The Life of Ely

But all the taunts and ass whooping's I received were all worth it when we won the league championship. And we won because of me.

Ely Carter

The gym was packed and the noise of screaming fans dominated the tense scene. This was the final match of the year. Kopachuck and Key Peninsula had a tied league score with five wins each and the winner of this match would be league champions. The score was 45 to 41 with Key Peninsula in the lead. Cisco had just pinned his man bringing the Key Peninsula Cougar score from 39 to 45 and the crowd was going crazy. It was a home match for the Cougars and it seemed that everyone from the school was in attendance.

Ely was crapping his pants. Not literally of course, but his stomach was churning and his heart pounded with nervous energy. His match was next and he stood behind Mr. Seljin's chair with an expression of barely concealed panic on his face. He was overwhelmed by the realization that whether or not they won the league title would be dependent on if he won or lost. His sweats were off and he was sweating profusely under his team sweat shirt. From his earphones Beethoven's 5th muffled the cacophonous sounds of the screaming crowd.

Jeff came up behind Ely and slapped him on the back, grabbing him roughly by the neck and pulling him in close so he could hear him above the crowd. Ely flipped off his head phones so he could hear Jeff better.

"You ready?" Jeff yelled.

"Yup," Ely said with little confidence.

"Listen, Ely, don't worry about the pressure. Just go out there and do your best. Just don't give up!" he yelled in his ear.

"Okay!" Ely yelled back.

Cisco stood on the mat with his hand raised in victory as the crowd exploded in applause. Cisco's opponent came over to shake Mr. Seljin's hand and Ely couldn't help but focus on the poor kid's face. His eyes were moist with tears of frustration and he wore an expression that seemed to be a mixture of shame, anger, and despair. *That's what I'll be looking like soon*, Ely thought.

Mr. Seljin shook the wrestler's hand and walked over quickly to Ely, coming around behind him to massage his neck and arms, the customary routine he practiced for his wrestlers before their matches, especially if it was an important match. It was almost a ritual. He shook Ely's arms to loosen them up and squeezed his shoulders and neck in his vice-like grip.

"Now listen, Ely, go out there and just do your best! When the whistle blows forget about all these people, forget about the score, just pay attention to what you're doing and try your best. We are up by four points. You don't have to win in order for *us* to win. Try not to get pinned, and if you lose by points, try to make it a decision. If your guy beats you by a major then we tie. If he beats you by a technical fall, or pins you, then we lose.

But I don't care if we lose as long as you've done your best, and as long as you don't give up. I know that you have it in you. I know that if you don't give up, that you can pull this off for us. That is all I can ask of you, and that is all you can ask of yourself." Mr. Seljin paused as he took Ely's hood off and turned him to face him. "You ready, buddy?"

Ely was nervous, but he was ready. All he knew was that he would not let this man down. If he lost, so be it. But he would not give up. "I'm ready."

"Take your sweat shirt off and get your head gear on, they're ready for you."

Ely quickly lifted his sweatshirt off. He was always concerned about how he looked in his singlet, but not this time. His mind was elsewhere. Screaming teammates patted his back as he moved to the referee's table to sign in. He could hear their encouraging shouts, "Go get 'em Ely! Don't give up! You got this guy!" The screams intensified as he moved to the center of the mat. The fans in the bleachers were howling equally loudly, and their combined cheers and stomping feet sounded like an earthquake. But all Ely heard was a muffled buzzing within his head gear, interrupted occasionally by shouts from his teammates.

Ely's opponent was big. That was a given since all the heavy weight guys were big, including himself. But this guy was taller than most, and he wasn't as fat as Ely. He looked like a football player.

Ely just wanted the match to begin so he could stop focusing on his opponent's size. They shook hands and the referee blew the whistle.

Round One:

The Kopachuck wrestler came at Ely like a freight train, hitting him hard enough to push Ely backwards until he finally tripped and they both went flying out of bounds. Ely's back hit the mat first and his opponent landed right on top of him. The referee blew the whistle and signaled out of bounds, no points awarded.

Ely gasped for breath as the force of the impact had knocked the wind out of him. He glanced over at Mr. Seljin as he struggled to pick his large frame up off the mat. Sel was showing Ely to drop to his knees if the kid charged again, and to take his legs out in a double leg takedown. Ely nodded in acknowledgement and moved back to the center of the mat to face his opponent. The kid's face was a mask of anger and he looked as if he would charge him again. *Okay*, Ely thought as he placed his foot on the line.

The whistle blew and the Kopachuck wrestler came at him again. This time Ely did what he was told to do. He dropped to his knees and the kid struck him hard in the chest. Ely wrapped his arms around his opponent's legs trying to take his body to either side, hoping to get a takedown. But this guy was strong and he had too much momentum going in his favor. When he struck Ely, and Ely wrapped his arms around his legs, it just caused him to trip over Ely, forcing him onto his back.

Oh crap, Ely thought in panic as he landed on his back, his opponent haphazardly lying on top of him.

Ely heard Jeff yell, "Get off your back!"

And that was what he did. Before the Kopachuck kid could get a good grip on him, Ely was able to get an arm through and scramble onto his stomach. Ely put his arms out in front of him as he had learned to do in practice, and tried to get a leg under him so he could work up to his hands and knees, to his base, where he could then work on standing up, which was pretty much the only move that Ely could do very well at this point in his wrestling career.

Ely heard the referee signal two points for his opponent. Luckily, since he had not managed to gain control of Ely, he wasn't given any near fall points.

The Kopachuck wrestler was controlling Ely pretty handedly, maintaining decent wrist control and boxing in his legs so Ely couldn't get to his base. Several times the guy had managed to grab his wrist and work his other hand under Ely's arm in an attempt to secure a half nelson where he could then turn Ely onto his back.

Mr. Seljin was screaming, "Look away and peel it off!"

It was a simple move and one that Ely had mastered pretty well. You just had to be careful that you looked away fast enough before your opponent could get a good grip on your neck and lift your elbow, gaining leverage by forcing your head down. If that happened then it was really hard to turn your head and peel it off. In fact, if your opponent sunk his hand in too deep on the half nelson, it would be almost impossible to counter it. At that point you either had to try to roll through, or hope that you were stronger than your opponent and fight off the half nelson.

Ely was able to lift his head up and peel his opponent's hand off his neck before he could turn him. They went back and forth like that for a while and Ely stuck to what he knew. He looked away and peeled it off, all the while trying to keep his head up and get to his knees. They both scooted around on the matt for a while, and several times Ely was able to get to his base, where he was promptly slammed back to the mat with a tight waist.

Ely could still hear the screams from his teammates. Even through the noise of the crowd, the pounding of his heart, and the sound of his own heavy breathing, he could hear the shouts of his teammates. "Get up!" "Move, Ely!, don't stop moving!" "You can do it!" "Stand up! Work your stand up!" That one came from Jeff.

Ely gritted his teeth and got his right leg under him again. He fought off his opponent's two-on-one just as the kid made his first mistake and tried to force a half nelson without having control of his wrist. A two-on-one was just like it sounded. It was when one wrestler knocked his opponent to the mat and then used both of his hands, reaching under his opponent's body, and grasping one wrist. From this position he would drive forward with his toes, hoping that his opponent would lift up his other arm to try and free his wrist. Then the offensive wrestler would slip in a half nelson and turn his opponent to his back. That was the goal anyway. But you only want to try this move while your opponent was on their belly. It was the classic mistake to attempt it while your opponent was still on their knees. And Ely was going to capitalize on that mistake. Ely felt the weight leave his body as his opponent shuffled to the side, trying to get his left arm under Ely's arm and his hand wrapped tightly around Ely's neck. But Ely, now unencumbered by the guy's weight, lifted up with both hands and popped up to his base.

"Turn in to him!" coach Seljin shouted. Ely looked up and saw Mr. Seljin who was frantically yelling at him. "Now! Turn into him!"

Ely vaguely remembered what he was talking about. But Sel's next move confirmed it. In a flash, Mr. Seljin jumped to his base, and showed him the move. Without any hesitation, Ely pivoted his legs out and turned his body towards his opponent, simultaneously lifting his head, pinching his own arm down, and preventing the kid from throwing a half nelson. Before he knew it, Ely was standing face to face with his opponent. The sound of the buzzer shattered Ely's own surprise. They broke apart and Ely saw the referee signal a one point escape.

The crowd went crazy and the Cougar bench erupted in cheers as everyone leapt from their chairs, screaming happily. The score of the match was now two to one with Kopachuck in the lead.

Round Two:

Ely was given the choice of starting positions second round and he looked to Mr. Seljin for advice, as all the wrestlers were instructed to do. Sel motioned for Ely to defer to the Kopachuck kid. What that meant was that Ely was giving the choice to his opponent for round two, enabling him to have the choice for round three, which could be a pivotal round in a close match.

As expected, the Kopachuck wrestler picked the down position. Of all the positions, Ely liked the top the best. He was generally heavier than his opponents so even if he didn't know many moves, his own weight was a pretty good defense against the bottom guy's movement.

The whistle blew and the Kopachuck wrestler exploded from the mat. His first instinct was to stand up, which he attempted to do. But Ely clamped down on his arm and pushed all his weight into him and they both crashed into the mat with a thud. Ely struggled to find a two-on-one but his opponent was tough, and fast, and Ely wasn't able to control either wrist. Within thirty seconds the Kopachuck wrestler had broken away from Ely and was standing facing him.

He was awarded a point for the escape, so now the score was three to one.

Ely was already tired. Sweat dripped from his body and his chest heaved as he tried to catch his breath.

Ely took two deep breaths before his opponent moved forward and locked up with him.

The lock up, or tie up, was when wrestlers held their heads side by side while each one grasped the back of their opponents head while using their free hand to work for arm control, hoping to line up various takedowns that can be done from that position. They moved back and forth across the mat; all the while Ely could hear the screams from his bench. As usual, the ones that made it through to his ears were from Mr. Seljin and Jeff. He heard Jeff say, "Break away from the tie up!" Then he heard Mr. Seljin, "Watch the head and arm!"

And just as he heard Sel's last comment, he found himself flying through the air. Time seemed to slow for those few seconds, then stopped abruptly as his back crashed onto the mat. For a second he was stunned. Then he realized that his shoulder blades were dangerously close to the mat and a surge of new energy rocketed through his body. He frantically lifted one shoulder off the mat as his opponent squeezed his arm and head together, slowly restricting the flow of blood to his brain.

Jeff was standing up, screaming as loud as he could. "Ely, keep your shoulder up! Hold on for thirty seconds!"

Thirty seconds, Ely thought. *I should be able to do anything for thirty seconds.* He fought for breath as he wrapped his arms around the body of his opponent, and tried as hard as he could to wrap a leg over the top of his opponent's leg. Ely remembered the move easily enough as it was quite simple. The idea was to hook the guy's leg so that the leverage and angle would keep his own shoulder off the mat.

And if your opponent tried to lean too far back to push your shoulder blade onto the mat, then you could roll him through when his center of gravity got too high. Ely knew he probably couldn't escape the move, but he thought it might be possible to keep his shoulder off the mat for the remaining thirty seconds.

Screams from his bench pushed through his daze and he struggled with renewed intensity to find the strength and energy to fight off his back. And he found it. Somewhere within himself, he found what he needed. Years of anger and frustration boiled to the surface and he squeezed his opponent harder, gasping for air as the Kopachuck kid continued to squeeze his head and arm. He imagined that it was his father on top of him. He visualized blow after blow from his dad's fists. Each strike caused Ely to clinch his arms tighter around his opponent.

Ely roared with anger, and as his opponent leaned back further, hoping to get a pin, Ely used his neck and legs and bridged through, rolling his opponent and smacking the guy's face onto the mat. Ely was now on top of him but his head was still trapped within his arms.

Then the buzzer rang, ending round two.

Ely felt the kid release his hold, allowing much needed oxygen to fill his lungs. He sat there for a moment, breathing deeply, trying to get as much oxygen as he could as the Kopachuck wrestler stood up.

Ely glanced at the score clock and noticed that his opponent had earned a two point takedown and a three point near fall, adding five points to his score. Ely didn't get any points for his reversal because he hadn't gotten his head out. He needed to show control before points would be awarded. *Damn*, he thought. *I just needed a few more seconds.*

He stood up and looked over at Mr. Seljin who was calling him over to the side of the mat. Ely walked over to him, his legs trembling with fatigue.

"Ely, the score is eight to one! Remember, if you lose by more than eight, we will only tie for first! Excellent job getting off your back! Break him down, two-on-one, and throw the half! You got it!"

"Yes,....sir," Ely said through gasps.

The referee motioned for them to return to the center.

"Go get em, buddy!" Sel said.

Ely turned around and caught Jeff out of the corner of his eye. He saw him mouth the words, *kick his ass.*

Ely took the down position as he was instructed to do. Generally, being in the down position was more advantageous for scoring. It was much easier to get an escape or reversal than it was to turn someone onto their back for near fall points. So Ely got into the down position, on his hands and knees with his butt sitting on his ankles, and within seconds he felt his opponent grip his arm and stomach as he took the top position.

Round Three:

Then the whistle blew. The Kopachuck kid went to work on Ely, going back and forth between a tight waist and a far ankle whenever Ely made it to his base. He threw the half on Ely several times but couldn't turn him onto his back. Ely kept his head up and kept working for a stand up.

Suddenly Ely felt nothing on his back. His opponent had jumped back, allowing Ely to stand up, giving him one point for an escape. Sometimes, if a wrestler was good at takedowns, or at least confident that he could get one, he would let his opponent get an escape. He could then take him down, netting him a point. And that was exactly what this kid was doing.

The score was now eight to two.

But before Ely could contemplate the score, the kid moved in fast and took Ely to the mat with a beautiful double leg takedown.

The score was now ten to two

Shit, Ely thought. *He is winning by eight and that is a major decision, which will earn four points for his team, tying the overall team score.* Ely couldn't let that happen.

Mr. Seljin was at the side of the mat screaming. The entire bench was yelling. Hundreds of people in the stands were yelling and pounding their feet, and the only thing Ely could hear was his heart pounding in his chest.

Then he heard something else. He began to hear his dad's voice. It was soft at first. Then it got louder. Soon it was drowning out everything else. "Come on, pussy," his dad said. "Get your fat ass moving." The barrage of insults continued for what seemed like minutes, and with every hurtful word Ely's anger grew, until it finally erupted in a roar of defiance.

He heaved himself up like a submarine breaking through an ice sheet. It felt as if his opponent weighed a hundred pounds, not two hundred. He was desperate to get his weight off, to throw off the very thing that was holding him down, which to Ely felt like the personification of every negative thing his father had ever said to him. He exploded to his feet like a volcano, lifting his opponent with him. The Kopachuck wrestler was frantically trying to maintain his hold around Ely's body so he wouldn't escape They spun around as they fought, Ely savagely trying to break away, still fueled by his rage.

"Head and arm!" he heard from the bench. He wasn't sure who said it, but it triggered a memory of him practicing the move with Cisco in the very same position he was now in. He remembered coach Seljin calling it a desperation move, a move to try when you had nothing to lose and the match was almost over. Ely figured that in his current predicament now was the right time to do it. So he reached back with his left arm and grabbed the kid's head, simultaneously gripping his far arm with his right hand. They were already moving forward as his opponent was trying to shove him out of bounds, when Ely heaved with all his might and threw his hip into him. He really didn't know how he did it, but in a blink, the Kopachuck kid was flying through the air as Ely threw him in a head and arm. They hit the mat hard as Ely tenaciously held onto his head and arm, squeezing as tightly as he could.

Then the buzzer rang.

Ely was in a daze but he did hear the referee signal a two point reversal. Technically it would have been a takedown. But since he did not get an escape first, it would be awarded as a reversal. And since the kid was only on his back for a second before the buzzer rang, Ely would not be getting any near fall points. But it didn't matter. He only needed two.

Ely released his hold and looked up and saw that the score was now ten to four. He lost, but only by six. That meant that the Kopachuck wrestler had only won by a decision.

The gym exploded into wild cheers as they watched the score flash up on the scoreboard, 45 to 44. Key Peninsula had just won the league title by one point and everyone was screaming at the top of their lungs.

Ely slowly lifted his exhausted body off the mat, a dazed smile slowly spreading across his face. He looked over at Mr. Seljin who was jumping up and down and screaming with joy, although Ely had no idea what he was saying. His eyes drifted to the others on the bench who were also howling with glee. Jeff was yelling at Ely and hugging John at the same time. Cisco was screaming something but he couldn't hear anyone. But he didn't need to hear a thing. All he needed to see were the looks on their faces. They were looking at him with joy, with happiness, with a *you did it* expression. It gave him a feeling he had never felt before.

The referee raised his opponent's hand in victory and all Ely could do was smile. He lost the match, but he won something greater. For the first time, he won respect.

***

The rest of the evening was a blur. He had never felt so much joy. Kids he had never met congratulated him and teammates who had rarely spoken to him patted him on the back.

His mom couldn't come to the match as she had to rest before her graveyard shift at the grocery store. But she picked him up just after the match and she planned on dropping him off at home on her way to work. Ely was excited to see her to tell her the news.

She was a little late so Ely had to wait outside the gym with Mr. Seljin, who had to wait until all the wrestlers were picked up before he could leave. Ely felt bad that he was keeping him.

"Don't worry, bud. I don't mind," Mr. Seljin assured Ely. "You wrestled great tonight, you know."

"Thanks…but I still lost," Ely said.

"True, but *we* didn't. And we would have without you. You handed us the league title. You should be proud. Besides, you had a good match. That kid was pretty tough and you wrestled the best I've seen you wrestle. That stand up was great. You countered his half nelsons perfectly. And that head and arm at the end was classic. You've improved a lot, trust me," Sel smiled.

"I guess so. It did feel good at the end of the match when I threw him in that head and arm," Ely said, returning his smile.

"I bet it did. You never know what could've happened. Another thirty seconds you might have pinned him. One step at a time Ely. You're getting better and you'll continue to do so."

"Did you ever lose?" Ely asked.

"Of course, everyone loses at some point. I lost a few matches when I was in middle school, but I didn't lose as many in high school, or college. But I can still remember my losses like they were yesterday. You know, you learn more from losing than winning. Just like in school, you never get better if you don't make mistakes. It's part of the learning process."

"I guess so, but it still doesn't feel good. Were you a state champ in high school?" Ely asked. He had heard that Mr. Seljin was some prodigy wrestler, that he had won several state titles and then went on to win some national titles, but no one had ever confirmed it.

"Yeah, I won the state title my junior and senior year."

"How did you do in college?"

"Two national titles."

"Wow. I can't imagine being that good at something."

"Everyone is good at something. You'll find what you're good at, don't worry. Is that your mom?" Sel asked, indicating a beat up Datsun 210 driving into the school parking lot.

"Yup," Ely said as he grabbed his backpack and headed for the car.

"Nice job tonight. I'm proud of you Ely," Sel said as he followed Ely over to his car that was now parked at the curb.

Ely turned and smiled. "Thanks." Mr. Seljin walked around the car to the driver side window.

Ely got into the car as Mary rolled down the window.

Mr. Seljin leaned down to speak to her. "Hello, Mrs. Carter, I'm Mr. Seljin, Ely's coach and teacher. I just wanted to introduce myself and let you know how well Ely is doing."

"Hello, I've heard so much about you. Ely really enjoys your class. And thank you for letting him borrow your books. I can't keep him supplied fast enough. He moves through books faster than apple pie," Mary said with a laugh.

"No problem. I'm glad I can feed his voracious appetite for literature. You know, Ely won the match for us tonight. We won the league title because of him," Sel said with a big smile.

Mary looked at Ely. "You won, honey? I'm so proud of you."

"Well," Ely stammered, "not exactly."

"He lost, but only by enough to award his opponent a win by decision, which gave the Kopachuck team three points," Sel explained. "We were winning 45 to 41 before Ely's match so the final score was 45 to 44. We won by one point because Ely didn't give up. He wrestled really well tonight."

"If I hadn't been there the team would have had to forfeit the match and Kopachuck would have received six points," Ely explained, trying to make his loss sound less like a loss.

"And they would have won the match by two points?" Mary interjected.

"Exactly. He lost his match, but he won us the league title," Sel confirmed.

Mary turned back to Ely and patted him on the leg, smiling broadly. "I'm so proud of you, son."

Ely returned her smile.

Ely was on cloud nine until the car arrived at his long dirt driveway. Apprehension about seeing his father grabbed a hold of him and began to smother his previous feelings of elation. His stomach began to knot up and his heart beat faster. If he was lucky he'd already be passed out. If not, depending on his mood, it might not go well for Ely.

Mary dropped him off with a kiss on the cheek and Ely walked slowly to the front door, his apprehension causing him to perspire even though the night was cool. He could hear the television but couldn't tell whether his father was up and about.

When he opened the door his heart sank. Bill was standing at the refrigerator grabbing another beer.

Ely put his head down, closed the door, and moved towards the hallway that led to his room.

"Hey, dad," he said softly as he tried to scoot by him without a confrontation.

"Well, how'd you do, boy?" Bill asked as he turned around and popped open the can, which fizzed briefly as Ely reluctantly stopped and faced his father.

"We won the league title. We beat Kopachuck by one point. It was a great match," Ely said with enthusiasm, hoping to sideline his father's next question, which would probably be about his own match.

Bill took a long drink from his beer. "That's good," he said. "Did you win your match?" he added after a loud burp.

"Well, sort of," Ely added apprehensively.

"What do you mean, sort of? You either won or you didn't."

"Well, if I hadn't been there the team would've lost by one point. But because I was there, and I only lost by a decision, we won the match," Ely added quickly.

"You lost your match, and you're happy about it?" Bill said, his voice rising a little.

"Dad, I wrestled my best match so far. I didn't get pinned and because of that we won."

Bill looked disgusted. "What the hell is wrong with you, boy! You lost, again, and you think that's a good thing?"

"I don't think it's good. I'm just trying to explain to you how the scoring works—."

"I'm not stupid, boy!" Bill interrupted. "I get it. But I don't give a shit about the team score. You lost. That's all that matters. Get out of my face. You disgust me."

Ely looked up at his father. He was going to say something else but thought better of it. Luckily for Ely, Bill wasn't too drunk yet, so his abuse was strictly verbal. Ely didn't want to push it so he lowered his head and quickly made his way to his room.

He wanted to shower but he knew his dad might yell at him. Instead he went into the bathroom, wet a hand towel, and proceeded to do the best he could to wipe the sweat off his body. He wasn't sure it did much to eliminate the residual musty odor of his body resulting from his hard fought match, but it was better than nothing.

In his room Ely put on a fresh pair of underwear, turned on his bed lamp, and clicked off the light in the room. He lay down in his bed and pulled the blankets up over his chest. He lay there for several moments staring at the ceiling and thinking about the evening. *Not a bad day*, Ely thought. His mind drifted to the expressions on his teammates' faces after his match. He could still hear the roaring of the crowd and in his mind's eye he visualized Mr. Seljin jumping up and down in sheer joy. He was responsible for that. He did something that he was proud of. It was a good night. He was going to bed happy, a relatively novel experience for him. He had suffered only the usual verbal abuse from his father, and bore no injuries from his father's fists. Ely smiled. It was a good day, and as he knew from experience, it could have been a lot worse.

It was still early for Ely to sleep. Usually he'd read a bit until he drifted off to sleep. But tonight he was tired, and he wanted to fall asleep thinking about this wonderful night. For once he didn't want to read to escape to another world, he wanted to stay right where he was, relishing the feeling of his accomplishment. So he reached up, clicked off the light, and closed his eyes.

Eighth Grade

Ninth Grade

Tenth Grade

Ely's eyes shot open as his alarm clock buzzed annoyingly. He reached up and slapped his hand on the clock, struggling to find the snooze button.

Over the past three years, Ely had thinned out a bit as he had lost some of the pudginess of youth. But he was still big, weighing over two hundred and fifty pounds, and a significant amount of it was still fat. He had grown several inches and now stood nearly as tall as his father, just over six feet tall.

Ely dragged himself up and sat on the edge of his bed, scratching his head. His shaggy brown hair failed to cover his left eye, which was still slightly puffy and tinged a light shade of purple. His swollen upper lip was adorned by a small bloody scab. He slumped over wearily, feeling about as bad as he looked.

He sighed, stood up, and readied himself for his chores. Bill had asked Ely to have all the wood chopped by the time he got back from work, which would be sometime around four o'clock.

For the last four months Bill had managed to hold down a job at an auto parts store. It only paid minimum wage, but at least it was something. The best part was that it got Bill out of the house, which meant he had less time to drink, and less time to harass Ely. And even though Ely had spent most of his summer performing various chores for his father, it was still one of the best summers he could remember. Bill had only hit him on several occasions, the other night being the worst. But all in all, Ely had avoided his father's anger fairly well over the last few months.

Ely ate a quick breakfast of toast and orange juice and made his way outside. There was a massive pile of wood that Ely had cut up several days ago and Ely's job was now to split and stack it. The woodpile was over four feet high and Ely knew it would take all day to finish the job.

He sighed, grabbed the splitting maul, and walked over to the woodpile. He turned on his CD player, placed his ear phones in his ears, and began splitting the logs. It was going to be a long hard day.

It was nearly one o'clock and Ely had managed to work through only about half of the woodpile. *I better get moving*, Ely thought, knowing that his father would be pissed if he didn't finish on time. He had picked up the pace a bit when the sound of a horn suddenly startled him, interrupting the monotony of the seemingly endless task of splitting and stacking wood.

He turned to see a blue Honda driving up the road, and Ely smiled as he placed another piece of wood on the stack by the barn. It was Jeff, and Ely walked quickly over from the barn to the edge of their driveway to greet him. It was a hot day, and Ely's shirt was drenched with sweat while rivulets of perspiration dripped from his eyebrows.

The car skidded to a stop and Jeff got out. Ely could see a cute blonde girl sitting in the passenger seat. Jeff was now five ten and weighed a hundred and sixty five pounds, most of it dense muscle resulting from over five years of wrestling. He had always been good looking, but was now downright handsome, with short hair and a genuine smile. Ely always thought he looked like the young men you see on the Abercrombie and Fitch bags and the posters in their stores. Jeff was wearing black and lime green board shorts, flip flops, and a white tank top.

"Ely, what up?" Jeff said, reaching out to shake his buddy's hand.

"Hey, Jeff. You slumming or what? What brings you out in my neck of the woods?"

Jeff had been to Ely's house before, but the visits were infrequent. They had slowly developed a growing friendship during eighth grade and it had continued into high school. They didn't really see each other much, but they sort of had an unspoken connection. Neither of them had ever really talked about it, and Ely often wondered what Jeff saw in him, but either way, they both regarded each other as a friend, that much was certain.

"I had to come deliver the good news personally," Jeff said.

"What good news?"

"I just got word that Mr. Seljin was hired to teach at Peninsula High School and he's going to be the head wrestling coach," Jeff said enthusiastically.

"What! You're kidding! What happened to Mr. Hobart?"

"He retired. And no, I'm not kidding. Now you have no excuse. You have to wrestle," Jeff reasoned.

"No way. Come on, Jeff, I already told you, I'm not going to wrestle. Christ, I didn't win a single match in eighth grade. I'm going to be a junior. I'm not an athlete and my previous record supports that fact."

"*And my previous record supports that fact*," Jeff said mockingly. "Dude, who the hell talks like that? Anyway, it's bullshit. We'll make an athlete out of you yet. I remember that final match in eighth grade, and I sure as hell know you remember it. There is an athlete in you somewhere; we just have to find him."

"You'll have to dig through a lot of fat to find him. And of course I remember that match. And yes, it felt good, but I didn't win, and I have never won a match so pardon me for saying that wrestling is not top on my list of things to do in high school."

"Whatever. Stop making excuses. Now that we have Mr. Seljin as our coach we might be in the running for a state title. We've got the talent, and now we have the coach."

"It's easy for you to get all excited about it. When was the last time *you* lost a match?"

Jeff paused for a second as if he were thinking. "I don't know," he said smiling. "Sixth grade I think."

"Go ahead, rub it in," Ely said with a smile. "We'll talk about it later. I have to get this wood chopped before my dad gets home."

Jeff looked at the stack of wood and back at Ely. "Hey, what happened to your face?"

"Ah, a piece of wood flew back and hit me in the face when I chopped that damn tree down yesterday."

"Ouch, that looks painful," Jeff said, looking at his face more closely. "That's a pretty bad shiner. You got bad luck, man. Seems like you're always getting hurt."

"It's fine. Hey, who's that girl in the car?" Ely asked, changing the subject.

"Lisa Collier, that fine ass cheerleader."

"Oh yeah, I know who she is. When did you start seeing her?" Ely asked.

"Since today," Jeff said, smiling conspiratorially. "Which reminds me, I've got to get going. We're heading down to the lake. She's kind of stuck up but I can't wait to see her in a bikini. She has a rockin' body. You sure you can't take a break and come with us?"

"Hell no, my dad will be pissed if I don't get this done. Besides, I'm allergic to bathing suits," Ely said, smacking his belly through his sweat stained shirt.

"Alright bro', take it easy. But think about wrestling, we need you, man."

"I'm having a déjà vu," Ely replied said as he recalled a similar conversation he had had with Jeff, John, and Cisco several years back. They, along with Mr. Seljin, had somehow convinced him to wrestle in the eighth grade.

"And the tactic worked if I recall!" Jeff yelled as he got into his car and shut the door.

"Yes it did," Ely whispered to himself as Jeff started the engine.

Inside the car, Lisa looked at Jeff, making no effort to mask her annoyed look. "Who's that fat kid and why did we have to stop at this shit hole?"

Jeff's smile disappeared as he looked at her. "That fat kid is my friend, and this shit hole is his house."

"Well let's get out of here. This place is depressing," she said, trying unsuccessfully to mask her disdain. Lisa had light brown hair with blond highlights and her stunning blue eyes complimented her tan skin perfectly. She was a beautiful girl with an equally impressive figure.

"And by the way, his name is Ely. And if you say one more negative thing about him or where he lives then you'll be walking home from the lake."

"Okay, Jeff. I'm sorry. I didn't mean it. Let's just go," she said, giving Jeff her best inviting smile.

"Okay," Jeff said, turning away from her and putting the car in drive.

Six

As an avid history fan, I've always found it interesting how one person can often impact the world in a monumental way. There are so many examples that it makes your head swim. Unfortunately we tend to remember the individuals that had colossal negative impacts on our society. People like Hitler, Pol Pot in Cambodia, Stalin, Pinochet in Peru, Mussolini, Ivan the Terrible, and the list goes on, every name symbolic of millions of people that died as a result of their actions.

But there are also people who have struggled to do good as well and the impact of their lives is equally impressive, people like Martin Luther King Jr., Gandhi, Mother Theresa, the Dalai Lama, and with many others less well known. The point is, history is filled with examples of individuals who have dramatically affected society. We see numerous examples in our history books, but I also think we can see it in our daily lives. And although the impact an individual can have on someone else's life may be on a much smaller scale than that of someone like Gandhi, I would argue that the people on the receiving end of this altruistic behavior would not view their experience as being less important. To that individual, it may have been the most important influence in their life, perhaps even lifesaving.

I was lucky enough in my life to see examples of this. People I met on my life's path helped steer me in the right direction. Without them, I cringe to think what could have happened to me. Every little thing that someone did for me slowly added a new brick to my foundation. At least that is how I think of it. Without their support, my life would have crumbled. To them, giving a single brick, or ten bricks, was probably not a big deal, but they sure do add up.

I try to think of this as I live my life. I have the power to give bricks. I can do positive things every day and it takes little effort. To me, the actions are very simple, but to someone else, they may be very significant. I was lucky enough in life to have crossed paths with others who, over time, provided me with enough bricks to enable me to rise from the muck. Without their gifts I'm afraid that I might not have had the fortitude or the skills necessary to build anything of value from my life. I thank these people every day. They have been the models for my own actions and have given me a template on how to live my life. Pay it forward; it's a great way to live.

Ely Carter

The rays of the mid-day sun had vanquished the morning chill from the air, casting pleasant warmth around Ely as he sat on the bench outside the commons area of Peninsula High School. This was his favorite place to eat lunch. He could read his books and listen to his music, which to him was the highlight of his day. Today he was eating a slice of pizza and drinking a coke, the lunch of champions. He had just begun reading a series of books by an author named Brent Weeks. He was only twenty pages into it and he was already solidly hooked, and once snared, it was tough for Ely to put a book down.

Suddenly someone sat down next to him. Ely looked sidelong from the pages, hoping he would not see Adam or anyone else who might cause him problems. Fortunately Ely was pretty big, so most of the ridicule came from comments and nasty stares rather than anything physical. But there were some football players and a few other large guys that occasionally gave him grief. But most of the nonverbal abuse came from indifference. No one seemed to make an effort to know him, or talk to him, and sometimes that hurt more than a punch in the face. John, Cisco, and a few others said hi to him, but that was about it, and their interactions were pretty minimal. Jeff on the other hand was the only kid who Ely classified as a friend. And Ely had a suspicion that Jeff had a lot to do with the fact that he was not pushed around much anymore. Jeff Hanson was the type of guy that others listened to, and if he said to lay off of him, most would leave him be.

But it wasn't a bully who had sat down next to him, it was Mr. Seljin. Ely took off his headphones, smiling warmly at his old teacher. "Hey, Sel."

"It's just the man I've been looking for. Still listening to classical music?"

"Is there any other music?" Ely asked, smiling as they shook hands.

"How are you, Ely?" Sel asked, laughing.

"I'm alright. What about you? How's the new job?"

"I like it. Teaching seniors is a little different than middle school, that's for sure. But it's been a nice challenge. The age difference allows me to dig a bit deeper into the subject matter, which I've really enjoyed."

"I can see how that would be a nice change. Less babysitting I imagine."

"Exactly," Sel agreed.

"I heard you're coaching wrestling this year. Maybe we'll get a decent team now," Ely added.

"I'm working on it, which is why I'm here."

"What do you mean?" Ely asked hesitantly.

"Well, I'm doing some recruiting. I just finished talking to Jeff. He said you'd be out here. It sounds like you two have become friends?"

"Yeah, I guess so. He's the main reason why I didn't get beat up every day when we all moved on to high school."

"Oh yeah?"

"I don't know, but I think he had something to do with it. We don't hang out much. Jeff has a lot of friends and he's pretty busy with all his sports, but we try to hang out when we can."

"That's good. So let's cut to the chase. I need some unlimited wrestlers again. I need you," Sel said matter-of-factly.

"Jeff warned me you wouldn't leave me alone."

"He's a smart kid. I have two heavyweights right now and I need more."

"Sel, I'm awful. I didn't win one match in eighth grade."

"Don't worry about that," Sel countered.

"Easy for you to say when you probably can't remember what it was like to lose."

"We'll work on your skills," Sel said, ignoring Ely's comment. "Besides, you have one thing that many people don't have."

"What? A fatalistic attitude? Layers of fat? A love of classical music? Com on Sel, tell me, the suspense is killing me."

"I'm serious, Ely."

Ely just shook his head and laughed. "Okay, I'll bite. What do I have?"

"You have heart and determination," Sel said quickly.

"Come on, Sel. Flattering Hallmark words are not going to be enough to have that referee raise my hand at the end of a match," Ely said adamantly.

"I mean it," Sel said seriously. "You just haven't convinced yourself that you can be tough."

"But I'm not tough. I'm not an athlete."

"How do you know?" Sel challenged.

"I just know."

"Ely, you've never tested yourself. You don't *just know*. You have to prove to yourself that you either are, or you're not. The only way you'll find out is if you push yourself. You have to try. I mean you have to really give it a chance before you can say that you *know*."

"I don't know, Sel. I did try, and I think my record indicated that I'm not tough."

"I disagree. I saw you improve over those two months. I saw potential. I saw someone who, if he really applied himself, could be a great wrestler. I still remember that stand up and head and arm that allowed us to win the league title over Kopachuck. Do you remember it?"

Mr. Seljin had him there. He would never forget that night. He would never forget the feeling of being the person that had guaranteed Key Peninsula the league championship. The smiles from his teammates, the cheers from the fans, were all still burned into his memory. "Yeah, I still remember that match," Ely replied.

"I thought so. Hey, are you still reading a lot?" Sel asked, changing the subject, or at least that's what Ely thought.

"Every chance I get."

"And are you still getting straight A's?"

"Ummm, yes, school is easy."

"Why do you think you're so good at academic stuff?"

"I don't know. I like to read, to learn, to understand things. It comes easy for me."

"Were you born knowing everything you know now?" Sel asked.

"Of course not."

"Well, how did you become such a good student?"

"I worked at it I guess. I read all the time. But I enjoy reading, it helps me forget things," Ely said softly.

Mr. Seljin didn't ask about the things Ely wished to forget, but the comment was not lost on him. For a long time now he had suspected that things at home were not great for Ely. He had also known that Ely had struggled to meet people and make friends. He wondered what *things* Ely wanted to forget. When he had learned that Jeff had befriended Ely it had made him very happy.

"I understand that. But you can use wrestling in the same way; as an escape. It doesn't matter if you're good or not," Sel said.

"What do you mean it doesn't matter?" Ely asked skeptically.

"What I mean is…just lose yourself in the sport. Every day at practice, work as hard as you can. Lift weights during the off season. Run off season. Practice off season. It's not the end result that matters, it's how you get there."

"Again, that's easy for you to say, but try losing all the time. Sometimes the end result is the only thing that matters."

"You're right, I was good at wrestling. But it was very hard for me to get through school. I had to get tutors and all kinds of extra help. I'd have to study twice as hard as everyone else just to get the C's I needed to continue to wrestle. You could get C's and not even show up to class. Having to struggle so hard in my classes was very frustrating to me. Do you understand what I'm saying?"

"Yeah, I guess so."

"Wrestling is one of the most difficult sports there is. For that reason it's the most rewarding. When you come out on that mat, you are doing something that ninety five percent of the student body here can't do, or more likely is afraid to do. You will develop a skill set that will get you through anything you face in life. You will learn about courage, loyalty, team work, working hard, diet and health, and you will develop a sense of confidence in yourself that will see you through life. Why don't you be a part of the five percent that isn't afraid?

What would Drizzt Do Urden say?" Sel asked with a smile.

Ely couldn't believe that Mr. Seljin had just brought Drizzt into the argument. Years ago, in eighth grade, Ely had borrowed a lot of books from Mr. Seljin. As it turned out, Sel was just as big a fantasy freak as Ely. One of Mr. Seljin's favorites as a kid was a series of books about a dark elf named Drizzt Do Urden, a character that had become one of Ely's favorites as well. In fact he had written an eighth grade report about the elf for his English class.

"He'd probably say exactly what you just said. Then he would vanquish his foes with ease and become the hero of the school," Ely added with a flourish.

"There you go. There's your answer."

"Alright, you win. I'll give it a shot," Ely said, shaking his head in defeat.

"Good for you," Sel said, smiling widely. Then he checked his watch. "I better get going. Class starts in five minutes."

"Take it easy, Sel."

"You too. Come into my classroom during lunch sometime and visit. I'd like to talk to you some more."

"Okay, see ya later."

"Take care of yourself," Mr. Seljin added as he turned and walked away.

Ely smiled as he watched him leave. "I can't believe he brought up Drizzt," he said to himself.

It was fifth period when Ely received a green slip to go to the office. It was his calculus class and they were taking a quiz which Ely had already finished. So Mr. Walker told him to go ahead and go.

When Ely reached the main office, Mrs. Jovell, the perpetually friendly office manager, told him to go ahead and go back to Mr. Nelson's office. Mr. Nelson was his counselor and Ely rarely talked with him, so he was curious what this was all about.

As he neared Mr. Nelson's office he could see that his door was open and that he was at his computer. Ely knocked softly on the side of the door and Mr. Nelson turned and smiled invitingly.

"Come on in, Ely, have a seat," he said, gesturing to a soft leather chair opposite him.

Mr. Nelson was about fifty years old and he wore silver narrow rimmed glasses. His gray hair was sort of unruly, which was in contrast to his immaculately trimmed beard and mustache. His hair was totally gray, almost silver, which made him look older than he actually was.

Ely sat down in the chair and handed him the note. "Hi, Mr. Nelson. I got a note saying you wanted to see me."

"Yes, I do indeed. We just got the tenth grade WASL tests back."

"Yeah?"

"Yes, and I think you'll be interested to know how you did," Mr. Nelson said.

"Why's that?" he asked. He didn't really think much about the test. He always seemed to ace them, and those standardized tests were really easy.

Everyone made such a big deal out of the WASL test but Ely never really understood why. The Washington Assessment for Student Learning was just another test.

"Well, you had a perfect score. You didn't miss one problem."

"Really?" Ely wasn't really sure why that was worth being called down from class. After all it wasn't his first hundred percent and it probably wouldn't be his last. If there was one thing that Ely was confident about, it was his academic ability.

"I don't think you understand what that means. Since we've been administering this test, I've never seen anyone get a perfect score. Ely, with a score like that there's a good chance that you have an IQ in the upper fifth percentile," Mr. Neslon said seriously.

"Really! Me? You're kidding, right?" Ely had known he was smart, but the top fifth percentile? That would mean he was a genius, literally, not figuratively. Even though school was easy for him, he had never really imagined himself to be in the upper percentile of anything.

"No, I'm not kidding. I want you to take the IQ test. If it's as high as I think it is then we need to make some serious changes."

"What do you mean…changes?"

"Ely, if you're as intelligent as your tests suggest, then you're just wasting your time here. Do you find your classes here easy?" Mr. Nelson asked.

"Well…yeah, I guess so."

"Do you ever study for anything?"

Ely thought about it for a moment. "Not really. I just listen and read the books. I've never had to study much. I remember most everything I read."

"Really? How long would it take you to read this book?" Mr. Nelson asked, reaching up and lifting a heavy, thickly bound book off the shelf. The book looked like it might be a history textbook.

"I don't know. Probably a day or two," Ely reasoned.

"You're kidding."

"No. I can basically skim the text and I remember everything," Ely said.

"That's incredible, Ely. I think we need to get you into the Running Start program."

"What's that?"

"It's a program where you get to take college classes during high school. You would be here for half the day and then go to the community college for the rest. And the classes you take there would count as college credits," Mr. Nelson explained.

"I can't do college stuff," Ely said quickly, without really thinking. Over time he had become accustomed to not really believing he could do anything well, and it had just occurred to Ely that he was really good at saying he couldn't do something, even though this was actually one thing that he believed he *could* do.

"Believe me, you could, and you will, very easily I would imagine," Mr. Nelson said with conviction. "I'm going to call you out of P.E. tomorrow to take the IQ test, okay?"

"Okay."

"Now, why don't you get back to class," he said as he reached over to write Ely a pass.

"Okay."

Mr. Nelson handed him his pass and as Ely got up and headed for the door he added, "Hey, Ely."

Ely turned around at the door. "Yeah?"

"Nice job. You should be proud of yourself. You have a gift."

Ely smiled at Mr. Nelson. He liked the sound of that. Mr. Nelson believed in him. Now he just had to learn how to believe in himself. "Thanks, Mr. Nelson," Ely said as he turned to leave, his mind a flurry of activity as he began to process what his counselor had told him.

That afternoon Ely was busy outside cutting down a large fir tree near their driveway. Bill had wanted the tree down before he got home so Ely had gone to work on it immediately after school. The saw blade was six inches into the two foot girth of the tree when Ely thought he heard a car horn through the noise of the chainsaw's engine. He backed the blade out and turned around to see Jeff's Honda pull up the driveway. Ely flipped the off switch and the motor sputtered to a stop. He wiped off his sweaty brow and walked to the driveway to greet Jeff.

Ely noticed something large sticking out the back of Jeff's hatchback and the trunk lid had been tied down with rope. Jeff and Cisco hopped out of the car.

"Hey, Jeff, Cisco, what up?"

"Hey," Jeff replied, greeting Ely with a firm handshake.

"Hey, man," Cisco said, smacking Ely's hand in greeting.

"Looks like you're slaving away again. Dude, all you ever do is work," Jeff said, indicating the saw Ely had set down on the ground.

"My dad's a slave driver. If I don't do what he asks he gets really pissed." Ely glanced to the back of Jeff's car. "What's that?"

Jeff smiled. "That's what I'm here for. Sel asked me to bring you some things."

"What things?"

"He had an old dusty mat and weight set he wanted me to bring you," Jeff answered.

"That's cool you're going to wrestle this year," Cisco added.

"Wow, word travels quick," Ely said.

"Sel told us right away. I knew he could talk you into it," Jeff said smiling.

"Yeah, he got me," Ely admitted.

"Good choice man," Jeff said.

"I don't know how it's good news though, I don't have much to offer."

"Hey, we need some bigger guys. I'll be at two fifteen this year and we always need more people to practice with," Cisco said.

"Besides, that's what all this stuff is for, to make you a better wrestler," Jeff said.

"I think it will take more than that rusty weight set and that old mat," Ely said.

"Stop being a pessimist and help us get this stuff into the barn," Jeff said as he moved towards the back of the car.

"Pessimist. That's Jeff's word of the day. He's been saying it every two seconds," Cisco said laughing. "He learned it in Mrs. Meyer's class and now he won't shut up about it."

"My new word is eat shit," Jeff said as he smacked Cisco in the shoulder.

"That's two words," Ely said.

All three of the boys laughed as they started to unload the gear from Jeff's car. It didn't take them too long to get it all set up. The mat was old and not as soft as it should be, but the size was perfect for two wrestlers to practice moves. It was six feet by six feet and was torn in several places, but it would do. The weight set was pretty minimal. There was a bench that could adjust from flat to incline and it included one bar with two forty five pound plates, two thirty five pound plates, two twenty five pound plates, all the way down to five pound plates. There was also a small set of dumbbells starting from fifty five pounds and going down to twenties in five pound increments. They were old, but weights were weights and age did little to hamper their effectiveness.

After they got everything all set up Ely thanked them and went right back to his chores and the boys took off. His dad would be home in an hour and he had to make sure the tree was down and limbed, so he set to work doing just that.

The hour went by quickly and Ely was nearly finished with trimming the tree when his dad arrived in his beat up truck. Ely turned off the saw as his dad approached from the driveway.

"You almost done?" Bill asked as he got out of the car and surveyed Ely's work.

"Yeah, about ten more minutes," Ely mumbled as he wiped the sweat from his face.

"Good. Tomorrow I want you to start cutting it into eighteen inch logs and then chop it. We need to get two more cords before winter," Bill added as he turned to leave.

"Hey dad, ummm, there are some weights and an old mat in the barn. Do you mind?"

"What do you mean? Where did you get those things?"

"Mr. Seljin gave them to me. He asked me to wrestle," Ely said.

"Really? After your pathetic attempt in eighth grade?"

"Yeah, even after that," Ely said softly.

"Shit, I don't care. Just make sure it doesn't cost us anything."

"I'm sure it won't. He'll take care of it. What about the weights and stuff?"

"As long as that shit is not in my way, I don't care. It might do you some good. Now hurry up and get that wood done," Bill said as he turned to leave. "Your mom home yet?"

"No, I think she works 'til nine tonight."

"Dammit," Bill mumbled to himself as he made his way to the door. "Get your ass moving then, I need you to cook me something to eat."

"Okay," Ely whispered as he turned back to the saw.

"What! Don't go mumbling at me, boy!" Bill yelled as he turned back towards Ely.

"I said okay!" Ely said louder, picking up the saw.

Bill glared at Ely briefly before he slammed the door behind him.

"And let the drinking begin," Ely muttered as he pulled the cord on the saw, the loud rumbling engine unable to drown out his angry thoughts.

That night Ely was deep into a book when he heard his mom pull up. He was almost done with the first book in the new Brent Weeks series and he was excited to get into the other two. He would check first thing if the local library had them as he knew his school library did not. Ely wanted to start looking for a job but his dad wouldn't allow it. He said he had too much work for him to do around the house. If he could work then he could afford his own books. He thought tonight might be a good time to approach his mom about getting a job.

The front door opened and Ely got up from his bed and walked through the kitchen and into the living room. The television was on and his father was lounging in his typical spot with a beer in hand.

Mary set her purse down on the kitchen table and without a word went to the refrigerator to get Bill another beer.

"Hey, Mom," Ely said as he sat down at the table.

"Hi, hon," Mary said as she kissed him on the forehead. "How was your day?" she asked as she walked over to her husband.

Bill took the beer and looked up at her. "Dammit, Mary, I don't like you coming home so late. Who the hell is going to cook me dinner?"

"Bill, I had leftover lasagna in the refrigerator. I told you that last night."

"I don't remember that. Shit, I had to have Ely make me something and that boy can't cook worth shit. I thought I was eating pig slop," he said bitterly as he took a long drink of his fresh beer.

"Well, I'm sorry. Did you even look in the fridge?" Mary asked.

"Don't get sassy with me, girl," Bill said as he grabbed her hand roughly. "When I get home from work I want a good meal, you got that?" Bill let go of her hand and turned his attention back to the television.

Mary didn't say a thing. She just walked slowly back into the kitchen. Ely was looking at her intently. "Why do you let him talk to you like that?" Ely whispered as he joined her in the kitchen.

Mary poured herself a glass of water and sat down next to Ely, sighing heavily. "Son, I'm tired. I don't want to talk about it. How was your day?"

Ely shook his head in resignation. He hated to see his father treat her like that. It hurt him worse to watch his mother be the brunt of his abuse than feeling it firsthand himself. "Fine, but you don't deserve it." His mother put her hand over his, smiling weakly at him as if she had no energy to respond. "My day was pretty good. I saw Mr. Seljin today. He asked me to wrestle again this year."

"I thought he taught at the middle school," Mary said.

"He did, but he got a job at the high school this year and he is going to be the new coach."

"That's great. Are you going to wrestle?" She asked.

"I think so. He sort of talked me into it."

"Well, what do *you* want?"

"I think I want to give it a try."

"Might be good for him!" Bill yelled from the living room

The two just ignored him. "We don't have much extra money, son." Mary leaned in and brought her voice to a whisper. "But if you need some, I've stashed a little aside. I might be able to help."

"Thanks, Mom, but I think Sel will take care of me. But I wanted to ask you about me getting a job. I'd like to look for some part time work. You know, so I could have my own spending money."

"I don't know. You know what your father thinks about that," Mary said.

"Thinks about what?" Bill yelled from the living room.

Mary shrugged her shoulders to Ely and turned to face Bill. "Ely was asking about maybe getting a side job for extra spending money."

Bill looked over at them. "I don't want anything interfering with your chores, boy!"

"You mean I can?" Ely asked excitedly.

"Shit, I don't care, as long as you get your work done around the house," Bill growled.

Mary gripped Ely's hand tighter, happy in her son's excitement. "Where do you think you'll apply?"

"You know the book store in town, Gig Harbor Books? I've already talked to the owner and he said he could use some evening help a couple times a week. It's just minimum wage, but I should be able to get fifteen hours a week and that should be enough for spending money.

"What about when wrestling starts?" Mary asked.

"I don't know, maybe I can work weekends then. I'll have to talk to Mr. Clawson about that. He's really nice so maybe he'll work with me for those few months," Ely said hopefully.

"How will you get to work?" Mary asked. Ely didn't have his driver's license as they had no money for the extra class. Besides, what would be the point considering they had no car that he could use anyway. Mary often worked late, and driving Bill's crappy truck was out of the question.

"I mentioned the job thing to Jeff once and he said he could probably take me to the bus stop."

"Oh, okay. That's nice of him. Well, I'm proud of you. That will be great. And plus, you'll be around books. I imagine you'll get some discounts or something."

"Yup, thirty percent off everything. It's perfect for me."

"Good for you. How is school?"

"Fine. Guess what?"

"Ummm…I don't know, what?"

"I was called down to the counseling office today and Mr. Nelson, my counselor, told me that I scored a perfect score on the WASL test," Ely said.

"Wow, that's great. Was it a hard test?"

"Not for me," Ely said with a smile.

"He must have got my brains!" Bill yelled from the living room.

Mary looked at Ely and they silently laughed together. "Yeah, sure," she whispered.

"He wants me to take an IQ test tomorrow. He thought that maybe I should be doing Running Start," Ely continued.

"What's that?"

"It's a program where high school kids take college courses early, and they earn college credit while they do it. I'd be at the community college half of the day."

"Wow, but will it cost anything?" Mary asked, not wanting to put a damper on her son's news. College was expensive, and she knew there was no way they could afford it.

"I don't know yet, but I don't think so."

"Better not!" Bill yelled, burping loudly.

"I should find out more later," Ely said, ignoring his father.

"I'm proud of you, hon," Mary said as she gripped his hand with her own. "But I'm tired. I need to take a bath and go to bed. Good night, my dear."

"Good night, Mom."

Mary got up and walked toward the bathroom while Ely left his seat and headed to his own room, excited to re-submerge himself in his book.

Seven

Wrestling is one of those sports that, when you are participating in it, you are constantly asking yourself, 'Why am I doing this?' It's very demanding and it tests your resolve in many ways. One, you constantly have to watch what you eat if you want to do well. You need to make your weight, while at the same time maintaining maximum health and strength. Two, you are constantly sweaty and exhausted, the drain on your body being both physical and mental. Three, when you compete, it's just you and your opponent. You can't blame anyone else for what happens. Good or bad, you and you alone are responsible for your performance. Four, your body is confined in a tiny, tight, wrestling singlet and exposed to hundreds of people. And five, for me, since winning was a luxury, you have to continue to push yourself, both physically and mentally, with no tangible gain. That really is the hardest part. For someone who wins matches, they can say that all that hard work and dedication was worth it. But for the kids who don't win matches, or win very few, they have nothing to hold onto at the end of the season to support why they just spent three months of their lives getting their asses kicked.

I didn't realize it at the time, but it was these guys, yes, even me, who were the real tough kids. It took constant support from my few friends and from Mr. Seljin to motivate me to stay on the team. Now I understand what they were talking about when they told me that the means justifies the end, but I certainly didn't then. Being tough is mostly a mental state. Combine that with physical toughness and you have a true warrior. There are very few people like that.

Some are mentally tough, others are physically tough. But there are few individuals who possess both mental AND physical toughness. They are the ones who stand out in any sport. Jeff was one of those people, and so was Mr. Seljin. I certainly was not. But now when I look back at it, I understand what Mr. Seljin was always preaching to us. It's not whether you win or lose; it's the process that matters. It's what you do. It's the choices you make. Mr. Seljin had a quote hanging up in his room that came from Albus Dumbledore in the Harry Potter movies, which I guess makes it a J.K. Rowling quote. It said, "It's not our abilities that make us who we are, it's our choices." He always brought up that quote when referring to people he knew that were very talented in a particular field, but blew it because they made poor choices. He said he knew a basketball player who could have gone pro. He was gifted with natural ability and talent, but he was lazy. He worked out as little as possible, and he smoked a lot of pot. He was basically a loser who just so happened to have a lot of inherent talent. But his natural talent didn't carry him beyond his sophomore year in college. Sel would go on to say that it's the people who are hard workers, tenacious, and never give up that excel in life. No one cares how many wrestling matches you won back in high school, but they will notice someone who never falters, and who never gives up when they face adversity, which is a skill one can learn on the wrestling mat. And for me, adversity was not having the ability to win many matches. But what kept me going was hearing Seljin in my head say, "It's not our abilities, Ely, it's our choices. It's the decisions we make that lead us towards success. Remember that." And with his words ringing in my head, I stayed on the team and tried my best to win. It was an uphill fight, but the skills I learned on that mat are still with me today, and I will forever be grateful for them.

Ely Carter

———————————————

Sixty high school wrestlers were spread out over the mat, some stretching and talking while others used the peg board and rope hanging in the corner. It was the first day of practice and there was an air of excitement about as the athletes got ready for a new season with a new coach. Some of the wrestlers on the mat had gone to Key Peninsula Middle School so they were well versed on who Mr. Seljin was, but there were others that had come from the other feeder middle schools who had only heard rumors. But everyone was excited to start the year off on a positive note.

The ceiling of the wrestling room was high, probably forty feet, so climbing the complete rope, up and down, was not something that Ely could do. He was just too heavy and didn't have the upper body strength to lift his two hundred and fifty five pound frame forty feet in the air. There were two other heavy guys on the team who could do it though. Cisco was one, and Adam, the asshole from middle school, was another. Adam was the varsity heavyweight wrestler and he had grown into a gorilla, with big beefy arms and powerful legs.

The peg board was even more difficult. You held two wooden pegs in your hands and the goal was to climb a wooden board bolted in the wall by sticking the pegs in the holes that were drilled into the wood. The board went up ten feet and was a great way to help the wrestlers work on building arm strength and, more importantly, grip strength. Ely couldn't do the peg board either, but he wasn't alone there. Some of the kids really struggled with the board and some even got hurt. If you leaned back too far, the peg might slip out and hit you in the face, or worse, you might fall if you lacked the strength to hang on. On the other hand, some kids could easily climb the board, up and down, ten times. Again, Jeff was one of those who could. In fact, at times he would discard the peg and just use his fingers to climb the board, inserting two in at a time as he progressed up the board. That took immense finger, grip, and upper body strength and very few could do it. Jeff was built like a wrestler. He had dense sinewy muscles, muscles that looked like they were constantly pumped up and ready to explode into action.

Ely sat with Jeff, John, and Cisco as they stretched their muscles and prepared for the first practice. Mr. Seljin and his assistant coach, Pat Jackson, sat off to the side going over the practice schedule. Ely had never met Mr. Jackson before, but Jeff said he was a good guy. He was the assistant coach last year and all the kids seemed to like him. It turned out he had wrestled for Peninsula fifteen years ago and now he sold real estate for a living. Jeff said he had placed third in state his senior year and he was pretty knowledgeable about the sport. Of course Jeff took fourth his freshman year, second his sophomore year, and was in position to win the state title his junior and senior years. Ely halfheartedly suggested that he should be coaching, but Jeff said it took much more than just talent to coach a winning team. Ely wasn't so sure, but he figured he would see what Jeff meant soon enough.

Adam walked by the group as they were talking quietly. "Hey, who dragged in the trailer trash?" he asked, laughing as he sat on the mat nearby.

"Something stinks around here," Cisco said casually, ignoring Adam's comment.

"Yeah, what could it be?" Jeff said, playing along.

"I think it's an asshole," John said, sniffing disgustedly. "Yup, it's definitely an asshole."

They all turned to look at Adam and he just looked away with a sneer, choosing to ignore them.

"Don't worry, Ely," Jeff said, "he's still a jerk. He hasn't changed much."

"Other than the fact that he is now a muscle-bound monster," Ely whispered so Adam couldn't overhear him.

"You got that right. Good genetics I guess, but he's lazy as hell," John added.

"Try not to worry about him," Cisco said. "He's not that good. He's more intimidating than anything."

Suddenly the whistle blew and Sel ordered everyone to get moving. "Alright everyone, weight line. Hustle up!"

All the wrestlers jumped to attention and scattered to various spots along the wall, trying to find which weight they best fit into. The new high school weight classes went from one hundred and six pounds all the weigh up to two hundred and eighty five pounds. Ely went to the end of the line behind Adam and another big kid named Sawyer. Ely had never met him but he seemed friendly enough. Jeff was sitting at the front of the one hundred and fifty two pound line, while Cisco was leading the two hundred and twenty pound line and John was first in line at the one hundred and seventy pound class. Even though there had not been any challenges yet, the veterans knew the pecking order for now, at least until the real order could be determined by challenges.

Sel and coach Jackson stood before them.

Sel looked at everyone intently before he spoke. "Thank you all for being here. I feel very privileged to be a part of this program. Many of you know me and you know how I work. Some of you don't, and you will find out soon enough. Just remember; respect, honesty, commitment, and hard work are all I'm asking for. I don't want you to have any illusions. This will be the toughest thing you have ever done. We will start at three o'clock sharp and end at five every day. We will have tournaments or practice every Saturday without fail, and the weekend practices will go from eight to noon. You will *think* wrestling, *sleep* wrestling, and *eat* wrestling for the next three months. The only thing that you will put before wrestling is your family and school, and they will be in that order. I don't care who you are, how good you are, or how good you aren't, you're a part of this team and you'll be required to meet several criteria. One, you'll work hard on and off the mat and you will meet the required two point GPA to wrestle. If you need help in school then I will find a way to help you succeed. I will not lose anyone because of laziness. Two, you will be required to meet certain standards outside of school. You must be a positive part of this community and you'll respect your classmates, your teachers, and your family. If anyone of you gets in trouble during the season you will wish you hadn't. I'll tell you right now, no one gets special privileges. I don't care whether we win or lose as long as we all put one hundred and ten percent effort in life and on the mat. If we do that, losing will not even be an option because you've already won. If you push yourself as an individual then you will be successful, and that means *we* will be successful. Every one of you is a link in the Seahawk chain. You all must do your part. If everyone standing in front of me does that, then I believe that we will have a championship team. Now, let's warm up!"

Everyone cheered and snapped to attention. Ely felt like he had just heard Mel Gibson's speech in *Braveheart* and he had to admit that he was already feeling proud to be a part of the program.

***

Ely was pretty nervous. The junior varsity kids, including Ely, were finishing up their last matches and people were now starting to trickle in to watch the varsity match. Being the heaviest wrestler meant that he was wrestling last, which normally wouldn't be that bad except there were now a lot more people sitting in the stands eagerly awaiting the start of the varsity match. More people watching meant more nervousness, which was something that Ely definitely didn't need. This was his third match and he still hadn't won one yet, but he did have to admit that he was getting better.

Most of the varsity wrestlers were in the stands, suited up, and watching the JV matches. Soon, Sel would ask them to head into the locker room to begin mentally preparing themselves for their own matches. But for now, they were cheering on the JV kids, something that Sel always requested of them. He believed that an entire team's success was dependent on everyone, and that the varsity would not be the varsity unless the junior varsity team hadn't constantly pushed them. Every week it was possible for a varsity wrestler to be dethroned, to be beaten in challenges by someone who had improved and worked harder. Therefore no position was safe and the only thing that kept you in the varsity lineup was skill, hard work, tenacity, and knowing that three other guys in your weight class wanted your job.

Jeff and Cisco were next to Ely helping him warm up and get psyched. He had thirty seconds left before his match would start. Ely took off his headphones, releasing the strains of classical music through the tiny speakers.

"How the hell can you get amped up listening to that crap?" Jeff laughed, fully aware of Ely's passion for classical music.

"It focuses my chi," Ely quipped.

"Whatever. Alright bud, just go out there and be tough. Don't give up. Try not to even think about the end result. Just go out there and wrestle."

Cisco smacked Ely on the back as he took off his sweatshirt and put on his headgear. "You got this guy!"

Ely nodded his head to both of them as the buzzer rang, ending the match. "I got this guy!" He yelled over the cheers, trying to sound more confident than he really was.

Ely jumped up and down a few times trying to shake out the nerves. His two hundred and fifty pound frame was still covered with an abundance of fat but he was starting to look a little tighter as some of it, through practice and training, had been converted to muscle. But he still had a long way to go to look good in a singlet.

Ely walked toward the mat and Mr. Seljin stopped him at the corner. "Remember what I said. Don't think about winning or losing. Just go out there and wrestle as hard as you can. That's all I ask and that's all you should ask of yourself."

Ely smiled inwardly thinking that Sel's speech sounded an awful lot like Jeff's. He had a feeling that Jeff had probably often heard those same words from Sel and was now just repeating them to him. "Okay," was all Ely said in return.

Ely walked out to the center of the mat where his opponent was waiting for him. The guy was as big as Ely, with muscular arms, short powerful looking legs, and a round barrel chested torso. He looked like a football player, but then again, all the kids he wrestled looked like football players; probably because most of them were.

Instead of thinking about how big the guy looked, Ely tried to focus on what moves he was going to do first, anything to take his mind away from the butterflies doing aerial stunts in his stomach.

They shook hands and the whistle blew.

In the stands, Ely's parents watched intently as Ely began to circle his opponent. Mary gripped the edge of the bleacher as she sat nervously watching her son. Beside her Bill sat scowling, clearly not impressed and showing no sign of enthusiasm or support for his son. Mary had talked him into going and he had made it very clear that he would rather be at home watching television with a beer in hand. His scruffy face and unkempt clothing reflected his foul mood. Mary didn't take her eyes off of Ely as both wrestlers moved about the mat, trying to find an opening.

Nonchalantly, Bill pulled out a flask from his coat and poured some of the golden liquid into a travel mug he had brought with him, presumably filled with coffee. But no one noticed as all eyes were on the match.

Ely's opponent moved in fast and strong, grabbing Ely in a tie up and shaking him around. He couldn't believe how powerful the kid was. It felt like he was being held by two pythons, and they were beginning to squeeze even harder. Ely frantically got a hand inside the kids arm, trying to fight for control, and as his opponent loosened up his grip, hoping to readjust, Ely used that hand to desperately push away from him.

Ely only had a few seconds before the guy quickly moved in again for another tie up. This time Ely tried one of the few moves he actually could do well, a head and arm. But his opponent saw it coming and ducked under Ely's arm, spinning around Ely and throwing him to the mat for a two point takedown. Ely's head hit the mat hard.

"Oh, my poor baby," Mary cried softly as she saw her son's head violently bounce off the mat.

Bill shook his head, making no attempt to mask his disappointment. "Pussy," he whispered disdainfully, taking another long sip from his mug.

Mr. Seljin was on his knees at the edge of the mat yelling encouragement. "Come on, Ely! Keep your head up!"

Jeff and Cisco were behind him cheering as well.

"Come on, Ely!" Jeff yelled. "Get out of there! Get to your base!"

"Let's go, Ely!" yelled Cisco in encouragement. "Get up! Explode off that mat!"

Ely struggled under the weight of his opponent. On top of that, he was also strong, and obviously knew what he was doing. It took him a few moments but finally Ely was able to get one leg under him and push upward with his arms, allowing him to get to his base. That was the goal of the down wrestler, to get on their hands and knees, and from there to work towards an escape or reversal. His opponent immediately leaped to the side, making his first mistake by trying a half nelson while Ely was on all fours. As soon as Ely felt the weight leave his back, he did what he had learned, hoping it would work. He posted his right leg out, pivoted his weight over it, and stood up. Sure enough, within seconds he was standing, and another second later he had stepped away and turned into his opponent, freeing himself and gaining one point for an escape.

The score was now two to one.

"Nice job, Ely!" Jeff yelled, smacking Cisco enthusiastically on the back.

"It's two to one!" Cisco shouted to Jeff. "Come on buddy…you got this guy!"

In the bleachers Mary was clapping her hands in excitement. "Look, Bill, he just got a point."

"He's still losing. Shit, Mary, why are you happy with that?" Bill asked, clearly unimpressed with Ely's progress. This time he caught the attention of a few people sitting nearby who gave him a puzzled look, wondering if they had heard him correctly.

Mary looked at him briefly, her excitement quickly extinguished by her husband's negativity. But she didn't say anything, knowing full well that it would just make things worse.

But Ely's teammates were on the edge of their seats, yelling encouragement as Mr. Seljin paced with excitement in front of the mat.

"Go after him!" Sel yelled. "Arm drag him!"

On the mat, the two big wrestlers tied up again.

"Hit it now!" Sel yelled again. "Arm drag!"

Ely heard Sel yell at him and he fought to gain some wrist control. Finally, just for a second, he was able to grab and hold onto the guy's left wrist. He had worked on this move hundreds of times with Cisco, and although he was not an expert at it, he considered it one of his favorites. As soon as he grabbed the kid's wrist, he released his hold on the guy's neck with his left hand, pivoted his body to the side, grabbed the kid's arm around his tricep with his free hand, and leaned back hard, pulling that arm down and forcing his opponent to stumble forward and fall down onto the mat. As soon as he smacked into the mat, Ely spun around for control, gaining two points for a takedown.

The score was now three to one, and Ely was actually winning.

"Nice job!" Sel shouted as he leaped into the air in excitement. "Textbook arm drag!" he yelled to all the kids behind him, many of whom were screaming just as loud as he was.

"Yes!" Jeff shouted to Cisco. "He's winning three to two."

"He might win this one!" Cisco yelled back.

The two wrestlers rolled around for a few short moments before the buzzer signaled the end of round one.

Both wrestlers got up and the referee approached Ely and asked him his choice for round two. Ely, who was trying desperately to catch his breath, glanced over at Mr. Seljin who quickly indicated for him to defer the choice. So that is what he did.

The other wrestler picked the top position, probably hoping he could use his strength and weight to pin Ely. Once the referee gave Ely the okay to get into referee's position, on all fours in the middle of the mat, it was only a few seconds later before his opponent was on top of him and the whistle blew, starting round two. In the split second before the whistle blew, Ely glanced quickly at Mr. Seljin who gave him a *you can do it* nod. Then, at the sound of the whistle, they both exploded into action.

Both wrestlers maneuvered around the mat for a while, neither getting the upper hand. Finally, Ely was able to get his legs under him and stand up again, earning a one point escape.

The score was now four to two.

The next minute was filled with lots of tie ups and half executed moves as both wrestlers began to tire and try to catch their breath. It was obvious that they were tired since they spent more than a handful of seconds tied up, leaning into each other as they both sucked in desperately needed oxygen.

Then the buzzer rang ending round two.

Ely picked the down position hoping that he could ride out his win for the third round. But just as Ely got into position, his opponent showed the referee that he was going to let Ely up, then he placed both his hands on Ely's back in a diamond position.

"Shit, he's going to let him up and try to throw him," Jeff said to Cisco.

Sel realized it too and yelled at Ely, "Watch the head and arm! He's going to try and throw you!"

Ely nodded his head at Sel but it was pretty obvious that he was exhausted and not really registering what they were saying. The buzzer rang and his opponent immediately jumped back, letting Ely stand up to his feet and face him. Ely was awarded one point just before the guy lunged in and grabbed Ely in a vicious tie up. They held the tie up for a while, circling each other, and leaning into each other as they tried to regain their energy and maneuver for a move at the same time.

"Watch for the head and arm!" Sel yelled again.

Just as he shouted his warning, the kid positioned himself differently, leaning into him and pushing Ely's head up.

"He's going for it, Ely!" Sel yelled again. "Look out!"

"Oh no, he's setting up the head and arm," Jeff said through clenched teeth as he nervously clutched Cisco's arm.

"He's too tired. I don't think he sees it coming," Cisco moaned.

In reaction to the kid's sudden position change, Ely did just what his opponent wanted…he pushed back hard, allowing Ely's opponent to set the move up perfectly and use his momentum against him by turning his body and throwing Ely in a head and arm. If you blinked you would have missed the move.

Ely was flying through the air before he realized what had happened. He landed hard on his back and felt the guy's python like arms tighten around his arm and neck. Ely frantically kicked his feet and used his hand to try and break the kid's hold on him. But his opponent was too strong.

The kid squeezed hard and settled his two hundred and forty pound body right on top of his chest. Ely couldn't breathe and he could feel his face turn red as he frantically fought for a way to free himself from his predicament. He could feel his shoulder blade inch closer to the mat and despite his efforts he couldn't stop its downward descent. His vision swam as he desperately tried to breathe. He was so tired that his oxygen depleted brain didn't even register the feeling of his shoulder blade touching the mat.

Two seconds later he faintly heard the ref's hand smack the mat, then the suffocating weight suddenly left him.

He had been pinned.

Ely laid there for a few moments, gasping for air, trying to regain enough strength to stand.

In the stands, Mary brought her hands to her mouth. "Oh my baby," Mary cried. "He almost had him."

"How embarrassing," Bill muttered. "I can't believe I even came to this."

"Oh, Bill. Don't say anything to him. He'll be hurt enough for losing."

"And he should be, god dammit; I'll make that kid tougher if it's the last thing I do. You can bet on that," Bill said darkly, draining the last of the liquid in his cup.

Ely slowly got up, shook his opponent's hand, and the coaches', and moved dazedly toward his own bench, a malignant tumor of deep despair slowly consuming him. Mr. Seljin patted him on the back as he walked by. It was pretty obvious that Ely was more than upset, and no one attempted to talk with him right away, knowing full well that when you lost a match sometimes the first thing you needed was a little solitude. Jeff, Cisco, and a few others, attempted some encouraging words, but everyone else left him alone as he walked past them, head hanging down, toward the locker room.

As Ely neared the locker room door, Adam appeared before him, standing casually to the side in his varsity warm ups. Ely walked by without looking up, but he didn't need to see Adam's sneer, for he heard his snicker clearly enough. Laughing softly, Adam moved toward the mat to get ready for the varsity match.

Ely didn't break stride, completely ignoring him, and walked into the locker room.

Jeff and Cisco watched him go as the varsity wrestlers started to prepare for their match.

"Damn it, he needed that win," Jeff said under his breath.

"He sure did. Let's go Jeff, we need to start thinking about our match," Cisco said as he left to join the rest of the varsity squad who were now starting to congregate, getting ready for their team warm-ups.

Jeff stared at Ely's departing figure a bit longer, shook his head sadly, and joined his team.

Ely sat on a bench in the locker room quietly sobbing with his head in his hands. He hated that he was crying, but he couldn't control the flood of emotions that had come after losing this match, a match in which he had actually, for a while, been ahead. And it wasn't just a loss, he had been pinned. Here he was again with another loss. He had seen other kids cry after they lost, so he knew it was pretty normal, but that understanding didn't make him feel any better. Just once he wanted to win, to feel what it was like to have his hand raised in victory. Ely wiped the tears from his eyes, grabbed his head gear on the bench, and threw it hard against the lockers.

"Ely?"

It was Mr. Seljin.

"Yeah, I'm in here," Ely murmured as his coach turned the corner into the locker room. Ely wiped the tears from his eyes as Sel sat next to him, putting his hand on his shoulder.

"Listen to me, Ely. You did good out there. I know it doesn't feel like it, but trust me, you are getting better. That was the best match I've seen you wrestle so far."

"What do you mean? I got pinned. I lost....... again."

"I don't care about that," Sel continued.

"But I do!" Ely yelled, louder than he wanted to. He wasn't mad at Sel, he was just mad at himself. "I'm sorry, I'm not mad at you."

"I know. Don't worry about it. Listen, you were beating that guy for most of the match and that arm drag was the best I've seen you do. It was textbook perfect. You're getting better, Ely, and that's what matters."

"I don't know," Ely replied, shaking his head in resignation. "I don't know if I can do this. I've never won a match. You don't know what that's like."

"Maybe not," Sel agreed. "But I do know what it's like to lose. You hang in there. You'll win. I guarantee it. Who knows, if you stick with it, maybe you could be a state champion."

Ely looked incredulously at Seljin who was now smiling at him. "Now you're a comedian," Ely said, matching his smile.

"I'm not kidding. You have the potential. I believe it. Now it's *your* turn to believe."

"Now you sound like a preacher. You are a man of many faces."

Mr. Seljin stood up and slapped Ely on the back. "You're doing great, Ely. I'm proud of you. I gotta take a leak, then I'll get the varsity guys warming up. Come out when you're ready and watch us kick some butt."

"Alright, Sel," Ely said, beginning to smile. "Thanks."

"No worries. See ya out there." Mr. Seljin moved toward the bathrooms in the back of the locker room as Ely began to put his stuff away.

Just as Ely opened his locker to put his gear inside, his father walked around the corner.

"God dammit, son. You got your ass kicked again." And without breaking stride Bill walked up behind Ely and smacked him hard on the back of the head.

Ely turned around to face his father. "I'm sorry, Dad. I tried really hard. I almost…"

"I don' care what you almost did," Bill said, his words beginning to slur. He was obviously drunk. Then he slapped Ely across the face with his open palm. "You lost. I'm wasting my time coming to these stupid matches." Then he slapped him again.

Ely's head jerked to the side as the sting of the slap echoed in the concrete room. But this time, his father had picked the wrong time and the wrong place. Ely was still stinging from the loss of his match and his dad was pouring fuel on the smoldering embers of humiliation and anger that had built up over years of abuse. This time Ely snapped as his anger boiled to the surface. He pushed out hard with both arms and sent his dad flying into the row of lockers behind him.

Still standing, Bill slowly gathered himself, his expression of shock quickly replaced by one of fury. "So you think you're tough? We'll just see how tough you are." He lunged toward his son swinging his right fist in a wide arc, smashing into Ely's left cheek with tremendous force. The blow sounded like a firecracker in the tight confines of the lockers.

Ely's head jerked hard to the right and slammed against the locker behind him, slumping limply to the floor. His father was now standing over him, having completely lost control, his face red with drunken fury.

"You fat piece of shit! I'll teach you to never mess with me!" he stormed as he kicked Ely in the side. He had just stepped back again, ready for another kick, when Mr. Seljin came barreling around the corner from the bathrooms. "Hey!" he yelled as he moved in fast.

Bill turned around as Mr. Seljin rushed him. Like a striking adder Sel grabbed Bill by his throat with his right hand while he blocked Bill's clumsy swing with his left. He then slammed him against the locker, held him there for a moment, then released his hold and stepped back. "Who the hell are you?"

Bill, still out of control, answered Mr. Seljin with another swing of his meaty fist. Sel ducked under the attack and in a blur slammed his fist into his stomach. Bill groaned, leaning over in pain, but this time his face met Sel's fist as he followed his first strike with a vicious upper cut. Bill flew violently back, crashing again into the lockers, then collapsed to the floor completely unconscious.

Mr. Seljin reached down to help Ely to his feet. "Who is that, Ely? What's going on?"

Ely slowly stood, regaining his footing on shaking legs. His emotions gained the best of him and he slumped into Mr. Seljin, sobbing onto his shoulder. "That's......my dad," he said through his tears. "Please help me."

Sel held Ely in his arms. "It's okay, son. I'm here. I won't let anyone hurt you."

Ely could barely hold himself up as he continued to cry on his shoulder, his head buried in shame. All of the emotions that he had suppressed for so many years finally erupted and Ely could not control the torrent of tears. The dam had broken and there was nothing he could do to stop it

"I'm here. It's okay, son. I will help you."

Eight

It's hard to explain how I felt about that incident. You are taught your whole life that your father is supposed to protect you, that no matter what happens you can always count on him to teach you to be a man, to help you get through life. When you're a child, and none of the happy endings you read about in fairy tales, or hear about at school, come true, you start to question why. You think maybe it's your fault. You think maybe you did something to deserve the things that happen to you. You can't understand why the very person that is supposed to protect you actually does the opposite. He beats you and hurts you both physically and mentally. You pretend that it doesn't affect you…that you can make it through your childhood with no scars, but you realize that is not true.

I tried real hard to believe that my father's actions did not affect me. I didn't want to give him that kind of power. But I was wrong. His actions, repeated year after year, reduced my self-esteem to dangerous levels. You can have all the skills and talents in the world, but none of it matters if you don't believe in them. And I didn't. Self-esteem, confidence, they are the glue that holds you together. Without them, you are just a shell, your unrecognized skills and talents floating around in limbo. You can't build anything for your life if you lack self-esteem. You might have the tools, but they will be useless without confidence. And that is what my father took from me. He made me question my existence, he made me think that everything was my fault; he made me think that I had nothing to offer the world.

Luckily for me, there were others who showed me my father's lies.

Ely Carter

The Burger King in Gig Harbor was slow for this time of the evening. Jeff and Ely sat together, more or less alone in the small fast food restaurant, eating a meal of burgers and fries. There was one other group, presumably a family, with two young kids, sitting in the far corner.

"So, it's been a week. What's going on with your dad?" Jeff asked.

Everyone of course had heard about that night. You can't really hide police cars and sirens at a school event, but Mr. Seljin had no choice but to call them after the attack in the locker room. Word of the event spread like wildfire throughout the school and within days everyone knew what had happened to Ely and how Sel had saved him from his own father.

"He's moving out," Ely said casually as he ate some fries.

"Really?"

"I told him that I wouldn't press charges if he moved out."

"What about Sel, what is he doing?"

"He pressed assault charges. He didn't really have a choice."

"Yeah, I guess not. So will he spend some time in jail?"

"I think so. I don't know. I just want him out of the house," Ely said, looking up at Jeff.

"Did he agree to move out?"

"Yeah, but he pretty much had to."

"That makes sense," Jeff said, taking a bite from his burger.

Awkward silence followed as both boys ate their burgers. Finally Ely spoke. "My mother's taking it hard though."

As Jeff and Ely continued their meal and conversation, Mr. Seljin was just pulling his car up to Ely's house. He got out and walked up the front steps of the trailer, knocking softly on the dirt smudged door. After a few moments, Mary Carter opened the door.

"Good evening, Mrs. Carter," Mr. Seljin said. "I'm sorry to interrupt your evening, but may I have a brief word with you?"

"Of course, come in."

"I won't take much of your time," Mr. Seljin said as he followed Mary inside. They both sat at the kitchen table near the door. Mary's eyes were swollen and red from crying and the interior of the trailer looked unkempt, obviously a reflection of how she had been feeling.

"It's okay. Pardon the mess but I have not had much time to clean up," Mary said as she cleared some bills and clutter off the table.

"I don't mind. Is Ely here?"

"No, he went out with Jeff."

"That's good because I want to talk with you alone. I tried calling but no one answered."

"I'm sorry, I was taking a nap. Can I get you something to drink?" Mary asked.

"No, I'm fine. I just wanted to tell you personally that I'm sorry for what happened, and that I'm here if you ever need anything. "

Fresh tears formed in Mary's eyes. She looked away briefly, trying to gain control of her emotions. Looking back at Mr. Seljin she said, "It's not your fault. You were just protecting my boy. As I said that night, thank you again for helping him."

"You're welcome," Sel said. "I care a lot about him. He's a great kid."

"I know," she said, choking back a sob. She looked away again as tears slowly streaked down her face. "I love him very much."

"I know you do."

"No you don't. You probably think I'm a sick woman for letting my husband beat us."

"Not at all. Before my father retired he use to work as a psychologist at the state prison. He said the prison was filled with men who abused their girlfriends and spouses. Unfortunately, this kind of thing happens more than you know," Sel tried to reassure her.

"You don't understand. I let it go on," Mary continued, now crying openly. "I allowed it to continue. I don't deserve a boy like him."

"We all make mistakes, Mrs. Carter. The good thing is, you can rectify yours."

"I thought he loved me. I convinced myself that he did," Mary continued. "I wanted to believe so badly that he actually cared for me, even if he seldom showed it. Look at me, Mr. Seljin, what man will want me? I don't want to be alone," she sobbed.

"It's okay…you don't need a man like that. You have a great son who loves you. That's more than a lot of people have."

Mary wiped the tears from her eyes. "I'm just scared. We have bills to pay. And now with this latest incident I'm worried that CPS could take my Ely."

"I know you're scared. Like I said, if there's anything you need, please don't hesitate to ask. I will vouch for you if you need me too. I know you love him. He needs you as much as you need him."

"Thank you. I can see why Ely thinks so highly of you. You know he talks about you all the time. Thank you for taking care of my son. It's meant a lot to both of us," Mary said through sniffles.

"You're welcome. As I said, I have a fondness for Ely. He's a very bright, kind, and caring kid who deserves the best. Be strong for him. He's going to need it."

"I'll try."

"I better get going. Don't worry, everything will work out. Remember, an amazing person raised Ely to be an incredible kid. And it certainly wasn't his father," Mr. Seljin said as he stood up from the table.

"Thank you for everything."

Mr. Seljin moved toward the door and walked out onto the front porch. Mary followed him to the door.

"You have a lot to offer someone, Mrs. Carter. Just be patient and don't give up on yourself," Sel said with a smile as he turned and walked out toward his car.

Ely and Jeff were nearly done with their meals when the conversation turned in a different direction.

"How come you never told me about your father?" Jeff asked softly.

"I don't know. It's not something that you just bring up."

"I know, but I'm your friend."

"Come on Jeff. What was I supposed to say? Hey Jeff, my father beats me and my mom. Oh, and by the way, all my life I've been told I'm a fat, lazy, good for nothing loser. I just thought you should know because you're my friend. Besides, we barely see each other anyway."

Jeff didn't say anything as he looked uncomfortably at his dwindling fries. Then he looked up again. "Ely, can I tell you something?"

"Sure, go ahead."

"You promise you won't tell anyone?"

"Yes, I promise."

"I'm serious, Ely. I've never told anyone this before," Jeff said emphatically.

"Okay, I'm serious, I won't tell anyone," Ely said earnestly.

Jeff leaned in close as if he didn't want anyone else to hear. "Okay, remember this is not to be repeated."

"I know, I know, now get on with it."

Jeff looked around one more time to make sure no one was near. "I'm adopted."

"Really?" Ely looked at Jeff as if there must be something else. Jeff nodded his head. "I'm sorry, Jeff, but why is that such a big secret?"

"I have two moms."

"What?" Ely asked.

"I have two moms. My parents are lesbians."

"Wow! That is a big secret. I always wondered why I had never met your dad and why you never invited me over."

"Well now you know."

"When were you adopted?" Ely asked.

"When I was a baby. Remember, don't tell anyone."

"Don't worry, I won't. As I see it, you don't have anything to be ashamed about."

"I'm not ashamed. I love my parents. It's just that most people look down on that stuff. You know what I mean?"

"Yeah, I guess so," Ely said looking down at his fries. "At least you have two parents that love you."

"Yeah, I know. I'm lucky. But your mom loves you too, Ely, and that's more than some people have."

"I guess so. Hey, we have something in common. Neither of us has a dad," Ely said with a smile.

"True. But I have to admit. Even after all these years, it kind of grosses me out."

"You mean the whole sex thing?" Ely asked.

"Yeah."

"Parents and sex is always gross," Ely agreed.

"No shit. Then picture them being gay and it's even worse."

"Sorry, dude, but two women together is hot," Ely said with a laugh.

Jeff threw a handful of fries at Ely. "Not when it's your parents, you jerk!" But he joined in Ely's laughter.

After they settled down Ely asked Jeff, "Why did you tell me about your parents?"

"I don't know. You're my only friend that would understand."

"You never know. Your other friends might surprise you."

"Yeah, maybe. But I consider you my best friend, Ely. I know I've never told you that before, but you are. I can trust you. I also know that we don't hang out that much, but I plan on changing that."

Ely looked up at Jeff. "Thanks, Jeff. But I understand. You're the popular kid. I'm not. You have lots of friends. I don't. You don't have to make time for me. I get it. I'm used to it anyway."

"Ely, shut up and stop the self-pity," Jeff said as he tossed another fry at Ely's face.

"Knock it off."

"You knock it off. Don't you get it? People do like you. You just have to give them a chance and stop pushing them away like you just tried to do with me."

Ely smiled at Jeff. "Since when did you become a psychiatrist?"

"That's what my mom does for a living."

"Which one?" Ely laughed.

"Shut up," Jeff said, laughing.

They continued to laugh and joke around as they finished the last of their meal. There were several moments of silence as they cleaned up their mess before Ely spoke up.

"You know the guys would think it's hot."

"What?" Jeff asked warily.

"That your parents are lesbian milfs."

Jeff kicked Ely under the table and they both laughed together again. "Shut up, you perv!"

***

It was five minutes before first period when Ely walked into Mr. Seljin's room. He found him sitting at his desk correcting papers and sipping a cup of coffee. Mr. Seljin, seeing Ely, smiled invitingly and leaned back in his chair.

"Hi, Sel. Do you have a minute?"

"Of course, come in. I'm glad you're here, I wanted to talk with you as well."

"I just wanted to thank you again for helping me," Ely said, obviously a bit uncomfortable about bringing up the subject.

"Ely, you don't have to thank me. I'm just glad I was there. How are things at home?"

"Pretty good, I guess. Mom's working really hard so I don't see her much. Dad hasn't come back." Ely sat on the edge of a desk facing Mr. Seljin.

"How do you feel about that?"

"I don't know. I've spent so many years hating him that it's weird not to have him around. I

151

don't know if that makes sense or not. It sounds sort of lame."

"I think it does. It sounds like you were so accustomed to feeling that hatred that when the object of those feelings was no longer around, it sort of made you feel like a part of you disappeared."

"Yeah, I guess you're right."

"You know your mom cares a lot about you. She's going to need you now more than ever. You look after her, okay?"

"I will," Ely replied, then hesitated a moment. "I also wanted to talk to you about wrestling."

"What about wrestling?"

"I don't think I can finish the season," Ely said quietly, looking down at the floor before bringing his eyes up to Sel.

"Why is that?" Sel asked gently.

"I'm just no good. I'm sick of getting beat all the time. Why would I want to continue to do something that's seldom fun for me?" Ely asked, almost pleading for an adequate answer.

"That's a good question. Would you like me to try and answer it?"

"Please do."

"Well, I want you to think about something. When I was a wrestler I was pretty good. I think you know that, right?" Sel asked.

"Yeah. You were like a two time national champ or something. Weren't you like a three time state champion in high school as well?"

"Yes I was," Sel answered with no hint of arrogance. "I lost three times my freshman year and I went undefeated the rest of my high school career. Wrestling was fun for me because I won matches. But let me tell you something. There were guys on my wrestling team that were tougher than I was."

"Come on, Sel. That's impossible. Did you have a four time state champ on your team or something?" Ely asked in disbelief.

"Nope."

"Okay, I'll bite. How were they tougher than you?"

"There were guys on my high school team who never wrestled a varsity match because they wrestled on the toughest team in the state. They worked hard every day, went to every tournament, yet never wrestled a varsity match. Some of them rarely won matches on the junior varsity team. I still remember the guys that wrestled under me," Sel said, leaning forward in his chair. "Mitch Wapner, Jack Sultan, and Mark Ladenburg. I could give you five other names from other weight classes that also fit that mold."

"I still don't understand what you mean. How were they tougher than you? I don't get it."

"Think about it, Ely. I was naturally talented, strong, quick, and very good at what I did. Don't get me wrong. I worked hard too, but wrestling came easy for me. I can't tell you all the state champs we had over the years, but I can remember the names of my fellow wrestlers who stuck it out every year with no foreseeable chance of ever having much success. They bled and sweat on the mat six days a week, three months a year, for four years, but rarely did they experience what it was like to win."

Ely thought about Sel's words for a moment. "Why do you think they did it?"

Sel shrugged. "Answer this…what does it take to be a man?"

"I'm not sure."

Sel took a sip of his coffee. "Think about it for a moment," he said.

"Ummm…strength, power…"

"Come on, Ely. I know you're smarter than that. Did Gandhi have physical strength and power?"

"No," Ely said immediately. Then the light came on and Ely's eye's flashed with understanding. "Honor, courage, tenacity…"

"Exactly!" Sel exclaimed. "These guys had courage, integrity, honor, and they were tough as nails. Not physically, but mentally. They were real men. It's easy to do something that you're good at. But it takes courage and integrity to stick with something you're not. Oh, and don't let me forget to tell you, that one of these guys I'm talking about was a state champ his senior year. Sometimes, if you pound on coal long enough…"

"…a diamond will appear," Ely finished Sel's famous phrase.

"You got it," Sel said.

"I think I understand."

"Ely, I won't hold it against you if you don't want to wrestle. But why don't you think about what I said. You have more talent than many of those guys that I mentioned. You just have to believe in yourself."

"All right. Fair enough. I'll think it over some more."

"Good. If you decide to continue, which I hope you do, then just show up for practice tomorrow. If I don't see you at practice, then I will assume that you decided to quit. I won't be happy about it, but I'll respect your decision."

The bell to go to first period suddenly rang interrupting their conversation.

"That sounds good," Ely said after the ringing stopped. "Thanks, Sel."

"No problem. Now get going so you're not late to class," Sel said as he stood up.

"Okay. Oh, before I forget, I wanted to thank you again for the mat and weights."

"No problem. Get some use out of them. If you hit those weights on a regular basis you'll turn into a gorilla," Sel said with a laugh.

"Is that a good thing?" Ely asked as he moved toward the door.

"It is on the wrestling mat."

Ely just laughed. "Thanks again, Sel. I'll see ya."

Ely turned to walk out the door when Sel yelled after him. "Hey, I almost forgot."

Ely was at the door when he turned around. Sel grabbed a book off his desk and tossed it across the room to Ely. Ely grabbed it with both hands. "The next Drizzt Do'Urden book. It just came out. Thought you might want to read it."

"Thanks, Sel," Ely said, exposing his teeth in a wide grin. "I'll bring it back when I'm done."

"No hurry. Enjoy it. Now get to class."

"Okay."

Ely walked from the classroom with his head down, looking intently at the cool cover of the book. He was still looking down at the book when he turned the corner of the hall and ran right into a girl. Her books flew from her arms and she stumbled backward like she had hit a brick wall. It probably felt like that to her since Ely was more than twice her size.

"I'm so sorry," Ely stammered. "Are you okay?"

"Jesus! Watch where you're going. You're big enough to actually hurt someone."

She was petite, maybe five foot one, with short choppy blonde hair. She had a quirky look, wearing mismatched clothes that looked as if she might have bought them from a thrift store. Her large blue eyes were framed in thick black glasses. She was very cute, in a sort of 'I'm not trying to be cute' kind of way.

Ely quickly bent down to pick up her books. "Man, I'm such an idiot. I'm always doing stuff like this. I'm really sorry. I was looking at my book, thinking about stuff. I just wasn't looking."

"It's okay. Really," the girl said as she knelt down beside him to help gather her stuff. She had clearly calmed down. "You just scared me. What's your name?"

Ely stopped what he was doing and looked at her closely for the first time. "What?"

"I said, what's your name?" she repeated as they both stood up with her things.

"You want to know my name?"

"Yes, that's what I said."

"My name's Ely."

The girl extended her hand toward Ely. Ely looked at her hand as if it might bite him. He hesitated for a second, then reached out and shook it.

"I'm Amanda. I just moved here from California."

"Really," Ely stammered. "I know what that feels like."

"You've moved around a lot?"

"Yeah, several times, six actually."

"Really? Your parents military or something?"

"No, it's mostly because my dad's a drunk loser who can't hold down a job." Ely couldn't believe he had just blurted this out.

Amanda laughed. "Really? Wow, tell me what you really think," she said through her laughter as she looked up at Ely for what seemed like the first time. "Hey, sorry about the *you being big* comment. I just thought I was going to get flattened."

"It's okay," Ely said with a smile. "I know I'm fat. No mystery there."

"You're not fat, you're big…"

"…boned? That's what all skinny people say."

Amanda laughed again. "You're funny, Ely. Look, I have to get to class. It was nice to meet you. I'll see you around."

"It was nice to meet you too. See ya."

"Hopefully," Amanda said with a lingering smile before she turned on her heel and moved down the hall. The bell rang, but Ely just stood there with his book in his hands and watched her walk away.

***

It was almost noon on Saturday and Ely had to get moving if he was going to make the twelve thirty show. He was reading a new book by Jim Butcher and had gotten lost in the story. Luckily he had just glanced at the clock and noticed the time. He knew his mom didn't work until late so he hoped that her car was available. He quickly grabbed his coat from the back of his desk chair and raced out the door.

He found his mom at the kitchen table looking over various bills. "Hey mom, do you mind if I take the car for a few hours?"

"What?" she asked irritably.

Ely looked at her more closely and noticed that her eyes were brimming with tears. She was clearly frustrated and upset.

"What's wrong, Mom?"

Mary wiped her eyes and took a deep breath. "I'm sorry, hon. I'm just trying to figure out how to pay these bills. When your father was here he was able to get unemployment when he wasn't working. When he was working, we had a second check. Now it's just me, and I don't make that much money."

"I have a little over two hundred bucks saved up from my book store job if you need it. You can have it, Mom."

"Thanks, honey. But I need more than that. What was it you asked me?"

"Can I take the car to go see a movie?"

"Sure. Who are you going with?" Mary asked, hoping that he was not going by himself.

"No one, just myself."

"Why don't you call Jeff?"

"He's on a date tonight."

"Okay, well, have a good time. I need to leave for work tonight at seven o'clock. So make sure you're back by six."

"Thanks, Mom," Ely leaned over her and gave her a hug from behind. "It's going to be okay, Mom. I promise."

Mary smiled and tapped his arm. "Thanks, hon."

Ely let go, grabbed the keys off the table, and left his mother staring at the pile of bills, trying to convince herself that her son was right, that everything was actually going to be okay.

Ely got to the theater in good time, giving him ten minutes to spare before the movie started. Instead of going inside the theater, he sat on a bench near the bathrooms and continued reading his book. It was too dark to read inside the theater room and Ely was in a good spot in the book. That's why he nearly missed the movie to begin with. The bench was located adjacent the concession stand where there was plenty of light.

He had only read several lines when an all too familiar voice shattered his brief moment of relaxation.

"Well, what do we have here?"

Ely looked up to see Adam standing above him flanked by two of his cronies. He hung out a lot with two other jerks, Cole and Nate, fairly big guys, but not nearly as big as Adam. Cole's hair was jet black, shaved short, and he had a "wanna-be" gangster look. Nate was a mulatto kid with a pretty impressive afro. He rarely smiled and he had a hard look about him, like he was mad at the world. Ely didn't say anything. He just looked back down at his book, hoping that they would go away.

"It must be discount night tonight," Adam laughed, smacking Cole in the arm as if he was the funniest guy around. Cole laughed while Nate sneered at Ely.

"You here with your mommy?" Nate asked.

"Hell no, he's by himself," Adam said.

"No he's not." A voice came from in front of the concession stand. It was Amanda, the same girl that Ely had met the other day at school. She walked over, sat down on the bench, and slid over beside Ely, kissing him on the cheek. Then she looked up at Adam and his henchmen, smiled and said, "He's here with me."

Ely dropped his book in his lap and stared at her with an expression of complete confusion.

"You came here with *him*?" Adam asked, equally surprised.

"Of course. I love big guys."

"If that's the case, you should hang with me. He's a fat ass loser," Adam said bluntly.

"Oh, but his intelligence turns me on." Amanda was clearly enjoying herself and Ely could still do nothing but stare at her as she leaned up against him, touching his leg and smiling at him like an adoring groupie. Then, she turned it up a notch, licking her upper lip seductively as she gazed into Adam's eyes. "Are you smart?" she purred.

"Sure," Adam said.

"Mmmmmm…can you quote Shakespeare?"

Adam's buddies laughed as if that was the funniest thing they'd heard all day.

"No," he said, "why would I want to do quote some stupid old dude?"

Amanda turned toward Ely, batting her eyes at him. He still had not taken his eyes off of her. "Ely?"

Without a pause, as Ely continued to stare at her, he spoke for the first time. "Love looks not with the eyes, but with the mind: And therefore is wing'd cupid painted blind: Nor hath love's mind of any judgment taste; wings and no eyes figure unheedy haste:"

"Ahhhh….so beautiful," she said with exaggerated passion, as she gazed at Ely as if he were the only one in the room. She was hamming it up big time and Ely didn't know how to respond. So she quickly tore her eyes away from Ely and turned towards Adam and his friends. "You boys run along now," she said casually, shooing them away with her hand as if they were pesky flies.

"Whatever. This is stupid. Let's go," Adam said as he turned to leave, his two buddies close on his heels.

Finally, Amanda lowered her charade and looked at Ely with her own eyes. "Very nice. I'm impressed. So the rumors are true?"

"What rumors?"

"That you're some kind of genius or something."

"That's a rumor?"

"Yup. So what movie are you watching?"

"That Jason Statham action flick."

"Cool. Me too. I'm here with my parents. My dad loves those kinds of movies. They're sitting in the theater now."

"I love them too, b...but I guess that's obvious since I'm here to watch it," Ely stammered,

"Yeah, pretty obvious." Amanda giggled. "You're a real comedian aren't you?"

"I don't try to be," Ely said seriously.

"Which is why you are so funny."

"Anyway, thanks for helping me out there. I hate that Adam guy."

"No problem. That was so much fun. What an asshole. Every school has some; I can spot them a mile away."

"Well your *asshole vision* was right on with this guy."

"I'm rarely wrong when it comes to assholes…" Amanda paused briefly and smiled. "That sounded kind of funny."

They both laughed.

"Yes it did," Ely agreed.

"The movie is about to start. Do you want to sit with me?" Amanda asked casually.

"Ummm….well…I don't want to impose," Ely mumbled.

"Impose? Jesus, are we in England? What's with the pomp and formality?"

"Pomp? Formality? Look who's talking," Ely laughed.

Amanda just grinned at Ely. "Touché', my good man. You know, I think I like you. You're fun. So how about it? Want to sit with me?" She asked again as she stood up from the bench.

"Okay, if you insist."

"Good," Amanda said as she grabbed his hand and pulled him off the bench.

"Wait, I have to grab my book." Ely turned around and walked back to the bench. He picked up his book, hit his palm with it, and smiled.

Ely walked back to his car in a daze. He was having a hard time digesting the fact that he had just sat through a movie with a girl, and a cute girl at that. This was definitely new territory for him. He didn't know how to feel about it. One thing was for sure, though; he felt happy. They had parted casually, with a simple good bye, but Ely thought he saw a lingering smile. No way, he thought. I'm just imagining it. Either way, he had a great time, and he was still smiling from ear to ear when he reached his car at the far end of the nearly deserted parking lot. It was dark and very few people were at the theater.

"What are you smiling about, fatty?"

Ely stopped as he reached for the door and saw Adam and his cronies emerge from the brush nearby. They fanned out and surrounded him.

"Nothing. What do you want, Adam?"

"What do I want? That's a stupid question for someone who is so smart!" Adam glared, his voice getting louder.

Ely looked around and noticed that there was no one else in the parking lot. The few people who had emerged from the movie with him had parked closer, and were already gone.

"Adam, she…was just messing around with you. We…we didn't mean anything," Ely stammered, as he watched Nate and Cole move in closer to flank him.

"Shut up, shit face!" Adam growled, stepping in close to Ely. Adam was mad, really mad. Ely could see it on his face. "Now this is what is going to happen. We are going to kick the shit out of you, and you are not going to tell anyone it was us. You will not tell Mr. Seljin about it, no one at all, or I will make your life even more miserable than it already is.

Suddenly Nate and Cole lunged forward and grabbed Ely's arms, throwing him backwards into the car. Then Adam stepped forward and swung his fist with all his strength into Ely's exposed stomach. Ely doubled over in pain, the air pushed from his lungs. Coughing violently, Ely was lifted up again and slammed back into the car. This time Adam hit Ely in the face, connecting solidly with his chin.

Ely's vision flashed as pain exploded in his jaw. His body, now free from the boys' grip, fell heavily to the ground. He reached out sluggishly and barely caught himself before his head smashed into the concrete. Blood dripped from his mouth and nose as he struggled to maintain consciousness. He slowly looked up at Adam. "Adam…please…I didn't mean…," but his plea was cut short as Adam kicked him in the side. Adam was not just big; he was also very strong. The kick was powerful enough to slam Ely into the side of the car, where he crumpled to the ground nearly unconscious.

"Shut up you fat pig! Don't you ever mess with me like that again!" Adam yelled as he squatted next to Ely. He reached out and grabbed Ely's hair, bashing his head into the side of the car. "Am I clear?"

"…yes…," Ely muttered, his head pounding with pain. Ely's jaw felt like it might be dislocated but he wasn't sure. If he didn't have so much body fat, there'd be a good chance that the kick to his side would have broken some ribs. As it was, they were surely bruised, as Ely could barely move without pain lancing through his body.

"Let's go, man! Someone might see us!" Nate said, grabbing Adam and trying to usher him away.

Adam jerked his arm away from Nate and spit on Ely. "Don't come to practice, dip shit! In fact, quit the team! I don't want to smell you anymore!" Adam spit on him again before all three disappeared into the shadowy tree line. Their laughter echoed in Ely's mind as he lay there, dazed and in pain as blood dripped freely down his face.

Slowly he sat up and leaned against the side of his car. He saw his book on the ground and picked it up, staring at the front image, wishing for the millionth time that he was that hero gracing the cover.

Tears were now running freely, joining with the crimson smudges around his nose and mouth. Ely used his sleeve to wipe the wetness from his face. Then he looked up into the night sky, wondering if the pain would ever go away.

Nine

In life, you are often presented with dilemmas and tough choices. It is how you handle those situations that mold who are you are, and who you will become. Every time we are presented with a difficult situation, we are poised to either better our self, or weaken our character, depending on the choices we make. The easy way out always seems so simple, but I guess that is why it is called the easy way. The difficult choice, however, which is often the right choice, never seems that easy. If you make too many bad choices, before long you will be caught in a downward spiral, immersed in a deluge of crap that makes it almost impossible to see the bright side of anything. People, especially kids, need help along the way to make the right choices. If they are not getting those tools from their parents, then they need to get them elsewhere.

That night, after I got beat up, I had some decisions to make. Would I let Adam intimidate me? Would I do anything about what happened? I will be honest and say that I did not make all the decisions that night, but I did get the ball rolling in my head, and all I needed was some support, any support. And I was lucky to have found it.

Ely Carter

———————————————

The morning came quickly. When Ely woke up he felt as if Mike Tyson had used his fat body as a punching bag. He made his way into the bathroom to survey the damage.

As he gazed into the mirror he wondered if he would be able to come up with a plausible reason to explain his appearance. Not only that, but his ribs were so sore that he could barely move. He had a deep gash in his lower lip, which had swollen to almost twice its normal size. His left eye was almost closed shut, and he had scrapes and bruises around his nose and mouth. He didn't look very good and he felt even worse. His ribs were definitely bruised and extremely tender to the touch, but he didn't think they were broken since he could turn and bend without the typical severe shooting pains one would experience with a broken rib.

Ely figured the best thing to do was to tell the truth, at least partially. He could say that he was jumped by some guys who were trying to rob him. That would explain the damage to his body and he wouldn't have to say anything about Adam and his gang being involved. As far as he was concerned, that part would remain a secret. He had enough problems as it was, he surely didn't need another run in with that jerk.

But one thing he did decide was that he would not let Adam dictate his choices. He had decided, before the movie, that he would stay on the wrestling team. What Sel had said earlier that day had really sunk in, and besides, he just couldn't let him down. This was one of Adam's threats he would choose to ignore.

Ely took a deep breath and looked at himself in the mirror. It's going to be an interesting day, he thought. He sighed resignedly, walked over to the shower and turned on the water. He relieved himself in the toilet as the water warmed. Then he took off his boxers and jumped in the shower, resignation turning to anxiety.

Things started off pretty typical that morning, other than the curious stares of students as they walked down the halls. He did get a few hushed comments slung his way during first period, but it wasn't nearly as bad as he thought it would be. Then he ran into Jeff at his locker after second period.

"Dude, what happened to your face?"

Ely shut his locker, knowing that he couldn't avoid him forever. "I got beat up last night."

"What!? You're not serious. Is your dad back?" He whispered the last question, knowing that it was a touchy subject and not wanting any kids nearby to hear him.

"No. I went to the movies and some kids jumped me and took my wallet."

"No way, did you get a look at them?"

"No, they were wearing masks." Ely hated to lie to Jeff. But he knew it was the best thing since telling him the truth would only lead to more problems. If he had told him what really happened he'd probably immediately go after Adam and kick his ass. Then he would get suspended and probably not be able to wrestle…and that was something Ely could not allow to happen.

"Did you tell the police?"

"Nawww…I only had four bucks in my wallet. Figured it wouldn't be worth the effort."

"I don't know man, I think you should tell the police in case it happens again. How many of them were there?"

"Three. They beat me up pretty good. I don't think I can practice today."

"Man, that sucks. Have you told Sel yet?"

"Nope. I'll tell him at practice."

"So you are going?" Jeff asked.

"Yeah...I'll just watch though." Ely obviously didn't tell Jeff that he wanted to show his presence so Adam would know that he hadn't beaten him. Well, technically he had beat him, Ely laughed inwardly, but he didn't beat his spirit. He was scared, but he figured what else could the bully do? He had already beat him up, and despite the fact that that really sucked, and it hurt pretty bad, he knew he could take another beating if he had to. But he didn't think it would come to that. At least that was what he was hoping.

"Are any of your injuries serious?" Jeff asked with concern.

"I think I bruised some ribs. That feels like the worst of it. My jaw hurts like hell but I don't think it's broken."

"Do you think they were kids, or adults?" Jeff asked.

"I'm not sure. They were pretty big so probably adults. But hey, on a positive note, guess who I watched the movie with last night?"

"You mean before you were beat up?" Jeff asked, intrigued.

"Yup."

"Who?"

"A girl," Ely said with a smile.

Now it was Jeff's turn to smile. "A girl, eh?"

"Yup, and she's cute. She's new here and I ran into her a few days ago, literally. I almost knocked her down. I was so embarrassed. But she was really cool, and then I saw her at the movies and she asked if I wanted to sit with her."

"Nice work, bud," Jeff grinned. "You going to ask her out officially?"

"Hi, Ely!"

Ely looked up from his conversation and saw Amanda walk by carrying an armload of books.

"Oh, hey, how's it going?"

It looked as if she was just going to walk by. Obviously she was in a hurry to get to class, but when she saw his face, she stopped, skirted through the crowd of students, and walked up to him.

"What happened to your face?"

Jeff looked at Ely, then back to Amanda. Then he reached out his hand. "Hi, I'm Jeff."

Amanda was staring at Ely, her face a puzzled look of concern. Then she turned to look at Jeff for the first time and shook his hand. "Hi, Jeff, I'm Amanda. Nice to meet you," she said before directing her eyes back to Ely. "So what happened to your face?"

Ely didn't know how he was going to get out of this one and he wasn't sure if his lie was going to work with Amanda considering she was with him at the movies last night. He had purposefully omitted his run-in with Adam and his cronies when he had told Jeff about the movie, but now Jeff might put two and two together, and that was not good.

"I, umm, sort of got beat up and robbed last night after the movie."

"What! At the theater?"

"Yeah." Just then the one minute warning bell rang. Ely capitalized on it, hoping to end the conversation. "Hey, we better get to class."

"Not so fast," Amanda said, grabbing his arm. "Was is that jerk, Adam?"

Shit, Ely thought, looking at Jeff. But he stuck to his story, hoping that he could curb Jeff's rising suspicions. "No, I don't think so. They were wearing masks and it didn't sound like him."

"You saw Adam last night?" Jeff asked, raising his eyebrows.

Amanda answered for him. "Yes. He's an asshole and he was giving Ely shit. I stepped in and got him to leave." Then she looked back at Ely. "You sure it wasn't him? You should tell the principal so they can question him."

"Hey, I got to go," Jeff said as he turned to leave. "But we are not done with this conversation, Ely." Then he turned and jogged down the near empty hallway.

"I have to go too," Ely said.

"Okay," Amanda said, her voice reflecting her concern. She reached out and briefly touched Ely's arm. "I better go as well."

"Do you have first or second lunch?" Ely asked as he began to move down the hallway.

"First."

"Me too. I'll see you at lunch," he said, hustling away from her as she looked at him with a puzzled look on her face

Jeff was worried. In fact he had a hard time concentrating in his history class as he kept thinking about his friend. What were the chances that he had had a run-in with Adam, and then that same evening was beaten up with guys in masks? Jeff didn't think the odds were good; in fact he was not so sure that Ely was telling him the truth. He seemed jumpy and agitated to begin with. Then there was the omission about seeing Adam. And why would three guys rob some kid who drove a run-down beater? It didn't really make any sense.

Everyone was working quietly on a worksheet, but there was some soft talking, so Jeff leaned over and whispered to Cisco who sat next to him, "Hey man, have you seen Ely yet?"

Cisco looked up from his paper. He was a handsome guy with glossy ebony skin, a shaved head and a strong angular chin. But it was his stark white teeth and beautiful smile that really made him stand out

"Nope. Why?"

"He got beat up last night, and robbed at the movie theater."

"Really?"

"That's what he said. But I have a feeling that it might have been Adam and that he's lying to me."

Cisco crinkled his forehead as he thought about what Jeff had said. "Why would he lie about it?"

"I don't know. Probably because he was worried about what I might do."

The realization struck Cisco immediately. "Which is…?" Even though he asked the question he fully knew the answer.

"Kick his ass." Luckily the talking in the room had gotten louder and no one heard him.

"That's what I thought. You'd get suspended for sure and you wouldn't be able to wrestle. It would be a really bad decision, dude," Cisco added, clearly hoping to deter Jeff from any stupid knee jerk reaction.

Jeff looked back at his paper and sighed. "You're right. But we have to do something. What if Adam does it again?"

"What if it wasn't Adam at all?" Cisco countered.

Jeff just looked at Cisco, his expression clearly saying, *really? You believe that?*

Cisco relented. "Okay, you're probably right. It doesn't make much sense that Ely was robbed, and the fact that Adam and his buddies were there definitely seems suspicious. But you can't just kick his ass. Besides, you'd probably need my help, especially if his sidekicks are with him."

"Are you saying you would help?" Jeff asked, raising his eyebrows.

"Does a bear shit in the woods? But I think we should just scare him, not fight him. I don't think it's worth the risk. And we definitely can't do it here at school," Cisco added.

Jeff nodded his head. "What about John? You think he'll join us?"

"Is the Pope Catholic?" Cisco added, smiling.

Jeff just laughed.

Ely was nervous about seeing Amanda again. He wasn't exactly sure what he was going to say to her. He didn't want to lie to her, and it seemed like her bullshit detector was in top form. But he didn't want things to get worse between Adam and himself, so after careful deliberation he figured he better keep up with the ruse. Besides, there was really no way she was likely to find out the truth anyhow. She might suspect that it was Adam, but that was as far as she could take it.

Even though Ely and Jeff were friends, and Ely considered John and Cisco to be friends, it was still unusual for Ely to sit with them during lunch. There were other guys and girls that were typically at their table that Ely did not know and joining them with the uncertain knowledge of how he would be accepted generally kept him away. But this time Jeff called him over as he was working his way outside to his typical spot where he could eat and read in relative peace.

"Hey, Ely, come sit over here!" Jeff hollered at him as he made his way to the commons door that exited into the courtyard. Ely turned to face Jeff and gave him a *I don't think so* look. But Jeff wasn't having any of it. "Get over, man! Join us!" Then John and Cisco joined in and at that point there was no getting out of it.

So Ely shyly made his way to their table with a piece of pizza in one hand and his book in another. "Hey, Jeff, Cisco, John…how's it going?"

"Better than you it would seem. What happened to your face?" Cisco asked. Cisco was feeling out the situation for himself before he made any concrete conclusions.

"Some guys jumped me last night after the movie."

"Jeff mentioned that. Hey, sit down and tell us about it," Cisco said.

Three other seats were taken besides the ones occupied by Jeff, Cisco, and John. Ely knew one of the kids since he was on the wrestling team. His name was Damon and he was nice enough, although Ely didn't know him well. He wrestled at the weight class below Jeff and he was a good athlete, powerfully built, with a short and stocky body, and a blocky head topped with strawberry blonde hair. He looked like he had just come right out of an Irish Spring commercial.

Two attractive girls occupied the other seats. Ely knew one of them was Cisco's girlfriend, Tanya. She was a petite dark haired beauty who looked like she had spent too much time in the tanning bed. Ely had never met her but he'd seen her around. Ely recognized the other girl, Lauren, from his math class. He had never met her either, but she was smart, at least she did well in math. She resembled the stereotypical cute honors student. She was not as stunning as Tanya, but when she smiled she looked almost angelic, exposing two dimples that made her appear both endearing and genuine. Both girls smiled and glanced briefly at Ely as he sat down, before turning away and going back to their own private discussion.

Ely sat down next to Damon and Cisco. "What do you want to know?"

"Start from the beginning."

Ely took a bite from his pizza. "Okay, well it happened when I got out of the movie and went to my car. I had parked at the end of the parking lot near the woods. There wasn't anyone around when they came from the shadows. Then they attacked me and took my wallet."

"What car were you driving?" John asked.

"My mom's."

"That beat up Datsun?" Cisco asked, looking briefly at Jeff.

"Yup."

"And they were wearing masks?" John asked.

Now the girls had ended their conversation, clearly interested in Ely's story. "Black ski masks. I couldn't see anything."

"That sucks, man. How much money did they get?" John asked.

"A couple of bucks."

"Seems weird to me. No offense, but why would some guys risk attacking a young kid in an old car for a couple of bucks?" Cisco asked.

"I don't know," Ely said a bit defensively, picking up on their obvious skepticism. "Who knows why thieves do anything? Maybe they were bored." Ely shrugged his shoulders and casually bit into his pizza, hoping they would just drop it.

"You should call the police," Tanya added, speaking for the first time. "Maybe they would have an idea who it was."

"I don't want to go through the hassle just for a couple of bucks," Ely countered.

"I'm Tanya by the way. This is my friend, Lauren."

"Nice to meet you," Ely said. "I recognize you from class," Ely said, indicating Lauren.

"Yup, I'm the one always asking questions. Calculus is so hard. How do you breeze through it so easily?" It was obvious that she at least knew who Ely was, and she had clearly noticed that he always finished his tests and quizzes first, knew every oral question, even the ones that stumped the other math whizzes. And he never asked questions, as if it was as easy as tying your shoes.

"I don't know," he said, "It just comes natural I guess," not sure how to respond to her. He didn't want to make her feel stupid, but that seemed the best way he could explain it. It did come easy for him. He remembered numbers, equations, recognized patterns, and made connections. For him, it was as easy as basic math.

"Lucky you," she said with a frustrated sigh. "Sorry about your face. It looks pretty bad....I mean it looks like it hurts," she added quickly, smiling.

"Supposedly Adam and his goons were there watching the movie, and they had given Ely some shit," Jeff interjected, attempting to bring the conversation back on course.

"No shit," John said, acting as if that was new information. "You think it could've been him with a mask on? He's always seemed to have it out for you."

"I don't think so," Ely said rather too quickly. "It didn't sound like him." He quickly went to stuffing his face with the last of his pizza.

"I don't know, Ely," Cisco added. "It does seem strange that you got beat up the same night that you had a run-in with Adam. You want us to have a *talk* with him?"

"No, please don't. I'm sure it wasn't him. Hey, I have to go," Ely said as he stood up quickly. "It was nice to meet you," Ely addressed Tanya and Lauren. "I'll see you guys at practice."

"Alright, bud," Jeff said, clearly skeptical.

"Cool," John and Cisco said in unison.

Once Ely had left Cisco turned to Jeff. "I think you're right, man. It just doesn't add up and Ely is acting weird."

"You think it was Adam, don't you," John said.

"Yup, I sure as hell do," Jeff replied.

"Hey, not sure if this means anything," Tanya said thoughtfully, "but I just had Adam in class last period and I noticed he had several band aids on his right hand."

Cisco and John looked at Jeff.

"Are you serious?" Jeff asked softly.

"Yeah, they really stood out. It was hard to miss. There were two big band aides over his knuckles and both had blood seeping through. I didn't think anything of it then. Thought it was just a wrestling injury, but now it seems a bit suspicious."

"It sure does," Jeff said, turning towards John and Cisco. "I think we need to have a talk with Adam…tonight."

They both smiled conspiratorially.

Ely found Amanda soon after he left the lunchroom. Well actually, it was more like she had found him. She had gotten her lunch late and saw him leave the guy's table and head outside. So she took her sandwich and followed him out the common's door and into the courtyard, where she saw him sit on a bench tucked behind some shrubs. It was a good spot if you wanted some solitude.

"Hey," she said as she approached. "Do you mind if I sit with you?"

"Not at all," he said, smiling. "As long as you don't grill me like Jeff and his buddies just did."

"I can't promise you that."

Ely just smiled as he slid over to make room for her on the bench.

"I had fun last night," she said.

"Me too, well at least up 'til the point where I got beat up. Everything up to that point was pretty great. Thanks again for helping me out last night."

"You're welcome." She paused as she took a bite of her sandwich. Then she added, "You sure it wasn't that asshole Adam that attacked you?"

"I don't think so," Ely said, sticking to his story. "It didn't sound like him." It felt like the questioning was going to start all over again. But he had to keep up the charade until everyone dropped it. Once they did, then it would be over and everyone would just forget it. Then he could move on and hopefully not have to worry about Adam again.

Amanda shook her head, as if she didn't quite believe him. "Okay," she relented. "But you should probably go to the hospital, or at least the nurse's office to make sure you don't have any serious injuries."

"I'll be fine," Ely said. He almost followed it up with, *'I've had worse'*, but he caught himself. That would be a hard statement to explain. "So, how do you like the school so far?" he asked, changing the subject.

Amanda shrugged. "It's not bad. I like most of my teachers, and I must admit, it sure is beautiful here. All the hype you hear about the Pacific Northwest is true."

"It is that, and if you don't mind the rain, it's a great place to live."

"What about you?"

"What do you mean?" Ely asked.

"Do you mind the rain?"

Ely thought a moment. "I don't. I like it actually. I love to read and reading is an indoor sport."

"Are you trying to impress me?" Amanda asked.

"If you're impressed with fat guys who like to read by themselves, then yes, I am. Is it working?"

Amanda laughed and almost choked on her sandwich. "I'm going to have to keep you posted on that question. I better go. Promise me you'll go to the nurse."

"I can't promise you that," he replied.

Amanda stood up and gave him her best mock pouty look.

"Okay, I'll go." Ely caved in easily.

She smiled and turned to go. Ely was getting ready to crack open his book again and get a few more pages of reading in before the bell rang to go to class when she turned back around. "Hey, you want to do something sometime?"

Ely looked up at her, then behind him, then back at her, then behind him one more time before he pointed at himself. "Are you talking to me?" He knew she was. After all, there was no one else near them. But her invitation had caught him off guard. Did she really just ask him out?

"Very funny. Yes, I'm talking to you. I could use a tour guide."

"That would be fun."

"Perfect. How about Saturday?"

"I have to work a few hours in the morning. But I can hang out with you in the afternoon."

"Awesome. Write down my number."

"It's okay. I can remember it."

"Such confidence. You sure?"

"Yup. Shoot," Ely said.

"554-6745."

"Got it. Hey, but there is a problem. I don't have a car. My mom will be using our car."

"That's okay. I have a car. I'll pick you up."

Ely felt a sudden panic. He didn't want Amanda to see his house. He would be embarrassed. So he quickly came up with a better solution. "Why don't you pick me up at work? It will be closer anyway as I live way out on the peninsula."

"Okay. Where do you work?"

"I work at Harbor Books right across from the park down by the water. If you go to the main docks in the harbor, you'll see Johnson Park. The bookstore is right across the street."

"Cool. Pick you up at noon?"

"Sounds good," Ely said with a big smile.

"See ya," she said, returning his smile. Then she turned, gave a little skip, and headed for the main door.

"Maybe I should get beat up more often," Ely whispered to himself.

Practice that evening came and went quickly. Adam gave Ely some pretty dirty looks, but he did a decent job of disguising them so others wouldn't notice. Adam was obviously pissed that Ely was there, naturally assuming that he would have quit after the beating they had given him. Luckily Sel was pretty busy so the uncomfortable conversation that Ely was dreading didn't last very long.

"Ely, seriously, have you seen a doctor?" he asked as everyone was warming up.

"No, I think I'm fine, just some bruised ribs."

"Have you at least seen the school nurse?"

"Not yet, but I did make a promise that I would."

"I want you to go right now. You hear me?"

"Yes, Coach, I hear you. I think I'll be okay to practice in a day or two," Ely said as he slowly got to his feet. He had been sitting on the ground leaning up against the gym wall, and the pain in his ribs as he stood up prompted Ely to cringe involuntarily, which did not go unnoticed by his coach.

"You're not okay. You might have cracked a rib. Listen, Ely, you should really report this to the police. Hey, we'll talk more about this later. Go to the nurse and let me know what she says."

"Okay, Sel."

Sel patted him on the shoulder. "I'm glad you didn't quit. Good choice, buddy." Then he smiled and turned towards the team to start the practice.

As Ely had suspected, the nurse didn't think he had any broken ribs. But he definitely had some sore spots, and she too recommended that he see a doctor to confirm her opinion. A physician would be able to x-ray Ely and examine him for any other related injuries. Ely told her he would, though he knew full well that he would not be going to any doctor. After fifteen minutes with the nurse he made his way back to the wrestling gym.

The rest of the practice went pretty smoothly, with Adam avoiding him altogether. The activity bus ride home went by quickly as Ely's mind was completely occupied by pleasant thoughts of Amanda. He could still picture her smile as she had turned and walked away from him. And it was the first time in a long while that he hadn't opened a book on the bus. For once he didn't want to escape to another world. He wanted to remain in this one, looking out the window and thinking of Amanda. He leaned his head against the glass window, closed his eyes, and let his mind drift away with the first pleasant thoughts he'd had a long time.

Adam was definitely pissed off. He scowled furiously as he made his way to his car after practice. Ely had some nerve showing up for practice after taking such a beating. The question was…what was he going to do about it? He could just ignore it, hoping that maybe Ely would eventually quit on his own. Or he could continue to make his life miserable, as an added incentive for him to quit. Either way he was glad that Ely had kept his mouth shut. Maybe he would leave him alone because of that. Man, he hated that fat know-it-all. He began to smile as he ran through the mental images of his fist connecting with Ely's face. But his thoughts were interrupted by a familiar voice.

"Hey, Adam!"

Adam turned around to see Jeff approaching, flanked by Cisco and John.

"Hey, what's up?" Adam asked, a bit apprehensively as he took note of their aggressive posture.

Adam knew he would be hard pressed to defeat Jeff, even though he had him by seventy pounds. Jeff was a natural, strong, quick, and utterly fearless. And against the three of them, there was no way Adam had a chance. The only thing he had going for him was he knew that if they started a fight, that they would be suspended, and none of them would allow that to happen during wrestling season. That knowledge bolstered Adam's confidence.

"How's your hand?" Jeff asked, indicating Adam's right hand.

Adam glanced at the scrapes on his knuckles, realizing that somehow Jeff was aware of last night's altercation. The question was, how did they find out? Had Ely told him?

"It's fine, just scraped it a few times while chopping wood last night."

"Was that before or after the movie?"

"Before. Why? What the hell do you want?"

"Cut the crap, dipshit," Jeff said.

"We know it was you who beat Ely up last night," Cisco said, stepping closer to Adam. Cisco was nearly Adam's size, but a much better wrestler and overall athlete. Adam certainly didn't want to tangle with him.

"Whatever, you don't know shit," Adam said, trying desperately to show the confidence that he didn't really feel.

"Listen, you asshole." Jeff growled, as he too took another step closer to Adam, forcing him back up against his car door. "We are going to tell you this once, and only once. You are never to touch him again. Don't even look at him weird. If we ever hear that you bullied him again, we will end you. Do you understand?"

Adam didn't say anything for a second as he looked at all three of them. They were definitely serious. "What is it about him anyway? Are you guys' gay lovers or something? A couple of mat faggots?"

Adam didn't realize that comment was a big mistake, probably the worst thing he could have said to Jeff. Before Adam could blink Jeff had his neck in an iron grip that threatened to crush his windpipe. He found himself slammed back against his car, struggling in vain to breathe as Jeff stood over him, his face inches from his own.

"One more word," he said through tight lips, the intensity of his rage reflected in his eyes as they bore into Adam. Adam, on the verge of passing out, vaguely heard Cisco and John tell Jeff to let him go. Suddenly the vice around his neck loosened just enough to allow him to breathe again, though the pain in his neck was still intense. By this time Adam was nearly paralyzed with fear. He believed that Jeff could literally rip his throat out. "Don't say another word. Don't ever touch Ely again. Am I understood?" Adam couldn't speak so he just nodded his head in affirmation. "And if one word of our 'discussion' here gets out to anyone, anyone at all, you will wish it hadn't."

With that Jeff released Adam and stepped away, visibly trying to control the intense anger which still threatened to subjugate his reason.

Adam slowly stood up away from the car, and rubbed his injured throat, breathing deeply to catch his breath. "Okay.....okay, I won't...touch him again," he gasped.

"Good," was all Jeff said. Then the trio turned and walked away, leaving Adam alone to nurse his bruised neck.

As they neared their own vehicles, Cisco nudged Jeff in the side. "Dude, where did you learn to do that?"

"No shit, man. That was like Bruce Lee shit," John said as he mimed a karate punch.

Jeff smiled, his anger now dissipated. "Saw it in a movie."

The morning came quick for Ely as he had enjoyed the best sleep that he could remember in a long while. No nightmares plagued his dreams, and it felt as if he had no sooner closed his eyes than the morning alarm had begun ringing in his ears. But he awoke, feeling invigorated and refreshed, better than he had felt in a long time, and he eagerly got up and prepared himself for the day ahead. This was the first time that he could remember that he felt excited to go to school, and he knew that the prospect of seeing Amanda again was the reason for this rare feeling. Besides, each day that went by brought him one day closer to Saturday, and Saturday was his date with Amanda. At least he thought of it as a date, even though he wasn't sure if she felt the same way.

His thoughts danced around in his mind as he made his way to the bathroom. Just as he was about to take off his boxers and jump in the shower he heard a deafening bang, echoing loudly throughout the small confines of the mobile home. Ely was so startled he nearly fell into the tub. And then he realized what it was. It was a gun shot.

"Mom!" he screamed, as he tore through the bathroom door and down the short hall. It took him only a few heartbeats to take in the scene. His mom was on the floor, lying face down, with a pool of blood slowly growing around her stomach. Bill, his father, was sitting in his chair in the adjacent living room staring at a blank television screen, a handgun held casually in his right hand.

"Oh my god! What have you done!?" Ely cried as he raced to his mom, kneeling at her side. "Mom! Mom! Wake up!"

Ely heard the shuffle of footsteps and turned just in time to see only the blur of movement before Bill's booted foot connected solidly with his face. Ely flew onto his back, blood spattering outward from his broken nose and lacerated mouth.

"Iss all yer fault!" Bill shouted, clearly intoxicated. "Look what you've forced me t' do. Now geddup!"

Ely slowly stood on shaking legs, shielding his shattered nose with his hand. He was badly hurt, but his tears were for his mother as he saw her lying, unmoving, on the floor. Then Bill hit him again, this time with the hand holding the gun, the blow violently knocking his head to the side as the end of the barrel smashed into his cheek, opening a deep gash. Fresh blood poured from the cut as Ely tried to catch himself from falling. But before Ely could regain his balance, Bill used his other fist to smack him in the face a second time. This time Ely collapsed to the ground next to his mother.

Lying there Ely looked at his mother through a fog of pain. Her eyes struggled to open, and he could see the fear in them, her fear for him. She coughed up a small amount of blood as she tried to move. But the effort was too much. Her eyes fluttered briefly as she tried to keep them focused on her son. But it was a losing battle, and she fell into unconsciousness.

As her eyes closed, it was as if a switch had been turned on in Ely, a switch that had finally converted all the fear, pain, and anger he had suffered into something powerful, something indestructible. He suddenly found the strength to stand up, anger and determination fueling his battered body, the pain receding into a deep hole somewhere as it gave way to something else. Rage. It exploded to the surface like a volcano and Ely had no desire to control it.

"Is that all you got?" Ely growled, his eyes boring into his father's as he stood up to his full height.

"You son of…"

But his words were cut short by Ely's fist. Ely struck his father with the full force of his rage. Bill's head snapped back, forcing him to stumble backwards. He managed to regain his balance and face his son, his lower lip split open and bleeding down his chin. He was smiling.

"Nice job, son. Finally you're standin' up like a man. But I think that was a fluke. I think you're still a pussy." He lunged toward his son, swinging the pistol hand again.

Ely held up his arm in defense, but the gun slammed into it, cutting a deep gash in his forearm. Before he could recover from the blow, his father kicked him in the side of the leg, connecting solidly with his right knee, releasing an explosion of pain. He collapsed to his knees, still dazed from the kick to his face.

"You got me kicked out of my own home you pansy piece of shit!" Bill stormed as he punched

Ely in the face, knocking him to the ground again. Ely grunted, fresh pain exploding in his head. But the rage was still there, and it managed to force the pain deep within his subconscious.

This time Ely got to his knees, and as he saw his father lift his leg up to deliver another kick at him, Ely threw himself forward, grabbed his leg, thrusting it upward and forcing his father to lose his balance and fall backward. Ely stood and moved forward quickly, jumping on Bill as he struggled to get up, his gun scattered across the kitchen floor. Like a crazed maniac, Ely released all his rage and allowed it to fuel his fists as he brought them down repeatedly. His father managed to get his hands up to block most of the blows, but several connected solidly with Bill's face.

Swinging blindly, his father managed to land a lucky blow to the side of his head as he blocked one of Ely's blows with his other hand. The punch hit Ely in the temple, momentarily stunning him and allowing his father to push hard and knock Ely to the side, giving him enough space and time to get to his feet.

Dazed, Bill used the back of his hand to wipe away the blood that was dripping freely from his battered nose. "Finally," he said, spitting a glob of blood on the linoleum floor. "Maybe yer not such a pussy."

Ely had also struggled to his feet. The blow to his temple had definitely done some damage, and his head throbbed from the pain. But all it took was a glance at his mother to get him moving again, the pain and all rational thought again retreating before his fury.

Ely instinctively went into his wrestling mode and came in low, going for his father's legs. He struck him hard, clasping his arms around Bill's legs and using all his strength to hoist him up. Their momentum propelled them into the dining room table, where they crashed hard enough to tip it over, scattering the table, along with the chairs, against the kitchen cabinets. Bill struck the ground first, the wind whooshing from his lungs. Ely, his full weight pressing down on his gasping father, brought his fists down again and again, his wild blows connecting solidly until Ely realized his father was no longer moving. Ely paused, dizzy with pain and exhaustion, then fell to his side. He struggled to stand, all the while glancing at his unmoving father. He grabbed the kitchen counter to keep himself from falling. His head pounded with pain and he felt a rising nausea. He stared down at his father, his vision so blurred he could barely perceive the blood dripping from his father's nose and mouth.

Something was wrong. He knew he was on the verge of losing consciousness. He had to get the phone. He had to get help. Stumbling forward, he went to the phone located on a lone end table by the door, and his trembling fingers somehow found the numerals, 911. By this time he felt as if his skull could no longer contain the pressure in his head, and the pain dropped him to his knees. "Hello…I need…help," he stammered. "My mom…", and then he collapsed into the merciful oblivion of unconsciousness.

***

Ely opened eyes, and as his vision slowly cleared he struggled to take in his surroundings. Through the haze, white walls materialized and he noticed a familiar antiseptic smell. Then it hit him. He was in a hospital.

As that realization dawned on him, a flood of memories suddenly overwhelmed him. He tried to sit up but his body ached all over and he collapsed back down onto the soft sheets of the bed. He reached up and felt the bandages over his nose and face. There was a dull ache in his nose, but it wasn't terribly painful. They probably had him on pain medication since he felt a bit groggy and his body was so relaxed he found it difficult to move. He turned his head slowly and saw Jeff sitting in a chair next to his bed, his eyes closed as he dozed. Then he remembered his mom.

"Jeff, what happened to my mom?"

Jeff opened his eyes instantly and looked at Ely in surprise. "Oh, thank god you're awake. You've been unconscious for two days."

"What happened to my mom, Jeff?"

Jeff swallowed nervously as he leaned closer to Ely's bed. "She's hurt pretty bad, Ely. But the doctors say she's going to make it."

"I have to see her." Ely tried to get up but his body wouldn't move. He was so tired and the effort nearly caused him to pass out.

"You were beat up pretty bad, Ely. You suffered a severe concussion. The doctors have you on some strong pain medication. Don't worry, I'm looking after her. Everything is fine, I'm right here."

"Thanks," was all Ely could say before he again succumbed to oblivion.

When Ely finally awoke, he didn't know how much time had elapsed since he had fallen into that deep sleep. This time it was Mr. Seljin who was sitting next to him.

"Hey, how do you feel?" Sel asked as stood up and leaned over the bed.

Ely's mind still felt a bit foggy, though he did feel better. "My head still hurts but I feel a little better now."

"Well it should. Your nose was shattered and you suffered a severe concussion."

"Is my mom okay?"

"Yes, she is doing better. The doctor said that the bullet passed through her abdomen. They had to do surgery but they said she was lucky it didn't damage any vital organs." Sel reached out and put his hand on Ely's arm. "I'm sorry this happened."

Ely looked away. "Me too."

"Why don't you get some more rest. We are looking after your mom, so don't you worry."

"Thank you," Ely said as he closed his eyes, sinking wearily into another deep sleep.

Ten

In history there are events called watersheds. These are events that are considered turning points in history, important transitions between two eras. An example of a watershed would be the Emancipation Proclamation, or WWI, any major event that marks a significant or radical change in our culture. I bring this up because when my father came into our home and shot my mother, beating me up in the process, this became my own personal watershed, one of several in my life. Even though it was a devastating event, it set me on a path that would change my life. It forever severed the ties between me and my father. It reinforced my relationship with my mother, and with my friends, both of whom helped to steer my life in the right direction. This was a turning point for me. Yet it could have been a turning point that turned me in the wrong direction. If my mother had died, then who knows what would have happened to me. That single event could have sent me spiraling downward into a dark abyss of pain and depression. But luckily that did not happen.

Ely Carter

It was a beautiful day, but none of its beauty could penetrate Ely's thoughts as he lay on his back on his favorite bench outside the cafeteria. His eyes were closed and he was having trouble dispersing the mental images of the fight with his father. He couldn't erase the sight of his mother, sprawled across the kitchen floor, blood pooling around her body. His father's drunken snarling face was burned into his mind, and despite his efforts he could not escape the nightmare images of that terrible morning. And later, when he saw his mother in the hospital, hooked up to the machines, her chest slowly moving up and down, he was forced to relive the whole terrible experience again. His own father had done this to her, and beat him, and turned his world upside down. Ely was so angry, that it was all he could do to hold it back, to keep it below the surface.

It had been a week since the shooting. His mom was still in the hospital but she was now awake. The doctors said that she would heal fully but that she needed to stay in the hospital for another week or so. Ely's own wounds still looked pretty bad. His nose was splinted and bandaged and there was bruising around his eyes and cheeks. And he had had to get stiches, twelve of them, to close the cut on his face caused by his father's gun barrel. He looked as if he had just gotten out of the ring with Mike Tyson. Jeff's moms had offered to house Ely until Mary was fully recovered, and she graciously accepted the offer. Ely was thankful as well. He couldn't imagine going back, particularly by himself, to stay in their mobile home. It housed too many bad memories.

The sound of two kids talking snapped Ely from his thoughts and he opened his eyes to the glaring sun, a rare sight in February. He was screened by the foliage around the bench and the two boys that sat on the adjacent bench on the other side of the clearing had no idea Ely was there.

"Did you hear about that shooting at that fat kid's house?" a red headed boy asked. "He's back at school today I guess."

Ely reached up and took the half-eaten sandwich off his chest. Then he sat up, the rising anger barely restrained. There were two young boys sitting across from him. They sat with their backs to him, eating their lunches. He didn't recognize them, but by their height and stature they must have been freshman.

"Must be one messed up family," his dark haired friend replied. "I heard it was his own dad."

Before he knew what he was doing Ely was up and walking towards the two boys. "What about that fat kid?" he said, his voice quivering with emotion.

Startled to see Ely materialize before them, they looked up, their faces blanching as they recognized who he was. "Nothing, man, we were just talking, that's all," the red head responded.

"You want to know what it feels like!?" Ely yelled as he lunged aggressively toward them. He had lost control. Whatever it was that was holding the anger at bay had crumbled and blew away like a feather in a powerful hurricane. It was as if another being had taken possession of his mind and body. The real Ely was no longer recognizable; he had been replaced by a rabid raving maniac.

He came at the nearest boy with a wide swing of his fist. The red head who probably weighed no more than a hundred and thirty pounds, didn't even have time to blink before Ely's fist connected solidly with the side of his face, the force of the blow throwing him from the bench as if he were a rag doll. The dark haired kid turned to run but Ely grabbed his shirt from behind, yanking him off his feet and throwing him hard onto the concrete.

"You piece of shit!" Ely screamed as he stood over the cowering boy. "You're not going to hit me anymore! Do you hear me!?" Ely reached down and grabbed the astonished kid, jerking him back up to his feet.

"What are you talking about!?" the terrified boy screamed. "Please don't hurt me! I'm sorry!"

But all Ely could see were the flashing images of his father hitting him again and again, ten years of repressed memories boiling to the surface. "I'll show you what it feels like!" Ely roared. He held the boy up with his left hand, slapping him viciously across the face with his right. Ely outweighed the unfortunate kid by a hundred pounds and his misplaced rage added even more strength to the blow.

By this time a crowd had formed around them. As soon as the fight had started students had flooded from the cafeteria into the courtyard to watch the spectacle.

The boy's nose was now bleeding and he was openly crying. "Don't cry, you pussy! Isn't that what you always told me!?" Again Ely hit the kid. This time the strike sent the boy flying to the concrete.

"Ely! Stop it!"

But Ely didn't hear anything except for his father's taunts in his head. He stepped toward the kid who was slowly trying to get up and get away from him. "You're not going to hurt me or my mom again! Do you hear me!?"

Suddenly Jeff was there and he tried to grab Ely from behind to keep him from striking the kid a second time. Ely, still possessed by his blind rage, pivoted away, swinging his right fist in Jeff's direction, and catching him solidly on his right cheek.

Momentarily stunned, Jeff stepped away from Ely, holding his hand up to his bleeding lip. "Ely! Look at me!" he shouted. Ely paused, then looked at Jeff more closely, as if he was seeing him for the first time. Maybe it was the sight of blood dripping from Jeff's mouth that finally broke Ely's trance.

Ely, dazed, looked around at the crowd of students surrounding them; there must have been close to fifty, their faces mirroring emotions ranging from surprise and horror to morbid interest and excitement. Ely's entire body seemed to deflate as the anger drained away as quickly as it had arrived. Amanda was standing behind Jeff, her hand to her mouth in shock. Ely blinked for the first time as his eyes focused on Jeff. Then, when he caught sight of Amanda, he fell to his knees, the violent anger of just moments ago transformed into utter sadness and defeat. He crumpled over and began to softly sob. "I'm so sorry…I'm so sorry," he cried as he buried his head in his hands.

Jeff walked over and kneeled down next to him, wrapping his friend in a tight embrace. "It's okay, Ely. Everything will be okay." Jeff's eyes were rimmed with tears as he looked up to see Amanda step closer, her eyes reflecting the same sorrow.

***

Six staff members sat around a conference table in a closed room in the Peninsula High School office. Soon after the fight, Ely and the other unwilling participants were sent home. And once Mr. Seljin heard about what had happened he had asked the principal, Paul Youngchild, to hold a staff meeting with Ely's teachers to discuss Ely and the recent events. He was even missing wrestling practice to attend the meeting, something that did not happen often. Sel wasn't too worried though, as his able bodied assistant coach would be fine running the practice. His immediate concern was Ely.

At the table were three other teachers and Ely's counselor, Mr. Nelson. Everyone was in a heated debate and Mr. Seljin seemed to be in the middle of it.

"For a fight like this, standard procedure is suspension for a full week," Mr. Youngchild argued. Mr. Youngchild wore a dark gray suit and a red and blue striped tie. He was in his early fifties and for the last ten years had shaved his head as he lost the baldness battle to resignation and a sharp razor.

"Come on, Paul, I think that's the worst thing we can do for this kid," Sel argued, "He's had no behavior problems in the past. In fact he has been an exemplary student in all respects, which has been particularly impressive given the abuse he's suffered at home. Look, we can't just follow the rule book because we think that's what we're supposed to do. Each student is different and should be handled accordingly."

This time Ely's French teacher spoke up. Lisa Sampson was a young teacher fresh out of college. She was cute, but her stylish conservative clothes gave her an executive look that seemed to tone down her beauty. "You know him better than I do, Rick. But you must admit that this is a classic case of the picked on kid exploding and losing control. What's next? We have to think of the safety of our staff and student body. Considering what this student has been through you don't know what he might do."

"I agree. We don't know what he might do next," Leslie Scott added, clearly in agreement with Mrs. Sampson. Mrs. Scott was Ely's English teacher, a slightly heavy set, matronly looking woman with short dark hair and dark rimmed glasses. "I really like Ely, but we have to think of the safety of our students. I mean he clearly has anger problems."

"You would too if you had been beat up by your dad all your life and had watched your mom be nearly murdered by the same man!" Sel's voice rose as his frustration began to take over. "This is bullshit. So he snapped once. Think about it. After everything that has happened to him he has had no behavioral issues, none whatsoever...that is up until now. That tells us something. Ely is a strong kid.

He is a smart kid. He's had virtually no guidance his entire life. He needs us to stand up for him now, when it counts. If we suspend him now then we really should be asking what he will do. He has no support at home, his mother is still in the hospital, and his mind is in a dark place. Let's keep him here, close by, where we can watch him." Sel looked at each one of them hoping to gain some support.

Mr. Youngchild sighed deeply and leaned back in his chair. "What do you think, John?"

Mr. Nelson slowly took off his glasses and rubbed his eyes. "I've known Ely for almost two years now and I've never seen a mean bone in his body. Not only that, he's a genius."

"What?" Mike Turner, Ely's math teacher, asked. Mr. Turner was the school's basketball coach, a tall lanky man in his early forties with light brown hair and emerald green eyes.

"A genius," Mr. Nelson repeated. "He earned a perfect score on his tenth grade WASL, which is something that I had never seen before. So I tested him. His IQ is off the charts."

"What was his score?" Mr. Turner asked, his interest piqued. Ely had breezed through his class and he suspected that there was something special about the boy.

"145…like I said, he is literally a genius." Ely was not yet privy to this information. If he had been he would have been pretty amazed, as he knew what that number meant. Of course he would know, after all, he was a genius. It's believed that Einstein's IQ was around 160, while Isaac Newton's and Leonardo Da Vinci's is speculated to have been around 190, although that would be pretty tough to substantiate since they were dead. But Ely would have known that the highest IQ score on record was held by a man named Abbesselam Jelloul who scored 198 on a test that included 13 dimensions of intelligence. There is some disagreement on what score is considered a genius. But most scientists agree that the category of genius would be marked by a score between 140 and 150, which clearly placed Ely's score in that category.

"Well I'll be damned," Sel said. "I knew he was smart, but I didn't know he was a Steven Hawking."

"What are his grades?" Mr. Youngchild asked.

Mr. Nelson looked through a stack of papers in front of him and quickly shuffled through them, stopping at his transcript. "He has earned straight A's all the way through so far. He had a 4.0 GPA in middle school as well. In fact he is ranked number one in his class, and that's with taking honors courses."

"Ely once told me that school was easy for him," Sel mused.

"I should think so with an IQ of 145," Miss Sampson said.

"I was just getting ready to enroll him in the Running Start program when all this happened. I think we need to do that right away," Mr. Nelson said.

"Good idea," Mrs. Scott agreed. "But right now we have to decide what to do about this situation."

"Well, I plan to monitor Ely very closely," Mr. Nelson continued. "And I must agree with Rick. We shouldn't suspend him for that long. I think it would be a bad idea considering his mental state right now."

"Besides," Rick interjected. "If I can keep him on the wrestling team, then it might be a good place for him to release any stored up anger."

Mrs. Scott was shaking her head. "Suspending him, no matter how long, will put him on honor level four, which also puts him on probation, and off the wrestling team for at least two weeks."

"We have to make an exception for Ely," Sel argued. "Let's put him on honor level three and keep him on the team."

Mike Turner, being a coach himself, was nodding his head in agreement. "I agree with Rick. Keeping him in school and wrestling might be the best thing for him right now. He needs an avenue of escape, something to keep his mind off of everything that has happened to him."

"Well, he has to be punished," Mr. Youngchild said. "I have the parents of those two kids breathing down my neck right now. One wants to press assault charges."

"I agree…just not a week," Sel pleaded. "And let me talk to the parents. I think I can convince them to not press charges."

"How about three days? And maybe have him perform some community or school service in lieu of the honor level four designation," Mr. Youngchild suggested.

"Sounds good to me," Sel agreed. "Don't forget about honor level three. We need to keep him on the wrestling team."

"Okay, I'll make an exception." The rest of the staff nodded their heads in agreement and began to gather their belongings to go. Mr. Youngchild had one more thing to say. "It sounds like this kid has lots of potential, but he's certainly at risk. Let's keep a close eye on him."

"I plan to," Sel said emphatically.

"Have a good day, everyone," Mr. Youngchild said, concluding their meeting.

***

The buzzing alarm seemed abnormally loud to Ely. He reached up to slam his big hand onto the clock to shut up the screeching sound, but his hand smacked onto the floor. Floor? Then Ely remembered. He was sleeping on the floor of Jeff's room. After the shooting Jeff's parents had asked Mary, once she was in a condition to talk, if it would be okay for Ely to stay with them until she was out of the hospital. She was delighted, and quite frankly so was Ely. He had no desire to ever go back to their mobile home. He could still hear the gunshot and see his mother sprawled on the linoleum floor. The sounds and images from that day had been deeply embedded in his mind and would be hard to forget, especially if he were sleeping there.

Moaning groggily, Ely pulled the edge of his sleeping bag over his head, trying to retreat not only from the annoying sound, but also from the thoughts that plagued him.

Jeff reached out and turned the alarm off, then slowly emerged from his blankets and sat up, stretching his arms high into the air. "Come on, dude, we have to get ready."

"I don't want to go. Not after what I did," Ely said, his voice muffled by the sleeping bag over his face.

"Come on, man. It's been three days and your suspension is over."

"I don't care. I'm too embarrassed. Everyone knows what happened to me and what I did. They all think I'm a freak."

"Didn't they already know that before?" Jeff laughed.

Ely peeked out from under the sleeping bag. "Shut up, jack ass! It's way worse now and you know it."

"Who cares? Besides, you have to get back on the mat. Sel is expecting you. You know if you don't come, he'll just come looking for you."

Ely, who had reburied his face, peeked out again. "And how does he know to come here?"

"I told him of course. And so did your mom when he went to the hospital to visit her."

"Figures," Ely sighed. "Fine, I'm getting up."

Jeff got out of bed and walked past him toward the bathroom, pausing just long enough by Ely to fart directly in his face. Then, laughing hysterically, he scooted away from Ely who had swung at him with one hand while covering his nose with the other. But Jeff was too quick, and easily dodged the swipe as he hopped out of the way. "That should get you moving," Jeff said as he laughed his way into the bathroom.

"Asshole!"

Fifteen minutes later Jeff and Ely were sitting at the kitchen table eating a bowl of cereal. Laura, Jeff's little sister, was sitting next to Ely rummaging her hand around inside the cereal box.

"Stop that, Laura! Wait 'til we serve the food before you start touching it all," Jeff reprimanded her.

"I have to find the magic ring," Laura replied, the tip of her tongue sticking out as she concentrated on the task at hand. She always did that. Any time she was really focused on something, she would stick her tongue out and it would twist and turn like a fish on a hook. Her habit was really pronounced when she was focused on a drawing. But it was cute at the same time and Ely was getting a kick out of watching her face as she eagerly sought her prize.

Cindy was a psychiatrist, but she dressed like a fashionable CEO of a big corporation; she wore a chic and stylish business suit in shades of navy accented with a white silk blouse. She exhibited a relatively unadorned natural beauty, wearing only a minimal amount of makeup, a little mascara and a light application of peach lip gloss. But she also wore an air of confidence that further enhanced her attractiveness. It was obvious that she could enter any room and turn a few heads.

"Good morning, everyone," she announced as she poured cream into her coffee. "Laura, get your hand out of the cereal."

"But, Mom," Laura whined. "I have to find the ring."

"Jeff, help her find the ring."

"Come on, Mom, I'm trying to eat," Jeff complained.

"I'll get it for her, Miss Hanson," Ely said. Ely took the box from Laura and began to look for the prize that was buried in its depths.

"Thanks, Ely," Cindy said as she grabbed a granola bar from the pantry and then plucked some grapes from the fruit basket on the counter.

"No problem. Thanks again for letting me stay here until my mom gets out of the hospital."

"Who are you, fricken' Eddie Haskell?" Jeff said, rolling his eyes.

"Ely, you can stay as long as you like. And Jeff…shut up." Cindy then threw a grape and smacked Jeff right in the forehead. Everyone laughed and Ely couldn't help but feel jealous. He had never experienced the type of family camaraderie that he was now witnessing, and he wondered, and doubted, if he ever would.

***

Ely pulled his hat down low over his face and moved quickly down the hallway, keeping his head down. But it wasn't easy for him to try and disappear. After all, he was now almost six foot two, and whether he liked it or not, people were going to notice him. But although he drew furtive glances from students in his classes and in the hallways, they usually looked quickly away and no one seemed to bother him. Maybe they were scared of him. After all, he did go crazy and beat up a few kids. Ely was so mad at himself for that. It was bad enough that they were so much smaller than him, but what really bugged him was that he had lost control. He had virtually no memory of what he had done, and that was scary. After all, if he had so easily lost control then, what was to prevent it from happening again? And Ely didn't like being out of control. It reminded him of his father.

He made it to his locker with no problems, quickly put his jacket away, and took out his books for his next class. He couldn't help but notice that some of the students seemed to be whispering as they cast tentative glances his way, but nobody said anything to his face. Maybe he was being paranoid and was just imagining things. He was beginning to think that his morning was going to start off okay, until he heard the familiar voice of an asshole.

"Looks like the crazy fat ass is back." Ely turned around to see Adam walking towards him in the hall. "I guess they let you out of the mental institution. Was your dad in the room next to you?" Adam asked as he stopped in front of Ely. Ely stood there and said nothing, forcing himself to suppress the familiar anger rising up in him. He stood there, mute, saying nothing, knowing that if he spoke even a word it might break the wall that he had built around his feelings, his rage. "What's the matter, you wanna hit me too?"

Adam just laughed and walked away down the hall.

"Don't listen to that jerk," he heard a voice behind him. Ely turned around to see Amanda smiling up at him. "Hey, how are you?"

"Okay I guess."

"You don't sound so sure."

"Well, I'm sure the whole world knows what happened," Ely said softly.

"Yes I know. I was there when you hit those kids. And I visited you in the hospital after the shooting, but you were unconscious."

"You did? I didn't know that."

"How is your mom?"

"She's okay. The doctors said she'll recover, but she needs to spend a couple more weeks in the hospital."

"That's great."

Ely didn't say anything. He looked away uncomfortably before looking back at Amanda. "Look, I can't believe I hit those kids, I wish this whole thing had never happened. I don't know what came over me. I'm not a violent…"

"Ely, it's okay," Amanda interjected as she reached out to touch his arm. "You don't have to explain everything to me right now. But maybe we could talk over coffee sometime. Ely looked up, his face reflecting a mixture of surprise, confusion, and hope. "You want to have coffee with me?…… after all that's happened?"

"Yes."

"Hang out?"

"Yes."

"Shoot the breeze? Discuss my messed up family and my deranged dad and how his abuse over the years has created some mental issues with me, including uncontrollable fits of rage, disassociation, and the classic *I blame my daddy for everything* syndrome?"

"Well, if you put it like that let's skip class and go for that coffee now. The suspense is killing me," Amanda said, smiling. "Do you always joke about everything serious?"

"Another syndrome I blame on my father."

"Touché," Amanda laughed.

"I'm just not accustomed to being asked to hang out. Actually, this is the first time it's happened, if you don't count the time when you asked me to be your tour guide. But I wasn't really sure what that meant."

"So, you're sort of a hanging out virgin."

Ely almost choked. "Umm, I guess you could say that."

At this point in the conversation Jeff had sneaked up behind Amanda, leaning casually against a nearby locker.

"So would you like to be de-virginized?" Amanda asked with a giggle.

Ely looked over her shoulder to see Jeff, smiling widely, with both thumbs up in the air. Ely quickly averted his eyes and smiled back at Amanda. "Are we still talking about hanging out?"

"Wow, he's bold, witty, and confident too," she replied, still smiling. "So what do you say?"

"I'd love too."

"Cool. You still have my number?"

"Yup, right here," Ely said, tapping his head.

"Okay, call me…soon," she said, giving his arm a gentle squeeze before disappearing down the hall.

Jeff jumped up beside him. "You crafty son of a bitch. Good for you," he said as he jabbed Ely in the shoulder. "I gotta run, but Sel asked me to tell you to stop by his room really quick before class." Jeff slapped him on the back as he turned to go. "She's pretty cute, bud. Nice work."

"Yes she is," Ely said softly as he turned and moved down the hall. This time he didn't notice the curious glances of the other students in the hallways. All he saw was the image of Amanda's smiling face, and he couldn't wait to see her again.

The door to Mr. Seljin's room was open and Ely walked inside. Sel had his back to him and was writing the agenda for the day on his whiteboard.

"Hey, Coach."

Mr. Seljin turned from the board and smiled at Ely. "Hey, Ely, thanks for coming. I wanted to speak with you for a moment."

"Yeah, Jeff just told me."

"I just wanted to make sure things were okay. I know it's been rough for you," Sel said as he sat on the edge of a desk near Ely.

"I'm okay. I'm just embarrassed. I still can't believe I hit those two kids."

"I'm no counselor, Ely. But you've been dealing with some serious stuff." Ely laughed inwardly. Sel might not think he was a counselor, but he most definitely was. He had helped Ely over the years in more ways than he could possibly explain. "You lost control," Sel continued. "Nearly everyone has that experience at some time in their life. Just be thankful that no one got seriously hurt."

"I know. I feel awful. Those two kids were like a hundred pounds soaking wet."

"You've been holding in a lot of anger. It was just unfortunate that those kids happened to be there when it erupted. Did you get those apology letters out to their parents?"

"I did. They agreed to not press charges. I'm thinking you might have had something to do with that."

Sel smiled. "Maybe...or maybe you're just a great writer and your letter persuaded them otherwise."

Now it was Ely's turn to smile. "Maybe so. But I know one thing. I'm really going to work on controlling my anger from now on."

"Now that you mention that, I'd like to discuss the wrestling thing. I'm hoping that you haven't changed your mind about wrestling after all that's happened."

"Well, I thought I would be off the team after the fight, but Mr. Youngchild put me on honor level three instead of four. He mentioned that he thought I should still wrestle. Did you have something to do with that?"

"Maybe," Sel smiled again. "Listen, he's right. I think wrestling would be the best thing for you right now. Forget the losing and winning thing.

Just use it as a way to blow off some steam. Work out hard, sweat hard, exhaust your body and your mind will calm itself. I hope you'll be at practice today."

"Well, I've been thinking a lot about it over the last three days, and I agree with you. I think wrestling will be a great way for me to channel my energy. I'm afraid that if I don't do anything I might blow up again."

"Good. Let's use that energy on the mat. Has the nurse cleared you to wrestle?"

"Not yet. But the doc did, and I have a note from him."

"Perfect. So I'll see you on the mat today?"

"I'll be there."

The sound of the bell interrupted their conversation.

"I better get to class," Ely said.

"Alright. I'll see you later this afternoon."

"Okay."

"If you need anything, I want you to make sure and ask," Sel said seriously.

"I will. Thanks Sel."

Mr. Seljin slapped Ely on the shoulder. "No problem. Good to have you back. Now get to class."

Ely smiled and left. Maybe the day wouldn't be so bad after all.

Eleven

Dating…the joy and dread of all adolescents. I think that biology has it all screwed up. During our adolescent years we humans are governed more by our hormones than by rationality. We are emotionally unstable, sexually driven cellular structures that walk around constantly thinking about people of the opposite sex, or same sex depending on one's biological preference. Biology has given us teenagers the drive, as well as the physiological tools, to enable "physical pair bonding". But it has not given us the ability to comfortably interact with these same members of society of whom we are constantly thinking. It would be perfect if we never thought about sex when we were younger, and then, right around college or even later, a switch is turned on and we are off to the races. Think about it. That would be perfect. Our bodies would still be young enough to allow us to enjoy each other physically, but we could also now link several coherent sentences together and actually talk to someone we might like. But all these inherent desires are wasted on adolescents who have no idea how to establish a relationship, let alone maintain one once they have worked up the nerve to talk to the object of their desire. Then, throw sex into the mix. You could blindfold a young couple, strip them down, tie their hands behind their backs, and toss them together in a pool of maple syrup for all the good it would do. No one would know what to do.

Here's where I'm going with this. So I had this girl. I liked this girl. And I think she liked me. But I had no idea what to do about it. Should I call her? If so, what do I say? Should I ask her out? If so, where should we go? What would we do? Even if everything goes well and she agrees to hang out with me...then what? Should I try to kiss her? I've never kissed anyone before. Well, except for my mother, but that's certainly not going to help me. I have no idea what I'm doing. Imagine being kissed by an inexperienced fat kid. Well that's what I'm thinking anyway. Tons of insecurities start punching me in the face, taunting me, convincing me that there is no way this girl would really like me, let alone want to kiss me. So what do I do? Absolutely nothing. Eventually it becomes habit. I inherently knew this, but breaking down the prison I had built for myself was not easy.

Ely Carter

"Dude, stop being a pussy and just call her," Jeff said rubbing his short hair in frustration.

Ely shook his head. "I don't know. Easy for you to say 'Justin Bieber', but come on, look at me. You saw Amanda. There is no way she would want to go out with me."

"Bieber? Come on, man, I would think Brad Pitt would be more fitting."

"Whatever."

Jeff and Ely were sitting in front of the television playing an Xbox game. Well, Jeff was playing. Ely was just watching and stewing over Amanda. It was Saturday night and it had been three days since Amanda had talked with Ely at his locker and suggested that they do something. Even though he knew, deep down inside, that it was Amanda that actually suggested it, that still didn't make it any easier to pick up the phone and call her. He had handled himself well enough when he had spoken to her previously, but talking on the phone was different. It was so alien to him that just the thought of it caused his stomach to twist and turn, as if a baker were kneading dough in his abdomen. On top of that his heart was pounding like the sub-woofers at a rock concert.

Jeff paused the game and turned to face Ely. "Listen, I understand you being nervous, but you just have to do it. You can't, and won't go your entire life without calling a girl. At some point it will happen. You might as well do it now. Besides, it sounds like she likes you, so now seems as good a time as any to take the plunge. Jump in the pool and learn to swim."

"Nice analogy."

"Thanks, man. We learned about those in class last week."

Ely took a deep breath and let it out slowly. "I know you're right, but I can't convince my body to get up and pick up the phone." He looked over at the phone by the television as if it were the embodiment of evil.

"I have a plan," Jeff said as an idea suddenly struck him. He got up and ran into the kitchen, returning briefly with the whiteboard they kept on the wall.

"I'll call her and put it on speaker phone. As you talk to her I'll write stuff on the board to say if you get stuck. It's brilliant," Jeff grinned and jumped over to the phone.

"I don't know…"

"You're doing it. What's the number?"

Perspiration began to break out on Ely's forehead, but he knew Jeff was right. Besides, it was a good plan and Ely was pretty confident that Jeff could get him out of any hole he dug for himself. Ely wiped his clammy hands along his pants, stood up, and walked over to the phone. "Okay, let's do it."

"Great! What's the number?"

"554-6745."

"Here we go," Jeff said as he dialed the phone and made sure the speaker was on.

As the phone rang, Ely could feel an apple begin to grow in his throat. And the baker had now become a witch with claw tipped fingers scraping the inside of his stomach. He took a couple quick breaths as the phone rang two, and then three times. On the fourth ring Amanda answered.

"Hello."

Ely looked at Jeff, frozen in fear. Jeff urged him on and wrote 'hello' on the board.

"Hello," Amanda said again.

Ely's eyes were wide and the apple in his throat blocked any attempt to say something.

Finally Jeff took the situation into his own hands. "Ummm, hello," he said as he coughed, trying to disguise his voice.

"Who is this?" Amanda asked.

Luckily for Ely, Jeff's attempt to salvage the situation broke him from his paralysis and he was finally able to croak something out past the lump in his throat. "Hey, it's Ely."

"Oh, hey, how are you? I was wondering when you were going to work up the courage to call."

Ely was relieved to hear the humor in her voice. He nervously cleared his throat and found his voice at last. "Well, as we speak there is a lump the size of a watermelon in my throat and the Olympic hockey team is having shooting practice inside my stomach, but other than that I'm fine."

Amanda laughed and Jeff grinned at Ely, giving him a thumbs up and mouthing the words 'nice job'. Then he quickly wrote something on the board and held it up to Ely.

"I love that wit of yours," Amanda said.

"And I thought it was my washboard abs," Ely replied as he looked at what Jeff had written. On the board were the words 'So how are you? I've been thinking about you.'

Amanda laughed. "I'm not into the jock types."

Ely, without really thinking, read the phrase out loud. "So how are you? I've been thinking about you."

"You have? How so?" she asked, clearly enjoying the dialogue.

Now Ely was stuck. "Well, ummm," he stumbled, looking for something to say as Jeff frantically wrote on the board. "I like…ummm…" and before Ely could say anything Jeff held up the board and Ely read it quickly. "Hold on a second."

There was a pause on the other end. "Oh…okay."

Ely put his hand over the speaker on the phone. "What are you doing?" he whispered frantically.

"Shhhh," Jeff admonished. "I'm stalling for time," he whispered quickly as he erased the phrase and wrote something else. Ely looked at it and smiled.

"Sorry, I moved into the bedroom for more privacy. I was saying that I miss talking with you. I've been thinking a lot about how much I've enjoyed our conversations."

"Like this one?" she asked.

"Well this one started off a bit awkward, but it's getting better now."

"Yes...it definitely is."

Jeff smiled and wrote something on the board.

"So what are you doing?" Ely asked.

"Nothing much. I'm actually painting my room. Nothing terribly exciting."

Ely read the note on the board and shook his head at Jeff, silently mouthing 'no'.

Jeff got serious and pointed his finger at him, then at the board, emphasizing that he wanted Ely to read what he wrote.

There was a long pause as Jeff and Ely had a silent standoff. "Hello?" Amanda asked.

Finally Ely broke down and read the board, mainly because he hadn't thought of anything else to say. "So, how about that date?"

"Date? I said coffee…now aren't you getting a little presumptuous," Amanda teased.

'I told you', Ely silently mouthed the words as he glared at Jeff. "Ummm, that's what I meant, sorry…I…"

"Ely, I'm just kidding. I would love to go on a date with you. When?"

Jeff quickly wrote something in bold letters and held it before Ely.

"Now," Ely said.

"Now?"

"Well, I was going to suggest tomorrow, but then I realized you were painting your room. And I'm guessing that you'd rather be somewhere else, even if it's with me, than stuck in your room painting."

Jeff nodded his head approvingly. "Nice work, buddy," he whispered softly.

"Well, that's true. But Ely, stop sounding like a pessimist. It doesn't suit you. I actually want to hang out with you. So stop having a pity party and come pick me up."

Ely grinned, but his smile quickly disappeared as he fully realized what she had said. Then, before he could get a word out, Jeff had reached into his pocket, pulled out his car keys, and was dangling them in front of his face. Ely smiled gratefully at his friend, whose own smile was as wide as the Cheshire Cat.

"Okay, that would be great. Where do you live?" He paused for a moment as she asked him if he had a pen and paper to write down the directions.

"No, I will remember it." She gave him the directions and then said goodbye. "See ya soon," Ely responded before hanging up.

Ely was still smiling from ear to ear. "I did it. She wants me to pick her up in an hour."

"See, I told you so. You did great. And like she said, stop being so negative about yourself. I've told you this before and she just reinforced it. Girls like confidence, so stop acting like an insecure pussy."

"Fine, I'll try to work on it. Thanks Jeff. And thanks for letting me use your car tonight."

"No worries. Besides, I'm into this damn game so I don't think I'm going anywhere tonight. Now go get ready."

Ely smiled and ran up the stairs. This was a momentous occasion. His first date.

He found her house easily enough and as soon as he pulled up she opened the front door and ran to his car. Ely had read that girls liked it when you opened the door for them, so he frantically unbuckled his seat belt and ran to the passenger door. There was no way he could make it look smooth and get there before she did, so he didn't even try.

She laughed as he quickly opened the door for her. "Ely, it's okay, I'm a twenty first century kind of girl."

Ely looked dejected. "Oh…okay…I'm sorry."

Amanda smacked him on the arm. "It's no big deal. Lighten up. Besides, it's the thought that matters. I don't need my door opened for me but the fact that you thought of it is nice…and really cute. Thanks."

Ely's smile returned as she got in the car. Ely got back in and buckled up. "Well, what do you want to do?"

Now it was Amanda's turn to look dejected. "You mean you don't have a plan?"

"Ummm, I'm not sure…I don't…"

"Ely, I'm still joking. Relax. Let's just hang out."

"That sounds good. Honestly, I was so excited you said yes that I only came up with one idea."

"And…?"

"Well, it's a nice night and the moon is out. I have some wood in the back of the car and I thought it would be fun to light a fire down by the Purdy Bridge. I have a thermos of hot chocolate and we could just hang out by the fire." Ely looked at her questionably, hoping she wouldn't think the idea was lame.

"You came up with that plan on your own?" Amanda asked.

"Well," Ely hesitated. "If you must know it was Jeff's idea."

Amanda laughed. "Either way, I love it! Let's go."

It didn't take them long to get to the spit. Puget Sound was a collection of numerous waterways. Bays, lagoons, inlets, and spits reached shimmering azure fingers into the heavily forested surroundings. It was truly beautiful and Ely had yet to explore much of it. But the Purdy Spit was a well-known thoroughfare. It was the main road connecting Gig Harbor to the Key Peninsula and stretched for a half mile or so over a manmade base of rocks and backfill flanked by Henderson Bay on one side and the Purdy Lagoon on the other. The Purdy Bridge spanned the waterway that connected the bay to the lagoon, and the beach that lined the bay side was a popular hangout during the summer and known to the locals as the Purdy Spit.

Ely parked along the side of the road just before the entrance onto the bridge. "Why don't you grab the blankets and I'll start hauling down the wood," Ely suggested as he got out of the car.

"Sounds good."

Amanda traversed the short rocky trail that went down to the concrete supports under the bridge. The tide was on its way in but there was plenty of room along the edge of the driftwood piles that lined the entire length of the spit. There was already a spot that had a fire pit dug and several big logs had been dragged up to it to form some make-shift benches. It was a perfect spot. The concrete base of the bridge blocked the breeze but you could still look out across the bay. The night was clear and calm and the ambient glow of the moon and stars was reflected off the glassy surface of the water.

Ely had to make two trips but it didn't take him long to get the wood stacked up and a blazing fire lit while Amanda wrapped herself in a blanket that he had brought. He found a stick that he could nudge the fire with and sat down next to her on the log.

"Have you been here before?" Ely asked. Amanda lived on the harbor side so she didn't have to cross the spit, but the high school was close so he figured she at least knew about it.

"I've obviously driven by it, but I've never been down by the water."

"Well, the weather's been pretty rainy and crappy since you've been here. During the summer this is a pretty popular hangout."

"Oh yeah? Do you come here in the summer?"

"Nope. I try to stay away from bathing suits and crowds if I can help it. Especially if the former is accompanied by the latter." Ely smiled as he poked a log further into the flames. "Besides, this is where the cool kids come to hang out. I wouldn't really fit in."

"I don't know, Ely. You're pretty cool," she said as she nudged him gently. "Besides, aren't you friends with that Jeff kid? According to everyone in the school he is definitely cool."

"He is that. Yeah, we are friends. But we don't really hang out much in public. He has other friends that he does that with."

"So you guys are like *closet* friends?"

Now it was Ely's turn to gently elbow her. "No, and I get your reference. I wouldn't be here now if that was the case."

"I see," Amanda said, smiling subtly, locking eyes briefly before Ely returned his stare to the flickering flames of the fire.

After several moments of silence, Amanda finally spoke. "So Ely, will you tell me about your father?"

Ely's face became serious and he took a moment to stir the fire again before looking up at her. "You sure you want to hear? It's not a pleasant story."

"I do. But only if you're comfortable with it; I'd like to know more about you."

Ely sighed. "Okay. I don't remember much of my early youth. I'm not sure why, but I think it was a defense mechanism. My earliest memories start around fourth or fifth grade. As far back as I can remember he's had a drinking problem. In fact, I have very few memories of him sober. He beat my mother first. I remember that part of my childhood vividly. I can still hear the slaps in my head, and the yelling, but the part that is really burned into my mind is my mother's crying. There were so many nights that I heard her crying as I lay in bed."

Amanda reached out and touched Ely's arm as he continued to stir the fire. "I'm so sorry, Ely. No child should have to experience that."

Ely continued staring into the burning embers, momentarily losing himself in the memories. "That's when I started listening to music. I remember hearing Mozart in fourth grade, during one of our music classes. The music sort of transported me away from my own reality. It gave me a feeling that helped me forget all the stuff that was going on at home, at least for a while. I made a habit of putting on my headphones every night.

Listening to classical music helped drown out the beatings."

Ely got up and threw another log onto the fire. "You want some hot chocolate?"

"Sure," Amanda said softly as she tried to imagine what it must have been like to witness that type of abuse, and have to hear your mom crying at night. It was almost impossible for her to imagine.

Ely picked up the thermos and poured each of them a mug of steaming chocolate, then sat back down next to Amanda. He took a sip, staring into the hypnotic flames, not sure where to continue.

Amanda looked at him closely. He was actually a pretty good looking guy, or at least he could be. If he lost a little weight she could see how his chin and jawline would be more defined and strong, which would in turn accentuate the fullness of his lips. She also found his eyes intriguing. Long dark lashes accentuated the deep brown color of his eyes, which managed to reflect not only a boyish innocence, but a maturity beyond his years. And she thought it was cute how he bit his lower lip when he was deep in thought, as he was now.

It was his hair, however, that she liked the most, soft waves of golden brown, with auburn highlights that most girls would pay a lot of money to have. There were just a lot of things she liked about him, things that somehow transcended his weight.

"Was that when you also started reading a lot?" she asked, hoping to restart the conversation.

Ely tore his eyes away from the fire and looked at her again. "No, I started reading when he started beating *me*." He looked away from her quickly, as if he were ashamed.

"Ely, it's not your fault you know."

"I know. I've read a lot of psychology books on the subject so I'm well versed on abuse, but despite it all I feel like it was my fault."

"But, Ely, how could your father's abusive actions be your fault?"

"It's not his actions that I blame myself for. I blame myself for my *inaction*. I did nothing over the years. I allowed him to beat my mother, and myself, and in the end it almost killed her."

"But you were a boy when it happened. What could you have done? No child is prepared for what happened to you."

"Maybe," Ely mumbled, continuing to nudge the coals around in the fire. "But I got older, and bigger…I could have done something then."

"If you had done something, then he might have shot you," Amanda reasoned, clearly trying to help Ely understand that he was not to blame for any of the things that had happened to him.

"Good."

Amanda looked at him sternly. "You don't really mean that."

"I'd rather have been shot trying to stop him from hurting us than to have my mother shot. I was a coward."

Amanda waited for Ely to calm down. It was clear that he was getting agitated, and that was the last thing that she wanted. They sipped their chocolate in silence, allowing the tension to dissipate.

"I'm sorry," Ely finally said. "Sometimes I feel so angry and frustrated

"And rightly so," Amanda replied. "Ely, what happened that morning when your mom was shot?"

Ely shrugged. "I heard a gunshot when I was getting ready to get in the shower. Even though my dad had moved out of the house and was ordered by the court to stay away from us, I knew that it was him. I ran into the kitchen and saw my mother on the floor with blood all around her. After that it was all a blur."

"What do you mean?" Amanda asked.

"Well, I remember being infuriated and attacking him. I hit him I think," Ely said, trying to dig up the memories from that morning. "Then he punched me several times…hitting me with the gun, and I think he kicked me in the face as well. I remember an anger building deep inside me…and it overwhelmed me. Anger displaced the pain and I vaguely remember tackling him to the floor, and hitting him over and over again until he stopped moving. But he had hit me pretty good as well. The doctor said I took a fist to the temple, giving me a severe concussion. I remember feeling nauseous, and dizzy, but luckily I made it to the phone before I passed out. The details are all still a blur."

"Well then, it sounds like you did stand up to him."

"Yeah, I guess so."

Amanda felt the need to change the subject. "So what's your mother like?" she asked.

Ely finally smiled. "She's incredible. She is the kindest person I know. I don't think she has a mean bone in her body. And despite all of the abuse, she still looked out for me, in her own way."

"And I bet you looked out for her."

"Why do you say that?" Ely asked.

"I don't know. Like I told you at the theater, I'm a good judge of character. You are strong person, Ely, to have survived all that relatively mentally unscathed."

Ely lifted his eyebrows and smiled at her. "Relatively mentally unscathed?"

She smiled. "Well, you did beat those kids up like a madman."

Ely chuckled. "That is true. Something I'm not overly proud of."

Amanda scooted closer and leaned her head on his shoulder. "Well, despite your mad fits of rage and your penchant for self-loathing, I like you. You're charming, kind, smart, and witty, rare traits to find in one person." Even though Ely could not see her face he could sense that she was beaming from ear to ear, smiling at her semantic brilliance.

"So that is what a backhanded compliment sounds like," he said wryly. "If it makes you feel any better, I like you as well, despite your attempts to downplay your looks because you don't feel secure enough to believe that people will take you seriously if you look beautiful. That insecurity is rather endearing, and although you try really hard to look geeky, with your thick rimmed glasses, carelessly coifed hair, and thrift store clothes, you fail miserably at masking how pretty you really are."

Amanda lifted her head from his shoulder and scooted away from him. "Now, Ely, *that* backhanded compliment was far superior to my own, and might just be the nicest thing a guy has ever said to me."

They laughed and Amanda moved closer to him, again putting her head on his shoulder. "You are really smart aren't you." She said it as a statement, not a question.

"I guess so."

"Come on. No high school kid talks like you."

"Look who's talking. Your verbal swordplay is just as impressive."

"Case in point."

Ely chuckled and reveled in the closeness of her body. He was so relaxed with her now, as if they were old friends. Maybe it had helped to tell her about his father, to open up to her, to share with her something that he had not really talked about with anyone else, except for Jeff and Mr. Seljin.

"You know, for someone so smart, you'd think you would know when the time was right to put your arm around your date. Didn't you read about that in a book?"

Ely grinned and reached his big arm around her, pulling her in closer. She snuggled up against him, and for the first time in a long while, everything seemed right in the world, like things would be okay.

A couple of days later Jeff and Ely were sitting around their kitchen table doing their homework. It was around seven in the evening, relaxation time for Jeff's parents, Cindy and Lisa. Relaxing usually involved the television and a foot massage. Lisa, a little more heavy set than her partner, had propped herself up in the corner of the couch with her *Time* magazine and her feet resting on Cindy's lap. Lisa was a local firefighter and despite the fact that she was a woman, most people who looked at her would not question her ability to pull a body from a burning home. She looked more than capable, with strong arms and powerful muscular legs. Her chestnut brown hair was streaked with blonde highlights, and cut short at her neck line. Cindy was watching television, absent mindedly rubbing Lisa's feet.

In the kitchen Jeff shoved the math book aside in frustration. "God dammit, I hate this shit!"

Ely looked up from his physics book. "What's the problem?"

"This dumb ass geometry is impossible!"

From the living room Laura yelled at Jeff. "We can hear you!"

"Sorry!" Jeff yelled back, shrugging and smiling at Ely.

In the living room Lisa lowered her magazine and nudged Cindy with her foot. "You know he gets that mouth from you."

Cindy laughed and playfully pinched her foot. "He does not…you bitch!"

Ely set his book down on the kitchen table, reached over and grabbed Jeff's homework and began to look it over.

"Why do we even have to know this crap anyway?" Jeff asked.

"Actually, of all the math disciplines, geometry is probably one of the most useful," Ely said as he continued to scan Jeff's work.

"Well I don't see anything useful about this stuff."

In the living room Cindy gave Lisa's foot a final pat. "Thanks, Cin, that felt good." The seven o'clock news had just come on.

"You're welcome, honey," Lisa replied, her attention now diverted by the television screen. "Oh great, looks like another accident on 302."

Lisa lowered her magazine and looked up to watch the news. Sure enough, a reporter was covering a head-on collision on Highway 302, the main thoroughfare to the Key Peninsula on which they lived. The road was notoriously dangerous, consisting of only two lanes that twisted and turned through dark unlit wooded areas. There were no passing lanes or left turn lanes, increasing the risk of head-on and rear-end collisions. And traffic had increased significantly over the years as more and more people moved out to the peninsula. This increase in traffic also meant larger number of young or intoxicated drivers on the road. With a speed limit of fifty five miles per hour, and the tendency of drivers to go faster, 302 was a recipe for disaster.

"This just in," the news anchor began. "We've just received word of a fatal car accident on Highway 302, about a quarter mile past the Ravensara Coffee Shop. We have Bob Wait on the scene."

The television scene switched to a reporter standing outside a coffee shop alongside the highway. Bob Wait, the reporter, spoke while a flurry of activity went on behind him. Law enforcement officers, firefighters, and medics moved about in the background, a scene dominated by flashing blue and red lights. "We have reports," the reporter continued, "that the female driver of a black SUV crossed into the other lane while coming around this dangerous corner behind me, hitting an on-coming vehicle head on and catapulting that car into the gully. Her own car spun several times and was launched into the trees on the other side of the road.

"Do we know the status of the drivers?" the news anchor asked.

"We do. Unfortunately the driver that was hit was killed. The condition of the driver that crossed the lane is unknown at this time, but she is alive and being flown to Harborview Medical Center."

Lisa and Cindy were now listening intently, their eyes glued to the television set. The location of the accident was very familiar to them. They lived only five minutes away from Ravensara, and often stopped there for coffee on their way to work.

"That damn corner is so dangerous," Cindy said.

"That's the second accident there this year," Lisa added as she set her magazine down on the table.

The report of the accident continued on the television. "Do we know the identity of the driver that was killed?" the anchorman asked.

"Yes we do, Dan," the reporter answered. "Tragically, the driver of the car that was hit was one of Peninsula's local teachers, a highly respected member the community."

"Oh my god," Lisa said softly, hardly able to speak.

In the kitchen Ely continued to look over Jeff's homework. Jeff sat waiting, a bored expression on his face. Up until now the sound of the television, though audible, was just white noise. Ely was still focused on Jeff's work, but Jeff was now listening to the reporter and when he heard that a teacher had been killed, he looked up from the table, turning his attention to the news report in the other room.

"The teacher has been identified," the reporter continued, "as Rick Seljin, the wrestling coach and history teacher at Peninsula High School."

Jeff snapped his head up, a look of utter disbelief on his face.

Cindy and Lisa had sat up from the couch, their bodies rigid with shock. "Oh my god. Jeff, Ely, please come in here," Cindy said, her voice rising with alarm.

Jeff jumped up and grabbed Ely's arm. "No…I didn't just hear that."

Startled, Ely dropped the paper and stood up. "Jeff, what's wrong? You didn't just hear what?"

They heard Lisa yelling from in the living room. "You guys, get in here! Quick!"

Jeff ran to the living room with Ely right on his heels. "Please tell me that I didn't just hear that," Jeff said, his voice cracking with emotion.

Cindy and Lisa stood up and faced the boys. Jeff reached the couch and stood behind it, his eyes focused on the news. Ely, still confused, stood beside him.

"What's going on?" Ely asked, quickly picking up on the tension in the air. He stared at the television as the anchorman continued, "Bob, do you know how the accident occurred?"

"We don't yet have all the details, but we do know that Mr. Seljin was driving home from work when a vehicle moving in the opposite direction crossed into his lane, hitting him head on. Witnesses say he had no time to react."

Ely's face paled as he stood stunned. "That can't be," he whispered.

"We just saw him," Jeff murmured, as if he were talking to himself. Lisa put a hand on his shoulder and he turned to look at her as tears welled up in his eyes, glistening in the dim light of the nearby lamp. "Mom, that can't be. He can't be dead."

She pulled him in close and hugged him tight. "I'm sorry, sweetie." Her touch seemed to confirm the reality of the tragedy, and he broke down, succumbing to choking sobs that shook his body. Lisa held him tighter, her own eyes streaming with tears as she too realized the enormity of this loss for her son.

Ely stood frozen, unable to see through his tears. He blinked several times, and felt himself sinking into a well of sorrow. The sounds in the room had evaporated into a meaningless muffled din, smothered by a fog of pain that permeated his being and pierced his heart.

Cindy reached out and touched Ely's arm, hoping to console him as best she could. Her touch startled him from his trance, and he stepped away from her, as if she were a spectre. "Are you okay, honey," she asked softly, reaching for him again, hoping to bury his pain in a tight motherly embrace.

"No, I'm not," he said firmly as he stepped back further, bumping into the wall behind him. He could feel himself begin to lose touch with reality; he wanted no part of this reality. But he couldn't escape it, and the shock of the news finally embraced him. But it was too much for him to bear and his body began to shake. "He can't be dead!" Ely shouted. "He just can't be!"

Jeff had collapsed onto the couch, still wrapped in his mom's embrace. She glanced up at Ely, her tear streaked face mirroring her concern.

"Ely, it's okay," Cindy said softly, "everything's going to be okay."

But Ely's mind was spinning, filled with emotions he was unable to process. Denial, anger, emptiness, and above all an overwhelming loss. He reached up and grabbed his hair, "He can't be dead!" he moaned. "Heroes don't die!" he cried, his voice rising in a crescendo of anguish. "They don't die like this!" Anger had now replaced all other emotions, morphing into a rage he could scarcely control. He turned and began slamming his fists against the wall behind him.

Cindy stepped closer, unsure if it was wise to try and touch him at the moment, thinking maybe she should let his anger run its course. But she wanted to be close to him when it did, and she knew it would. "Ely, it's okay. Calm down," she said in a reassuring voice as she stepped a little closer. "Come here, honey."

But Ely continued pounding on the wall, cracking the drywall and sending white sheetrock powder to the carpet below. "No! No!" Ely sobbed, "He was my friend! He helped me! Why did he have to die?"

Cindy waited patiently as his anger began to subside and the pounding of his fists became weaker, until finally he stopped, collapsed to the floor and buried his head in his hands. His anger had succumbed to numb exhaustion, and a feeling of complete emptiness and despair. "Why him? Why?" His grief stricken voice was now a soft murmur, and his body felt deflated and empty, as if nothing could ever again restore its substance.

Seeing that Ely's anger had run its course, Cindy went to her knees and wrapped her arms around his body in a protective embrace. "I'm so sorry, honey. We're all here for you. It's going to be okay."

The air in the room was thick with the intense grief they were all feeling. Their muffled crying mingled with the noise of the television as the news continued, moving to the weather, as if the world would go on as before.

Twelve

Death. It can be such a tragic event. Few are prepared for it, especially those who are young. It's so unfamiliar to most young people that the reality and finality of it seldom enters their minds. But as we get older, we find ourselves thinking of it more…it becomes a reality that begins to appear within our eyesight, contrary to our view of death in our youth, when it seems so far away that we couldn't even see it with a telescope.

Needless to say, I wasn't prepared for my first run in with death. It nearly crushed me. The bond that I had developed with Mr. Seljin was so strong, that when I lost him, I almost fell apart. But it was the relationship that we had created together that got me through it. He taught me so many valuable lessons, lessons that provided the strength and confidence I needed to cope with his death. It wasn't easy, however. My mother was there to help me. My friends were there to help me. I think back on it now and I know that without their help, even with Mr. Seljin's lessons, I might not have been able to climb out of the hole of depression. But I did, and it made me even stronger.

What I needed was something to grasp onto, something on which to focus my energy, something to keep me from drifting into a sad meaningless existence. I needed a lifeline, and I found it in wrestling. Wrestling was the primary activity through which I had connected with Mr. Seljin. In my own way it became my avenue to honor him, and to help me keep his memory at the surface of my consciousness. In fact, it was the one thing I could do where I could actually hear his voice in my head. He was my hidden trainer, my invisible coach.

I can still remember the day when I decided to end my mourning. It was the day I realized that if I continued slipping down this waterslide of grief that I would eventually drown in my own self-pity. It was the same day I heard the familiar voice in my head. "Ely, how do you know what you're capable of if you have never tested yourself?" And that was it. This time I was truly going to test myself. I would do what I should have done when he was alive. I was going to put all of my energy into wrestling…I was going to test myself…I was going to find out what I was made of. I made this promise to Mr. Seljin, but more importantly I made it to myself.

But before I could come to this realization, a friend had to help guide me there.

Ely Carter

————————————————

The sun was just getting ready to set behind the tree line as Ely walked out onto the long dock that was nestled at the end of Von Geldern Cove. This was one of his favorite spots to go when he wanted to think, or to just get away by himself, and he was doing a little of both this evening. He took off his shoes, rolled up his pants, and sat at the end of the dock with his feet in the water. It was early spring and the water was still cold. But he didn't care. It made him feel alive, and that was much better than how he had been feeling lately.

It had been over two months since the accident, but   Ely was still depressed, weighed down by a feeling of despondency and apathy that he just couldn't seem to shake. He had missed a lot of school lately. His grades, despite his high scores on exams, were beginning to slip. Completing homework assignments seemed trivial and he was falling behind. Normally he would never have let that happen, but at this moment in time he just didn't seem to care. It just didn't seem important.

He was doing better now, though, than he had after that first week following Mr. Seljin's death. For a brief time he had completely withdrawn from everyone, and the only interactions he had had with any of his friends, even his mother, had been accompanied by either anger or indifference.

"Hey, bud."

Jeff's voice interrupted Ely's thoughts, but he didn't turn around. "I don't want to talk, Jeff."

"Sorry," Jeff said as he stood next to Ely, looking out at the tranquil waters of the bay. "Friends don't let friends rot away."

"How did you know I was here?"

"Your mom told me."

Ely got up and put his shoes back on. "I told you I don't want to talk about it."

"Come on, Ely. You have to move on. We all do."

"I don't have to do anything," Ely snapped as he finished tying his shoes.

"It's been over a month. You hardly go to school anymore, your grades have got to be falling, and you've withdrawn from everyone."

"Who gives a shit? I never talked to anyone before. Why does it matter now? I doubt anyone is missing me."

"If that were true I wouldn't be here. Cisco and John both ask about you. And Amanda keeps bugging me as well. She says you're not returning her phone calls and you're avoiding her at school."

Ely sighed wearily, "I can't deal with any of that right now. Can't I just be alone and think without being bugged?" Ely turned his back to Jeff and gazed vacantly at Mt. Rainer, unmoved by its grandeur.

"I know how you felt about him, Ely. I miss him too."

Ely quickly turned around and stepped toward Jeff. "No you don't! You have no idea what he meant to me! You don't know what it's like to be beat up by your father. To be constantly told by your own flesh and blood that you're a worthless piece of shit! You start to believe it after a while. Mr. Seljin made me feel like I was somebody, like I had something to offer. You've always been somebody, the popular kid, the great athlete. You can't know how I feel."

Jeff sighed. "I'm sorry, Ely. I really am. But you're wrong. Just because I haven't experienced what you went through, doesn't mean I don't miss him. He was a father figure to me as well, something I too have never had. I miss him just as much as you. Everyone does."

This time it was Ely's turn to sigh, as Jeff's words began to sink in, penetrating the wall of anger and self-pity that Ely had built around himself.   He shook his head and looked away. "I'm sorry, Jeff. I know you're right. Besides, you're the last person I should be angry at."

Jeff walked over and stood next to him and together they looked out over the bay. "It's okay, Ely."

"I wish he had been my father," Ely whispered. "I'd rather have had him for a father even if he had to die, than to have my real father…who's still alive," he added bitterly. "I just miss him. I feel so empty."

"I know. Me too." Jeff looked at Ely. "You know, it's funny, but I keep hearing him yell things in my head."

"Me too." Ely smiled, remembering all the catch phrases that Mr. Seljin was so fond of.

"How about this one. 'Pain is temporary. Pride is forever'."

Ely laughed. "Yup, that was one of his favorites. I like this one. 'Square wheels stack fine but they don't roll worth a damn.'"

"I still don't even know what that means," Jeff snorted. "What about this one, 'Mess with the best…'"

"…get pinned like the rest," they said in unison, laughing together. Ely paused a moment, then added, "I think my favorite is a question he asked me once. 'How do you know what you're capable of if you don't ever test yourself?' "

"That sounds like something he would say."

That's when it clicked for Ely. That's when he knew what he needed to do. He would test himself, he would find out what he was truly capable of. Ely didn't say anything, he just smiled, new energy lighting up his face. He felt as if he were suddenly released from a prison, the one he had built around himself, the walls of despondency broken by a new resolve.

"What is it?" Jeff asked, sensing the change in Ely.

"Nothing. A work in progress. I'll tell you later. Thanks for coming out here."

"No problem. Are you ready to come and join the living?"

Ely didn't respond. He just looked out at the beautiful sunset. The sun had nearly disappeared behind the trees and it was getting dark. But the sun wasn't giving up so easily. Bright pink tendrils stretched across the darkening sky, casting shimmering shards of light across the calm waters of the bay. "I find it so peaceful here," Ely said, as he watched the final play of light give way to night.

"Will you hold me?" Jeff asked, his voice dramatically plaintive.

Ely elbowed Jeff in the side. "Shut up."

They stood for a while, both immersed in the peaceful beauty of their surroundings, and lost in their own thoughts and images of Mr. Seljin. But now they were smiling, and Ely, for the first time since his death, felt like he was going to get through it.

FOUR MONTHS LATER

A rhythmic clanking sounded from Ely's barn. It was an early July morning and despite the rising sun the air was still brisk with the chill of night. The barn sat in a field, hugged by thick patches of tall grasses and weeds, its large double door ajar. The old barn had seen better days. Only remnants of its red paint remained, chipped and peeling over the worn gray of the exposed cedar. Rays of sunlight broke through cracks in the wood, casting fingers of golden light that danced inside like a laser show.

One such beam of light illuminated the rhythmic movement of Ely's dumbbells as he repeatedly lifted them up and down from an inclined bench, the heavy metal plates crashing together loudly as Ely brought the dumbbells together at the top of the extension. An old worn wrestling mat lay splayed across the barn floor. In the corner a hundred pound punching bag swayed lazily back and forth, remnants of kinetic energy left from Ely's recent bag work.

And that was just part of Ely's daily Routine. Every morning he would get up, eat a bowl of steel cut oats with honey, and wash it down with cold water. Then he would go into the barn to work out. His workout usually consisted of two minutes on the punching bag followed by a set with the dumbbells, or sit-ups, push-ups, or pull-ups, followed again by another two minutes on the bag. His sets were always to burn out, until he couldn't do anymore. He would do this for thirty minutes before he spent another thirty minutes shadow wrestling on the mat. He generally would start off slow, moving through various moves as if he were wrestling a shadow, focusing on the precise movements that would make the move perfect. Then he would pick up the pace until he could do the move so quickly that it became second nature. After thirty minutes of this he would go for a run. At first he could only run a mile before he had to stop. But that was three months ago. He was now up to three miles a day and his goal was to be up to five miles a day by the end of the summer.

Jeff had been working with him as well. A couple days a week Jeff would come over and they would work together on various moves. Ely still outweighed Jeff by a hundred pounds, but it didn't really matter. Jeff was so adept, and so strong, that he was able to work on proper movement and positioning despite the weight difference. On the days when Ely wanted the experience of actually wrestling someone, they would bring Cisco over.

It was difficult at first for Ely to maintain this new regimen. The early mornings, the new diet, the workouts….his mind and body didn't always want to cooperate. He would often wake up sore and tired and it took all of his willpower to force himself out of bed to do it all over again. On the mornings when he felt like quitting, he would just look up at the ceiling and read the quote that he had posted there…*How do you know what you're capable of if you don't ever test yourself?* And that was all it took.

Maintaining his diet proved to be the hardest part of his training. Luckily his mother wanted to be a part of it. She not only supported him, but she joined him on his diet. It helped Ely tremendously knowing that they were doing it together. Ely read book after book about health and nutrition, and once he felt like he knew everything there was to know, he created a diet plan for them both. After a week he was already tired of tuna and spinach salads, egg white and spinach omelets, dry unsalted chicken breast, and plain old water. But after a month he had lost thirty pounds, and his mother had lost fifteen. Then it started getting easier. He was feeling better, stronger, healthier, and his body was adapting to the workouts.

As his body got healthier, so did his mind. He had rekindled his relationship with Amanda, and although they had been taking things slowly, and he didn't really know the exact status of their relationship, he did know that they were more than friends. He didn't want to admit it to himself, but he was afraid to take it any further, the risk of rejection ever present in his mind.

Amanda was content for now to take things slowly as well. She gave him some space, concerned that too much pressure might push him away. And with the combination of their own idiosyncratic insecurities, it was no wonder that their relationship was moving at a snail's pace. It was also clear to Amanda that Ely was on a mission, and the last thing she wanted to do was throw emotional and hormonal wrenches at him while he was concentrating on his goal, to make the varsity wrestling team and place in the state tournament. That was his goal, a promise he had made to Mr. Seljin, and to himself, and Amanda did not want to be the distraction that got in his way. Besides, she would rather just let the pieces fall where they may than force something that possibly wasn't meant to be. But the hard part was that she felt maybe it *was* meant to be. She thoroughly enjoyed his company and there was no other guy that she wanted to be with. They hung out often, spending evenings doing homework, running together on the weekends, or just relaxing at her house to a movie. But they had yet to kiss, let alone take their 'friendship' to the next level. But she felt that he was worth the wait.

The summer was a blur of activity, days filled with running, lifting, wrestling, working at the book store, and hanging out with Amanda or Jeff and the guys. By the end of August Ely had lost nearly fifty pounds and he was weighing in at 215. He had to admit, he was looking pretty good. He was still big mind you, but not BIG, and the thought of putting on a singlet was no longer anathema to him. And not only was he a lot stronger, but Jeff and Cisco had taught him a lot over the summer. With his improved skills, increased energy, strength, and stamina, he was beginning to feel that he just might win some matches. But the most important result of all his efforts was the fact that he was gaining some confidence. He was no longer the pessimistic fat kid who loved to host his own *pity parties,* as Jeff loved to call them.

When wrestling season started his senior year, Ely had never felt such a strong dichotomy of emotions. On the one hand he was dreading the day, knowing full well that his thoughts would inevitably drift to Mr. Seljin. How could they not? He couldn't even hear a coach's whistle and not think of him. The smell of a wrestling mat, everything about the sport, stirred up memories that were constant reminders of Mr. Seljin's absence. But on the other hand he was excited to start practice. He was ready to test himself, to put his hard work into action and see what he was made of. The start of wrestling season was definitely a double edged sword. For although the memories carried with them a sense of loss, they were also a source of inspiration, a way to honor Mr. Seljin by helping him focus on his goal.

That first day of practice came and went more quickly than Ely had expected. The entire day was an amalgam of sounds and emotions. And he wasn't the only one experiencing the poignancy of the day. It was hard for most of the wrestlers to imagine the start of the season without Mr. Seljin. But they were lucky to have Mr. Jackson, their assistant coach, take over the program. He was a good guy, well liked and respected, and he made the transition much easier. He was an experienced wrestler in his own right, and had learned a lot from Mr. Seljin, running practices the same, and using similar techniques as his predecessor. As it turned out, it wouldn't be the first day of wrestling that would pose a problem for Ely. It would be the first day of challenges, an event that brought Ely more anxiety than he had wished.

When the first morning of challenges came, he awoke early, ready to tackle the day and the ensuing emotions head on. He jumped out of bed, quickly dressed, then went into the kitchen where his mom was preparing breakfast for both of them, an omelet made with egg whites, turkey sausage, low-fat cheese, and spinach. He chased it all down with a hot mug of green tea and honey, then proceeded to pack his lunch, a healthy meal of chicken breast, rice, and more spinach, in the form of a salad.

Like Ely, his mother was also showing the benefits of the changes they had each made in their diets. She was down to a hundred and eighty pounds, fifty pounds lighter than her previous weight. Her face had thinned out, revealing more of her bone structure. She smiled more and moved with a lively bounce that displayed her new found energy and sense of purpose.

Jeff would arrive in a half an hour to pick him up, so Ely kissed his mom on the cheek, grabbed his bag, and ran into the barn for some quick sets on the bench. The barn was a place of solace for Ely. It had been his sanctuary, his healing place, and every time he opened the rickety double doors a sense of peace came over him. The smell of the mat, the sound of the dumbbells clinking together, the creaking noise the bag made as it swayed back and forth…those were the sounds that gave him a sense of serenity. It was here where he had begun to heal.

A honking horn interrupted Ely's flat bench rep and he heaved the heavy bar back into its resting place with a grunt. He sat up and looked around the barn. "Here we go," he whispered to himself. Then he grabbed his backpack and headed outside.

Jeff was there in his Honda and Ely leaped into the passenger seat. Ely looked at Jeff and Jeff looked back at him, his expression serious, but there was a slight upward curve at the corners of his lips which belied his stoic look. "You ready to do this?"

"Yup. I'm ready."

"Good," Jeff said as he pressed the gas pedal down and tore out of the driveway, leaving a trail of dust in the air behind him.

"What were you doing in the barn?" Jeff asked.

"Just a quick workout."

"At six thirty in the morning? The day of your big challenge?" he asked, raising his eyebrows.

"Yep."

Jeff paused and smiled. "You're the man."

"I think I'm ready. I must admit, I'm pretty nervous to take on Adam. But I've got to make varsity this year. My plan won't work if I can't do that."

"You'll beat him. You've worked really hard, and besides, Cisco said you've gotten better than Adam."

"I know he's said that, but that's just it, he might just be saying it to make me feel better, maybe make me feel more confident."

"No way. Besides, don't forget I've wrestled you as well, and I've seen Adam wrestle. You're better than him. Ely, he's not that good. He's just big, strong, and intimidating. Once you get past that, and use the skills you've learned, you'll kick his ass."

"You really think so?"

"Yup." Jeff grinned and slapped the steering wheel in excitement. "Oh man, I can't wait to see his face when you beat him. It's going to be priceless."

Ely looked out the window as he digested Jeff's words. After a minute or so he looked back at Jeff. "Hey, Jeff, do you think I could ever win state?"

Jeff didn't answer right away. "I don't know, Ely. It's a lofty goal. But here is what I do know. There is no way you could've worked any harder than you have. So whether you beat Adam, whether you make it to state, whether you place at state, whether you win state...none of that really matters. What matters is that whatever happens you can rest assured in knowing that you did your best. Do I think you can win state? Why not? Anything is possible when you apply determination, hard work, and steadfast will, and you seem to have all three traits in great quantities."

"Damn, dude, have my linguistic skills rubbed off on you? You sound downright pedantic."

"Downright what?"

Ely laughed. "Never mind. Thanks, Jeff, I appreciate the vote of confidence. Now let's stop talking and crank up some tunes. You have any Mozart or Bach?" Ely asked smiling, knowing full well he did not.

"Yeah, right. How about some White Zombie?"

They both smiled as Jeff leaned over and turned up the volume. The heavy metal rhythm blared as they both sang along, shaking their heads and pounding on the dashboard to the beat. They drove on, enjoying the camaraderie of their early morning ritual, its familiar sounds and movements dissolving any remnants of Ely's anxiety.

But when Ely got to school, he could hardly concentrate on anything other than the upcoming challenges. He went from class to class, barely conscious of the lessons. He had to beat Adam. If he didn't earn the varsity spot there was no way he could make it to the state tournament, let alone win it. *One step at a time* he kept telling himself as his mind jumped to the future where he couldn't help imagining himself wrestling at the state tournament in the Tacoma Dome, or standing at the podium holding his first place bracket. He knew it was dangerous to think too far ahead. He had to focus on making varsity, and not get distracted by what might happen afterward. He spent all day locked in this mental battle, trying to keep himself from thinking too far ahead, while forcing himself to focus on all the hard work he had done over the last six months and how he would beat Adam, step by step, round by round. He thought about everything he had learned from Mr. Seljin, and mentally reviewed the general plan that Jeff and Cisco had helped him devise to beat Adam. By the end of the day that plan had completely occupied his thoughts. But when the challenge came, no amount of preparation could keep the nerves at bay.

Seventy three wrestlers were lined up against the wall in a stacked weight line. The lightweights were on one end while the heavyweight wrestlers were on the other end. Coach Jackson addressed everyone while their assistant coach, Lars Anders, stood behind him. Lars was short and stocky, with a wrestler's physique. It was easy to tell that at one point he had probably been a pretty formidable wrestler, but now, in his mid-forties, he had added a bit of excess weight to his sturdy frame. And although he looked as if thirty seconds on the mat would do him in, he was knowledgeable and everyone really seemed to like him.

"All right everyone," coach Jackson began, "listen carefully. We've been practicing now for two weeks. Today and tomorrow are challenge days. Coach Anders and I will be refereeing all of the scheduled challenges. You have several options. You can work on moves on the empty mat or you can watch the challenges. Remember, this is for the varsity spot this week. Coach Anders, who's up first?"

Coach Anders looked on his clip board. "Looks like we have Luke Meyers and Evan Johnson on my mat. On your mat we have Jason Kendrick and Levi Forland."

"Okay, let's get going. We will end the challenges today with our heavyweight challenge." Coach Jackson looked over at Ely at the back of the heavyweight line. "Ely, you still want to challenge Adam for the varsity spot?"

"Yes, sir," Ely answered.

Adam was sitting at the front of the line, the position reserved for current varsity wrestlers. He snickered quietly and elbowed one of his friends sitting next to him. A few other wrestlers chuckled as if that were the most ridiculous thing they had ever heard.

Ely glanced uncertainly at Cisco who was sitting near him at the head of the next weight class. Cisco gave him a reassuring nod and a thumbs up.

"You got it," Coach Jackson said. "Let's get things going."

With that said, everyone scattered as wrestlers prepared for their matches and others practiced various moves on the only available mat.

The challenges went by quickly, just as the day had. Ely wanted to keep a sweat up, but not get too tired, so he shadow wrestled, slowly going through various moves as he mentally prepared himself for his upcoming match. Then he heard it…

"Ely, you're up!" Coach Jackson shouted.

Ely looked up and saw that Adam already had his sweats off and was shaking out his arms on the side of the mat. He couldn't help but notice how big the guy was. His arms were huge, every inch of them covered with dense muscle. Adam returned Ely's look with a defiant glare. Ely looked away and moved to his side of the mat where Jeff, Cisco, and John were already waiting for him. His sweatpants were already off so as he approached them he took off his sweatshirt and snapped on his head gear.

"Now you listen to me," Cisco said as he grabbed his shoulders and brought him in close. "I've been wrestling with you the last six months, and believe me, you can beat him."

John smacked him on the shoulder. "You got him, bud. Take it to him."

Jeff stepped in front of Ely and got in his face. "You can take this guy," he growled seriously. "You know that, right?"

"Yup."

"Get pissed. Use your anger. Channel it into every move. Use it to beat down any doubts that enter your mind. You're a warrior. It's that simple."

"I'm a warrior," Ely repeated.

"Good. You go in there and rip his head off. He's just an obstacle in your path. What did Leonardo da Vinci say about obstacles?"

Ely smiled. He had told Jeff one day that this quote was his favorite. "He said every obstacle must yield to stern resolve."

Jeff smiled. "You got it. Now go get 'em!"

Ely walked out onto the mat. He was wearing a t-shirt and sweats while Adam was wearing a tight singlet, looking every bit like the varsity wrestler. They came together at the center of the mat and Adam looked at him and smiled.

Coach Jackson was there and after one look to make sure that his timers were ready he addressed them both. "You guys ready?" They both nodded. "Okay, gentlemen, shake hands." They shook hands and then Coach Jackson stepped back and blew the whistle.

ROUND ONE

Both wrestlers slowly circled each other. Then Adam moved in confidently and tied up with Ely. Ely shook him off and stepped back a bit, not excited about tying up with someone who was stronger. Cisco had told Ely that Adam would try to tie up and attempt to use his upper body strength to control the match. So they had worked out a plan.

Adam rushed forward again, his hands out and reaching again for the tie up. Ely, expecting the move, reached out as well, but at the last minute he dropped low and shot forward, attempting a double leg takedown. The move was textbook perfect and in a blink Adam found himself on the mat with Ely behind him.

"Yes! Nice takedown, Ely!"

John smiled and smacked Jeff on the arm. "Dude, that was perfect!"

"You bet it was. I worked with him on that for hours."

Back on the mat Ely was struggling to keep Adam, now enraged, on the mat. Within fifteen seconds Adam was up and had earned his escape. The score was now two to one. They circled each other again. This time Adam was more cautious, watching Ely warily, not as confident as he had been before the start of the match. Adam quickly lunged in and tied up with Ely, roughly shaking him with his powerful arms, trying to thrown him off balance while looking for an opening. Ely, momentarily stunned by the strength of the attack, hesitated, giving Adam enough time to set up his move. He jerked his arm forward and slightly lifted Ely's head, setting up the dreaded head and arm, a favorite of the heavyweight wrestlers. Ely felt it coming, but was too slow to duck under the arm to counter it. Horrified, Ely felt his body flying through the air.

"Roll him through!" Jeff yelled.

Ely, moving on instinct, wrapped his arms tightly around Adam's body as he soared through the air. They both hit hard but Ely used Adam's momentum and rolled him all the way through. Ely popped his head out from Adam's grip and came up on top, earning two points for the takedown.

Jeff, John, and Cisco were screaming like maniacs, and at this point there was quite the crowd assembling around the edges of the mat as word of the current score had quickly spread.

"Four to one, baby!" Cisco screamed.

Within seconds the whistle blew to end round one.

Ely stood up and shook out his arms. He felt good. He was tired, but that was to be expected. His eyes, radiating determined anger, focused on Adam as if he were evil incarnate, remembering the physical and mental pain that Adam had inflicted on him. But, at least for now, the tables had turned; he was winning by three points. *Don't get too ahead of yourself,* he silently reprimanded himself. There were still two rounds left, and a lot could happen in two rounds.

"Nice job, Ely!" Jeff screamed.

Adam won the coin toss and chose the down position.

ROUND TWO

As the whistle blew Adam took off like a rocket. Ely held onto him and managed to keep him in the down position, but it was a struggle. They moved across the mat like scurrying ants as Adam tried various moves hoping to get an escape or reversal. Ely defended most of the time, but he did try to break him down on several occasions. But Adam was just too strong and when Ely went to hip into him and break his arm down at the elbow, it felt like he was hitting the knotted trunk of an oak tree. No matter how hard he tried, he just couldn't break him down to the mat. After thirty seconds or so Adam was able to break away and stand up for his escape. The score was now four to two.

This time Adam didn't hesitate. He moved in quick, hoping to take Ely off guard, which he did. He under hooked Ely's arm, lifted up hard, leaned back and threw Ely through the air. Landing hard on his back, it took Ely a second to realize what had happened. But luckily he had worked with Cisco on this move as well, and even though Adam had caught him in one of his favorite throws, Ely had worked hard on how to counter it. No sooner had Ely landed than he bridged up hard, using his neck and legs to lift his back, and Adam, off the mat. Then he pushed his arm through and spun around to his belly, countering the potentially deadly throw by giving Adam just the takedown points and not the near fall, points he would have earned if he had kept Ely on his back for longer than two seconds.

"Damn! Now it's tied up!" Jeff muttered in frustration.

"No problem. Ely's in better shape. He'll get him in round three," Cisco said.

On the mat, Adam broke Ely down several times but couldn't seem to turn him for any near fall points. The crowd of wrestlers were all screaming now, moved by the excitement of the match.

Ely was sweating profusely and sucking in air, but he was able to constantly keep his body moving, preventing Adam from any near fall moves and nearly getting several escapes in his own right. Then the whistle blew ending round two.

Adam and Ely stood up slowly. They both looked tired, but Ely was the first up, pacing around the mat and shaking his arms out, trying to bring life back to his tired muscles. He was tired, but Adam looked worse. Ely knew that Adam was not a hard worker, relying instead on natural ability and strength. And he also knew that he had not spent the last six months preparing for this one event, getting up early every morning to run and work out. That knowledge alone gave him the confidence he needed to go into round three with the thought that he could beat him. As he looked at Adam drag his tired body up off the mat, Ely finally realized what Jeff felt in every match. Confidence. He saw Adam and knew that he could beat him. Sel had always talked about how the 'process' was what mattered, not the result. That if you showed up every day, worked as hard as you could, that things would fall into place, and eventually you would get the results you were looking for. Now he knew what he meant, and he smiled as he thought how much Sel would be enjoying this match.

"Come on, Ely! Shake it out! One more round!" Jeff yelled.

"He looks good," Cisco said. "You can do it, buddy!"

Jeff smiled and looked at Cisco and John. "He's going to take this punk."

On the mat, Coach Jackson approached Ely. "Alright, Ely, its third round and it's your choice."

Ely looked over at Jeff who signaled for Ely to take the down position. The down position was the scoring position. Earning points for escapes or reversals was generally easier than turning someone for near fall points, especially if they were a good wrestler. But it was a risk at the heavyweight level. Some of the guys were so strong and heavy, that getting away was an unlikely occurrence. And if you ended up on your back, that kind of weight could make it really difficult to not get pinned. But Jeff and Ely had talked about this in case he was given the choice third round. They both felt that he would be in better shape than Adam, and they had constantly drilled defensive moves, as well as offensive moves from that position. Ely dropped to his knees, his eyes intense as he went over the moves in his head.

Coach Jackson approached the wrestlers. "Bottom man set?" Ely nodded his head. "Top man, take your position." Then he felt Adam's iron grip on his elbow and belly. And then the whistle blew.

ROUND THREE

Ely erupted like a volcano, moving so quickly he caught Adam by surprise. Adam was barely able to hold on to him as Ely bolted upright, twisting and turning as he tried to break away. Adam, fearing he would lose his grip, pushed Ely out of bounds.

Coach Jackson blew the whistle and they both moved back to the center of the mat.

Jeff smacked the mat hard trying to get Ely's attention. "Ely! Do it again!"

Ely glanced at Jeff and nodded his head before he dropped back to referee's position. Within seconds the whistle blew again and Ely exploded to his feet. Grunting and growling, he focused all of his energy on trying to break Adam's grip and turn into him. Ely was hoping to earn his escape and bring the score to five to four. They danced around the mat for a while but Adam couldn't hold onto him. Ely arched his back, broke his loosening grip, and spun into Adam, earning his one point escape.

They continued circling each other, their chests heaving as their tired muscles demanded oxygen.

"He's up by one!" John yelled. "What should we do, Jeff?"

"Take it to him! Don't stop moving! Wear him out!" Jeff yelled as he nervously jumped around on the edge of the mat.

Ely lunged toward Adam, but this time Adam used the last of his strength to take the initiative. As Ely moved forward, Adam dropped low and shot his body forward and to the side, hoping to snag Ely's leg and take him down with a single leg takedown. Ely tried to sprawl, but just wasn't quick enough. Adam spun by him, coming up hard and jerking Ely's leg into the air.

Jeff was now kneeling by the side of the mat, frantically pounding his hands on it. "Damn it!" Push him away! Move out of bounds!" Jeff screamed. His heart felt like it was in his throat. He didn't want to watch, but he also didn't want to look away.

But Ely heard him and did just that. He used his hand to push Adam's head away, while using his arm and his held leg as leverage to try and gain as much distance as he could between Adam and himself. If Adam closed the distance, then he could use pressure, or a leg sweep, or various other ways, to take Ely's only leg out and put him on the mat for a takedown. Ely knew that he couldn't let that happen. So as he pushed his head away, he hopped backwards, moving closer to the edge of the mat. When he was close, he spun around and kicked out with his held leg, launching his body forward and tumbling out of bounds. Adam tried to hang on and follow Ely, but it was no use. Coach Jackson blew the whistle, indicating they were out of bounds.

"That was close," Cisco said to Jeff as he wiped the sweat from his forehead. "What about the arm drag? Adam is tired and it's Ely's best move. He'll walk right into it," Cisco suggested.

"That's what I was thinking," Jeff agreed. "Ely, look at me!" Jeff yelled.

Ely heard him as he was walking back to the center of the mat. As Adam briefly looked down, tired and breathing deeply, Jeff motioned for Ely to do the arm drag, pantomiming the move with Cisco.

Ely, clearly tired, but still moving with confidence, gave an affirmative nod.

Adam and Ely faced each and then the whistle blew. Sluggishly, Adam moved in to tie up with Ely, a move typically used by tired heavyweight wrestlers.

"Ten seconds left!" Coach Thompson yelled.

Adam, hearing Coach Jackson, frantically pushed hard into Ely, hoping to line up his famous head and arm.

"Hit it now!" Jeff screamed.

As Adam pushed forward, Ely grabbed Adam's wrist, stepped quickly to the side while simultaneously gripping the inside of the same arm, under the bicep, and leaning back hard as he jerked the arm forward. The move, perfectly executed, caught Adam completely off guard. His body weight was already leaning forward as he moved in for the tie up. Ely jerked Adam's body forward so hard that his head smacked into the mat, making a sound similar to a cracking whip. Just as Adam hit the mat, Ely quickly spun around his prone body, coming up behind his hips and earning two points for the takedown.

Then the whistle blew and the gym exploded in applause. Ely jumped up with his arms in the air as Jeff, John, and Cisco cheered excitedly. Ely's smile took up his entire face as he locked eyes with Jeff.

"You did it, buddy! You did it!" Jeff shouted.

"Nice job, Ely!" John yelled.

Adam got up slowly and walked to the center of the mat, his head lowered, avoiding eye contact with everyone. Coach Jackson directed Ely to the center of the mat where the two wrestlers shook hands before he lifted Ely's arm into the air in victory. Ely grinned happily, the cheers of his teammates reflecting his own joy.

Cisco stood beside Jeff, smiling with his friend. "Man, I sure wish Mr. Seljin was here to see this."

"Me too, buddy, me too."

Thirteen

Let's fast forward a little. So as a varsity wrestler I did pretty well. I lost some, but I won more, and as I won I continued to learn more about the sport, and more about myself. I worked harder, I studied my opponents, and I researched techniques. When most kids were sleeping I was up running, and with a smile on my face. It was like my drug, I couldn't get enough.

Then, more quickly than I thought possible, the district wrestling tournament arrived. I took second place, which guaranteed me a spot at the regional tournament. Eight months ago I would have been ecstatic with this accomplishment, but not now, now I knew that I could achieve more. Mr. Seljin was right. Once you begin to test yourself…once you begin to really work hard, to achieve your own personal best; that's when you create the mindset, the know how to achieve even more. The phrase, 'It's a vicious cycle' is usually applied to negative experiences, such as physical or emotional abuse, substance abuse, poverty, or crime. But this was a cycle that was not at all negative. I think we need a new term, like 'radical roundabout', or 'circle of awesomeness' to better explain how one positive step can lead to another, then another, making the 'circle' of one's life better and better. The harder I worked, the more I realized what I could do, and the more I realized what I could do, the harder I worked. My outlook became more positive, allowing me to take on even bigger challenges. I think most people have no clue of this simple cycle. They are happy with mediocrity. Now, because of my 'circle of awesomeness', I was not content to be like most people. I wanted to be the best

I could be, and I knew that I would not be satisfied until I really tested myself.

So at the regional tournament I kept pushing myself. I needed to place in the top four in order to continue on to the state tournament at the Tacoma Dome. Now keep in mind, if I placed in the top four in my region that would mean that I was one of the top sixteen best wrestlers in my weight class in the entire state. That in itself would be a great accomplishment for anyone, let alone myself. But I tried to remember what Sel had taught me. Don't worry about things in the future that you can't control, just focus on one match at a time and see where it takes you...you might be surprised. And I was. I took third at the regional tournament, which brought me to my goal, the state wrestling tournament.

Ely Carter

———————————

A green van pulled into the entrance of the Tacoma Dome. Eight Peninsula wrestlers made it to the state tournament and those eight sat in the van along with the two coaches. As they pulled into the driveway, Jeff, who was sitting next to Ely in the back, jabbed his elbow into Ely's side and pointed out the window. On the billboard were the words 'Welcome schools to the state wrestling championships!' Ely smiled excitedly. The van was quiet, everyone either too excited or too nervous to talk. Ely was both, excited to have made it this far, but nervous as well. But he had to admit, he was not as nervous as some of the others. After all, he had already surpassed what most people thought he could do. Most of the others however, including

Jeff, were expected to do well, and that added pressure was enough to get the butterflies flying around in their bellies. Ely was just excited to see how he would stack up to the other regional qualifiers.

The rest of the day was spent weighing in, getting a light breakfast, and then putting on their gear and heading out onto the mats that covered the Dome's massive floor. There were sixteen mats total and the entire Dome was a bustle of activity. Wrestlers from hundreds of teams warmed up while workers, refs, coaches, and scorekeepers moved around like worker ants trying to get everything ready. But Ely didn't notice any of it. He had his headphones on and the sweet notes of Beethoven drowned out the chaos around him, enabling him to slowly stretch, warm up, and prepare for the matches to come.

Ely had already spotted his mother. She was sitting near mat two and nearby was Amanda who had come to watch with a friend of hers.

Once the matches had started, things got even crazier. There were thousands of people in the stands cheering and yelling, wrestlers milling about trying to figure out when their next match was, and coaches scurrying from mat to mat, looking for their wrestlers and trying to organize which coach was going to watch which wrestler.

Jeff won all of his matches that day placing him in the finals. Ely won his first match, and then his second match, putting him in a position to possibly make it to the state finals. He pinned the first kid, catching him in a head and arm and squeezing him tight until he couldn't breathe. Ely knew he would win when he leaned way back and looked at the lights above him, his arms, like a boa constrictor, cinched around his opponent's head and arm as he lifted the wrestler's head. His opponent squirmed and fought, but Ely's weight, now consisting mostly of solid dense muscle, finally broke down his defenses; Ely was able to press his shoulder blades against the mat for over two seconds. The second match was a close one. It came down to round three when Ely scored a point for an escape. The score was now six to five, with Ely down by one point and only fifteen seconds left. But his opponent was tired, and he leaned into Ely with his legs straight and his arms out wide, a position that leaves you open for attack. Ely was thankful for all his hard work, all his early morning runs, as he still had some energy left, and he used it to launch into his favorite move, the arm drag. The guy didn't know what hit him. It was not a common move for heavyweight wrestlers since it required a certain amount of speed and finesse, traits not typically prevalent with the big guys. It was the same move that he had used on Adam, and it worked like a charm this time as well. Ely scored a takedown, earning two points, and winning the match by one point.

When it came time for the semi-final match Ely was now nervous. He couldn't believe he had come this far, and now that he realized that he had a chance to actually be in the state finals, his stomach began to churn with nervous energy. To be honest, he had really not expected to make it to the semifinals. Now there was only one opponent and six minutes separating him from possibly being the top wrestler in the state.

He had never been more nervous about anything in his life. Luckily, once the whistle blew, training and instinct took over, converting nervous energy to focused energy. His opponent was tough, really tough. He was big, strong, fast, and knowledgeable. Ely wrestled well, countering his moves, and executing some perfect moves himself. But in the end he lost by one point. He was down in the third round and all he had to do was get an escape to tie it up. But every time he tried to stand up his opponent broke him down, immediately applying head pressure and working for a two on one or a half nelson. It went on like this for an entire minute with no wrestler scoring a point. Ely could hear his teammates screaming. He could hear his coaches yelling at him. The sounds and their movements seemed to be in slow motion as he focused intently on working to his base, standing up, and getting away. Every time he was knocked down he would try again, never stopping, grunting and growling his way through the third round. No matter how hard he worked, his opponent relentlessly matched his own intensity. When the whistle finally blew, ending the match, Ely stood up proudly. He didn't want to show that he was tired. And at the same time he wanted to show respect to his opponent who had earned the victory.

It had been a tough loss, losing by just one point, but it wasn't the most difficult part of the tournament. Ely now had to battle his way through the loser's bracket on the second day to wrestle for either third and fourth, or fifth and sixth. Ely's goal that day was to just focus on each round, one at a time, and do the best he could, to try and not think about the matches, his opponents, or the possible outcomes. He lost himself in his music and concentrated on every move he was going to unleash on his opponents. The tactic worked. One round after another, Ely powered through his opponents and ended up taking third place. He won his next match by a major decision, placing him in a position to take third or fourth place. That match was another close one. It came down to round three and the score was tied four to four. Both wrestlers were standing and Ely performed another brilliant arm drag, taking his opponent down in the last few seconds for two points. He had never been more proud in his entire life. He was the third best wrestler in the state, all because he made a decision, a conscious decision to not be a victim, to go out and tackle life. Every step of this new path had given him new confidence, and each ounce of confidence had allowed him to access his abilities and to test himself further.

The matches had been an endless dance of moves and counter moves, the instinctive actions that were the result of hard work and training. He could hardly remember any specific moments. Yet the time he spent on the awards stand was burned into his mind. The screaming from the crowd, the flashes of cameras, the smell of the mats mingled with the sweat of his fellow wrestlers standing with him on the platform became permanently etched into his consciousness.

In the crowded stands Mary Carter looked down at her son standing on the third place stand. She wiped the tears from her eyes and cheered wildly for her son, this marvelous boy who had, for the last year, been her inspiration. She marveled at his newfound dedication. He had taught her that anything was possible. She had lost almost sixty pounds and was feeling better than she had in a long time.

"Here you go," a voice came from her left. Mary looked up to the bench behind her and saw a man handing her a tissue. He smiled as he gestured for her to take it. The man was large with a solid bulk around his mid-section. But if you had just looked at his face you would not have guessed that he weighed two hundred pounds. His defined jaw belied his weight, and his chocolate brown eyes softened his biker look defined by his black and gray goatee and shaved head. He looked strong and powerful, but when he smiled he looked like a cuddly teddy bear.

"Thank you."

"Sure. One of them must be your son," he said as he indicated the awards stand below them.

"Yes, third place. His name is Ely."

"You must be very proud."

Mary laughed. "You have no idea."

"My name is Bob." He smiled warmly and presented his hand to Mary, who took it and smiled in return.

"Nice to meet you."

"I bet your husband is proud as well," the man said.

Mary hesitated and smiled awkwardly. "Well, he hasn't been around in a while. We're divorced."

"Me too," he said. Their smiles lingered for a moment before Mary shyly turned her eyes back onto the podium where her son stood.

Ely was staring into the crowd in the stands, his entire face a massive smile. He looked up and saw his mom cheering wildly for him. Amanda was there too, jumping up and down and screaming his name. Ely gazed into the crowd, hoping to take mental snap shots of the moment so he would never forget it. The only thing that was missing was Mr. Seljin. But he didn't let that thought sully the moment. He couldn't let it, for as surely as the sun sets he knew that Mr. Seljin would never have approved of such morose thoughts while he stood on that stand. He knew that he would want him to enjoy the moment, to soak it up like a sponge. And that was exactly what he did. He created a memory scrapbook in his mind, complete with photos and captions. This was an event that he would never forget.

***

Five months later Ely found himself in another situation that had again kick started the butterflies. He was sitting in the front row of the school auditorium with Jeff, Cisco, John, Amanda, and others from his graduating class. He wiped the sweat from his forehead and he reached up to adjust his tie, hoping to loosen it up just enough to give him some relief from the heat building up under his button up shirt.

"It's okay," Amanda whispered as she rubbed his knee. "You'll do fine."

Ely smiled nervously. He wasn't so sure. It was the night of their high school graduation ceremony and the gym was packed with students, parents, teachers, and friends. The graduating class all sat in chairs on the gym floor while the bleachers were filled with parents, friends, and family members.

Mr. Youngchild, the principal, stood at the podium addressing the crowd. "I'd like to thank you all for coming tonight to share this wonderful occasion. It's a great opportunity to celebrate the accomplishments of this year's graduating class. I know you didn't all come here to hear me speak so I'd like to pass the microphone over to this year's valedictorian, Ely Carter."

The students and parents clapped and cheered as Ely stood up from his chair. His friends in the front row, and others sitting nearby clapped even more excitedly for Ely, screaming his name and cheering him on. Ely took a deep breath and walked to the podium.

In the audience Mary Carter clapped enthusiastically for her son. Bob, the big guy she had met at the wrestling tournament, sat next to her, cheering and whistling loudly. As it turned out, Bob was from North Kitsap, which was pretty close to Gig Harbor. He had a nephew that had wrestled in the state tournament and he had come to watch him wrestle, meeting Mary in the process. They had struck up an easy conversation that day that had progressed to an invitation to go out for a cup of coffee. Since then they had begun seeing each other on a regular basis and were now officially 'dating'. When the applause subsided Bob reached over and held her hand, smiling at her as she wiped a lone tear from the corner of her eye.

Ely stood before the podium, took several deep breaths, and began his speech. "I'm glad you could all make it here tonight," then he took another deep breath, hoping to push down the nervous lump that was forming in his throat. "Sorry. I'm not very good at speeches."

"You got it, Ely!" someone yelled from the audience. More yells of encouragement rang out from other students, mingling with the cheers of Jeff, Amanda, and the rest of his friends in the front row. Ely smiled and continued. "I would like to start off by telling you a story. It begins in front of an old run-down store. A fourteen year old boy is sitting on a curb, his head in his hands, hiding his face. You see, his nose is broken and bleeding, and his eyes are a bit black and blue. He reaches under his sweatshirt to grab hold of something hidden under the old worn out garment, when a young kid, around his age, comes over and asks him if he's okay."

Jeff shifted uncomfortably in his seat wondering where this was going. Amanda leaned over and whispered in his ear. "Do you know about this?"

Jeff shook his head as Ely continued.

"The young boy introduced himself as Jeff, and you all know him as Jeff Hanson." At the mention of Jeff's name everyone in the graduating class screamed and shouted, but not Jeff, who sat still, smiling awkwardly, unsure about where Ely's story was going. "You see, that young fat boy with the bloody nose was me. I can still remember what Jeff said to me. He said, 'My name's Jeff. I don't recognize you. Are you from around here?' I answered shyly that I had just moved here a couple weeks ago. He went on to ask if I was going to Key Peninsula Middle School. It was the day before school was to start and I didn't know what to say, so I said 'Yes'. At that moment I simply wanted him to go away. I had other things on my mind. Then he said a few simple words, but for me they were very profound. He said, 'In that case, it looks like I'll see you tomorrow.'" Ely paused for a moment to gather himself. Everyone in the audience was deathly silent, listening intently to Ely's story, wondering where he was going with it. "You see, Jeff showed me an act of kindness that day when no one else would. Jeff, who is now my best friend, whom I've never told this to, or anyone else for that matter, literally saved my life that day four years ago. Jeff went back to his car and brought me out a towel from his backpack to wipe my face. He said to me, 'You can have it. I'll see you tomorrow.' Then he turned around and went back to his car to join his family. I can still hear him say those words in my head. '*I'll see you tomorrow*.' What Jeff didn't know was that under my sweatshirt was my dad's gun. I hadn't really planned on *anyone seeing me tomorrow."*

Jeff sat frozen in his chair, staring at Ely through the blur of his tears. Amanda reached over and gripped his knee, her face reflecting a mix of emotions, as tears welled up in her own eyes. In the stands Mary gasped and held her hands over her mouth, trying vainly to control her own emotions. Bob said nothing; he simply put his big arm around her and pulled her in close.

Ely paused again as he struggled to maintain his composure. He glanced at Jeff, and managed a smile as he directed his gaze back up to the rest of the audience, the silence in the room broken only by muffled sniffles and the nervous shuffling of feet.

"I am standing here today because of someone who did something seemingly insignificant. Tonight I would like to take this opportunity to thank Jeff for showing me kindness when very few did. I would like to thank him for saving my life. His words didn't erase the problems in my life, but at the time they were enough to hold onto, providing me with the distraction of hope. It wasn't much, but it was enough to make me put the gun away. I've never told anyone this story before. As things got better for me I felt like it wasn't necessary. But there's an important message here that's worthy of sharing, especially now, before we all go our separate ways after graduation. Simply put, it's important for all of us to realize that everything we do can make a difference in the lives of others. Something that seems small and insignificant to you could mean the world to someone else. You might even save a life.

A simple smile, a friendly greeting, a small act of kindness can have an unexpectedly positive impact on someone. Conversely, thoughtless and mean behaviors, like a shove in the halls, name calling, malicious teasing, bullying, or merely ignoring someone can, over time, have devastating consequences for them. When you leave here today, think about that. Everything you say and do *does* make a difference in people's lives."

Mary was crying openly now, tears pouring down her cheeks as Bob continued to hold her tight.

Ely took another deep breath before continuing. "There is one more thing I would like to say before we all move on to the next stage of our lives. But first, would all the teachers in this room, including the audience, please stand up." Ely paused as people looked around, wondering what was coming next. "Please, all the teachers here stand up." Slowly, the teachers that were sitting behind him stood up, followed by a handful of educators in the audience who hesitantly followed suit. "I want every student to look at those who are standing here today. These individuals are unsung heroes. We tend to look up to firefighters, police officers, and the soldiers who defend our country, as well we should. They all deserve our respect and praise. But we also must not forget the silent heroes among us, those who are in the trenches each day, nurturing, mentoring, and doing their best to educate those who will one day make decisions not only for themselves, but for our country. There are few jobs where an employee is responsible for up to a hundred and fifty students each day, many of whom would rather be elsewhere. Then they are given the daunting task of educating these students, often finding it necessary to take on the additional role of friend, counselor, coach, or surrogate parent. And then, after spending eight to ten hours at school each day, our teachers continue their jobs at home, planning lessons, correcting papers, contacting parents, or even attending classes or seminars. They give their sweat and their hearts to all of us and they deserve our gratitude." Ely paused and took a sip from the water bottle that he had brought, providing a moment of silence for students and parents to digest his words as they looked around at the teachers who continued to stand self-consciously. "I would not only like to thank all those who are now standing here, but I would also like to take this opportunity to dedicate this night to a teacher who saved my life as much as Jeff and my mom did. I want to thank Mr. Seljin, who as you all know, passed away last year in a car accident." Ely paused as he tried to keep his voice steady. "I want to thank him for believing in me and for giving me the confidence and the skills that I needed, that have helped me achieve things I never thought I could. Mr. Seljin, if you can hear me, you are the dad that I never had." Ely took a deep breath as his voice again began to abandon him. *Just a few more minutes* he told himself.

  "I would like to conclude by asking everyone to give a big round of applause not only for our teachers, but our parents, our friends, and anyone else who has helped us overcome the fears and obstacles of our lives. May we all be worthy of their effort and dedication." Ely held his arms out to the audience, then turned and spread his arms to encompass the teachers behind him. "Thank you...thank you all very much."

There was a brief moment of silence as everyone was unsure if he was really finished. Finally Jeff stood, followed by Amanda, and they began to clap. Within moments the gym exploded in a deafening sound of cheers and applause. Ely smiled and looked out into the crowd, then made more direct eye contact with Jeff, Cisco, John, Amanda, and his mother, all of whom returned his smile tenfold.

***

Fifteen years later a solitary sparrow flitted across an August sky over the small country cemetery in Longbranch, darting in and out of a copse of fir trees before landing softly on one of the gravestones. Etched into the stone were the words, 'Here lies Rick Seljin, a man who dedicated his life to the service of others. To many he was a teacher, to some he was a friend, but to all he was a hero.'

The voice of a young boy interrupted the sparrow's reverie. "Papa, what are we doing here?"

Ely Carter, now thirty three, walked hand and hand with his six year old son. They stopped before the gravestone and Ely looked about, breathing in the clean air and the serenity of the scene. He looked down at his boy who was waiting expectantly for an answer. "I want to give an old friend something."

"Who, Papa? Who's buried here?"

They stood still for a moment, looking at the gravestone, the sparrow adamantly maintaining its perch. "A long time ago someone helped me. He died when I was young and this is where he was buried. I want to give him a gift."

Ely reached under his arm and removed a hardback book. The sparrow fluttered away as he walked slowly forward and placed the book gently on the top of the grave marker.

"Do you miss him, Papa?"

"I miss him very much." The little boy, sensing his father's sadness, was quiet as they turned around and walked hand in hand back to their car. The little sparrow watched from the branch of a nearby fir tree, and seeing that the intruders had finally left, flew back to its resting spot next to the book. The book was a hardcover fantasy book, the cover depicting a mighty warrior in silver armor holding aloft a glowing sword, and in the background a city of white stone glittered in the sun. The title of the book was, 'The Lost Hero', and underneath it were the words, 'Written by Ely Carter.'

THE END

More books (fantasy) by Jason L. McWhirter

The Cavalier Trilogy
Look for them at www.twiinentertainment.com
or online at Amazon and Barnes and Noble

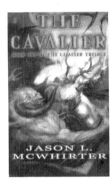

Visit Jason McWhirter's Facebook at
https://www.facebook.com/TwiinEntertainement

About the author

 Jason McWhirter has been a history teacher for eighteen years. He lives in Washington with his wife, Jodi, and dogs Meadow and Macalan. He is a certifiable fantasy freak who, when he wasn't playing sports, spent his childhood days immersed in books and games of fantasy. He'd tumble into bed at night with visions of heroes, dragons, and creatures of other worlds, fueling his imagination and spurring his desire to create fantasies of his own. When he isn't fly fishing the lakes and streams of the Northwest, or wine tasting and entertaining with his wife and friends, he spends his spare time sitting in front of the computer writing his next novel or screenplay.

CPSIA information can be obtained at www.ICGtesting.com
Printed in the USA
LVOW01s2125280514

387703LV00010B/90/P

9 780985 155193